Colored Sand

Colored Sand

a novel by
Nadia H. Reimer

Printed in the United States of America

Packaged by Selah Publishing Group, Bristol, TN. The views expressed or implied in this work do not necessarily reflect those of Selah Publishing. Ultimate design, content, and editorial accuracy of this work are the responsibilities of the author.

ISBN – 978-1-58930-024-8
Library Congress Catalog Card Number –2001089214

To my father, Issa M. Hazboun,
to whom this novel means a great deal

Acknowledgements

Deep appreciation to those who helped and continue to help in my endeavors:

Cover photo – Greg Reimer

Proofreaders – Michael Lynch, Clara Reimer, Greg Reimer, and Lois Bartel.

Resource persons – Issa M. Hazboun, Viola and Carol Basil, Rima and David Far.

Author Photo – Charles and Karen Meye from C. Meye Photo.

CHAPTER 1

"Hey, *Lizard Boy, come look at this!* "

"*Look at what?*"

"*Look at this.*"

"*It's a shard of clay, Jim. Look around you. Thousands are scattered everywhere.*"

"*A shard of history, Lizard - history of ancient civilizations.*"

"*Right.*"

Jim, the professor of archeology, gave me the name Lizard Boy when he couldn't pronounce my name. He had seen me climb up and down the High Place of Petra, the ancient Nabatean city at the edge of the Jordanian desert. He said I knew nothing about climbing. To him, I slithered like a salamander. I told him we had no salamanders in this part of the world; we had lizards. Since then, I became Lizard Boy.

That was forty years ago when I first saw Jim. He looked older than the muezzin, Sheik Khader, who was supposedly the oldest man in the village of Wadi Moussa. His voice came out of the minaret of the old mosque like a loud hiss with streaks of thunder every now and then, and his chants lacked the soft, soothing tone of prayer. Instead, they irritated the listeners like long fingernails driven against a chalkboard. But the reason Jim looked so old was because I was so young back then, and anyone past forty years of age seemed ancient to me whether he exceeded one hundred years, like the muezzin, Sheik Khader, or barely cleared fifty five, like Jim.

Now, forty years later, and, as I approach that age, I condemn the old ideas, and I think of Jim as a young, ambitious person, who came to our village looking for a set of caves and found me first. It took us a good share of a year to discover history. It is a long story, and I have procrastinated long enough and run out of excuses to make. The story of Jim and me has to be recorded and kept in a safe place, away from rodents, earthquakes and wars.

Jim and I waded through masses of dirt-slides while we excavated in the folds of the ruins; crushed rock and fine sand, layers of natural and man–made records. We uncovered reptiles and rodents of various species. They had taken care of all the chewable parts of the human story, but we also found solid antiques, true antiques, that actually made it through time. Jim and I found them all. They waited two thousand years for us to discover and record.

The ancient city of Petra itself, however, had already been discovered. It was concealed in colored sandstone monoliths that towered like a team of giant phantoms, just beyond the village. The Seeq, the only entrance to Petra was no more than a narrow winding canyon, carved by centuries of water. It meandered for two kilometers before it reached the ancient city, and its sides ascended vertically and touched the clouds. Huge rocks bulged above the path here and there, leaving eerie shadows to dim the brightness of the colored rocks and erasing the sun rays that tried to pierce its deep colored corners.

Chapter 1

This narrow path had haunted archeologists from many parts of the world. Like a conduit, it led them deeper and deeper into the narrowing rocks, until they finally reached the ruins of the Nabatean civilization early last century, and, for the first time since the collapse of that Civilization in the early centuries A.D., did Petra reveal to the world its art, the art created with hard and soft sand, colored sand.

Then Jim arrived.

CHAPTER 2

"Raji." The name echoed in the valley.

"Raji." It echoed again, but I ignored it.

"What a goofball," the voice mumbled gruffly.

I chuckled and walked around the corner of the guest house making an appearance before the tall figure. Abu-Zeid, the owner, stood by the main entrance like a palm tree. His crooked smile told me he had hoped I heard his last words. We stood there for an endless while, staring at each other, communicating in silence, my eyes reassuring him that, this time, he would have to pay dearly to get me to run his errands for him. Then I turned around and walked away feeling his eyes on my back.

From a distance, the semi arid portion of Jordan revealed to the naked eye a mass of dull, pale yellow hills brushed with some browns – burnt sienna and burnt umber, smeared with streaks of cadmium yellow and highlighted with blotches of bright ivory here and there, where the sun rays hit directly. A few monumental rocks arose from the hills to break the monotony of the view. However, a closer look at the scene exposed more than earth tones and rock formation. There were caves, ancient tombs, wild goats, and hyenas that usually helped minimize the boredom and the feeling of emptiness.

Green grass, on the verge of turning brown, and patches of wild flowers covered the lower hills. They added rich colors to the landscape that stretched as far south as the town of Ma'an. There were red poppies with delicate petals, each naturally brushed with a touch of onyx black at the center; there were wild iris in all shades of blue, white daisies, yellow mustard plants that attempted to cross the border of the semi arid zone but stopped, sharply. Beyond the town of Ma'an, the absolute desert, the ruthless tyrant, reigned. It consumed all signs of life and replaced them with hot scorching sand, which traveled on all the way south to the city of Aqaba on the tip of the Red Sea. The one hundred six degrees Fahrenheit usually marked the peak of the season in this part of the country, but the August weather arrived in early June that year and caused major sections of the pasture ground to dry up prematurely.

In spite of all that dryness, the echo of sheep and goats could still be heard all around the village of Wadi Moussa and the outskirts of its two thousand year old majestic neighbor, the ruins of Petra, many of which continued to stand tall and straight despite the harsh surroundings. Also, the sound of tourists emerged from the mouth of the Seeq, the narrow entrance of the ancient city. The human noise joined the neighing of horses from the clearing in front of the Guest House, where my brothers had ended the horseback tours and proceeded to lead the animals to their stalls for the night.

They looked weary; the animals did, for they had spent another day carrying tourists through the rough path. Now that they were allowed on smooth ground, they galloped in agile steps toward home. As for my brothers, they always looked the same, serious, dutiful and cold. Their life had been chained to a routine they would never trade, work, sleep, and back to work. At the moment, they were on their way to sleep.

Several tour guides rounded up their groups by the buses. They jabbered steadily, and the tourists didn't seem to care anymore. To me, city tour-guides looked more foreign at times than the tourists themselves. They usually recited what they had memorized during training and quickly moved on to the next site, before any of their audience had a chance to absorb the information and become curious enough to ask profound questions.

These guided tourists would either continue their journey south and finish the tour in the city of Aqaba by the Red Sea or go back north to Amman, the Capital, where the scenery would be greener, the weather cooler, and therefore, the breathing much easier.

Other unguided visitors were getting ready to have supper at the restaurant of the Guest House. These tourists usually traveled on their own. They would spend the night at the Guest House and continue on with their expeditions, research, and other endeavors early next morning.

A sudden, gentle breeze early in the evening brought cool weather to the place. Men pulled down the wet handkerchiefs tied around their heads and wiped their greasy faces. Women mimicked with their scarves, smearing them with make-up and a pasty mixture of sand and sweat. Deep breaths were inhaled slowly, with ecstasy, and then exhaled as their takers collapsed on the boulders in the front yard of the Guest House under the poplar trees. Some people poured the last drops of water in their canteens on their heads; others drank the final portion in relief, knowing that the supply is finally at hand.

Everybody had evacuated the ancient city and its ruins and rushed to the safety of modern civilization before nightfall, all except the old man. He was walking against the flow of traffic, back into the rough and winding path, back to the Seeq that led to the ruins of Petra, all alone.

"Now, where did this one come from?" I asked one of the guides.

"Which one?"

"That old man down there." I pointed toward the narrow path, and the guide squinted so he could see the hunched figure before it disappeared in the Seeq. "He's not one of your group, is he?"

"My group is already in the bus," said the guide firmly. He talked in a city accent and with a tone full of efficiency and pride. He looked neat, well organized, and much too stiff to acknowledge a little merriment in life.

"But what does that man think he's doing – going back to the ruins at this time of the day?" I asked.

"None of my business," the guide concluded. "I have enough weird species to contend with and need no more; thank you."

"But …."

"No buts, kid. I'm on my way home."

"He needs to be reported."

Silence.

"Have you ever seen anybody go back to the ruins so late in the evening? He won't make it back before dark."

"I told you. That is none of my business," the guide insisted. "I am through for the day."

He tucked his canteen in his bag, checked the contents in the side pockets and zipped everything shut. My mind wandered through the Seeq accompanying the strange man.

"Could he be a loner?" I mumbled.

Chapter 2

"He looks like he could be one of them," said the guide. He lifted his brushed eyebrows and smiled at me. "You know – the stray ones, the kind you seek and chaperone." He nudged me on the shoulder with his fist. "Go for it, young man. Tell him Petra is not Paris in case he misread the word. Make sure he knows there's a slight difference between the two cities. For one thing, tell him the road to Petra is not paved, and it is Eiffel hard to get there at night." He laughed at his own joke, grabbed his bag and headed for the bus. "Au-revoir, my friend," he yelled and waived his hand in the air. "Don't worry too much."

No one else noticed the old man disappear in the cleft, and I couldn't let the miserable wretch go down the wicked road by himself. I had to follow him. If nothing else, it would be entertaining just to see what he had up his sleeve.

I crept up behind him, quietly at first, like a reptile. He walked like a turtle in full gear, watched every step he took and never looked back. After he cleared the Seeq, he continued on the main road to the foot of the High Place. The old man had guts. I did feel the urge to stop him, but I allowed my curiosity to take over for a while. I wanted to see how far he would go before he sensed the souls of the ancients surrounding him and screamed for help.

Many tourists hesitated to climb the High Place, even during the day when the sun provided ample visibility and the place rumbled with crowds, and, to hike the steep, rocky hill so late in the evening, when chances for receiving help were reduced to a zero, had to be insane. But the old man did not seem bothered by such thought. He had a mind of his own, all set on one path. I stared at him to confirm his reality. The elderly folks in the village always talked about ghosts appearing and disappearing, luring men to follow them to ominous caves.

He was definitely a tourist. Who else would attempt to climb the High Place in a brand new pair of stiff, blue jeans? I stood there shaking my head, wondering whether to interfere or not. Maybe the man was mad, I thought, or maybe his last wish included a hike to the High Place of Petra, all alone. One slip of the foot, and his last wish would be confirmed as last.

I continued to follow quietly until following became tiresome. So I moved closer and, in the process, made enough noise to get his attention. He anchored himself against the cliff and gripped its edges tightly until the veins on the back of his hands bulged. Then he lifted his head up and looked at me. I nodded in a greeting gesture and passed him, pretending to be on my way up too. He nodded and resumed his climbing, while I advanced all the way up and waited for him. When he didn't come, I climbed back down to check on him and found him climbing, still. So I went back up again and continued to practice my climbing up and down, appearing and disappearing before him like a ghost myself. He maintained his upward motion with perseverance on the verge of hazardous insanity.

A large backpack rested on his back and bent it enough for his nose to meet bulging rocks at certain points. It took him over an hour to climb the Place. I wore out, just waiting for him; he wore out, just watching me whiz by him up and down. He crept on each rock like a turtle that had lost a leg now. Each time he set his foot down, I pretended to give him a push from the rear to help his body follow before it dropped down and resumed a second attempt.

The Department of Tourism had opened a trail of a sort, so that people could climb on step-like boulders to the High Place rather than rough their way up. Although the old man tried to follow it faithfully, he still appeared hopeless. He stopped every once in a while to make sure his feet had not wandered off the trail, for there were no bold marks, and it would be too easy to drift off into a neighboring mass of rocks. I never even tried to follow the trail myself. My imaginary paths sufficed. I usually took off in small, fast steps that made me look as if I slithered over the rocks. The old man looked at me with contempt and disgust. It wasn't my fault I was born forty years later than he and in this part of the world, where I had a chance to practice climbing more than he did all his life in his own country. I told him that – but after I came to know him better. For the moment, I had to approach him with civility to avoid scaring him, since there was no room to jump on this perfidious ground.

I had been looking for something to do, and this fellow looked like he could use my services, strong hands and nimble feet for a clumsy old man, short sighted with eyes so distorted you'd wonder if they were all there behind his thick glasses. I had never seen glasses so thick. The lenses surpassed the frame by a centimeter or so and looked as if ready to fall off. His half-bald head glistened in the evening sun. What was left of his hair stuck out the sides of his head like wet feathers of a chicken half plucked.

"What's your name, Son," he finally asked.

"Rajaiiddin," I said.

"Rajjjj … It should be Salamander."

"Lizard," I corrected.

"I beg your pardon?" he asked, and with the tips of his fingers, he pulled his left ear toward me for better hearing.

"Lizard," I repeated. "Salamanders do not live here. This is not the Amazon Jungle."

He laughed until the tears streamed under his glasses. "Okay. Lizard Boy," he said.

Nobody else could pronounce my real name either, or at least, nobody wanted to, not even my own brothers. They called me Raji. They thought my full name was too old fashioned, long and awkward for our times. They said that Father would have given me a shorter name had he been living at the time of my birth. How could I blame the tourists? I might as well tell you what my full name is right now and get it over with. And, like I said to the old man - don't feel obligated; Lizard Boy will do.

My full name, as given by my mother was Rajaiiddeen Mansour Al-Muhtadi. I still had three more months to spend in my mother's womb when my father was killed in a car accident on the desert highway somewhere between the Capital, Amman, and the village of Wadi Moussa at the mouth of Petra. He had gone to Amman to bring supplies for his home improvement projects. Mother said that he used to have endless projects, and whenever he made extra money, especially during tourist seasons, he would make a trip to the Capital and bring home building supplies to expand and improve our living quarters. As a result, he left the family in a fairly comfortable situation, although, many of his dream projects remained incomplete.

When I was born I joined three brothers, and in my mind I grew up calling them boss 1, boss 2, and boss 3. That gave them even shorter names than the ones Father had given them. Our relationship had become irksome, mostly after I finished sixth grade - compulsory education. My brothers thought I should join them and help them run Father's business, leading tourists on horseback through the Seeq that led to the ruins of Petra. But I said no.

During school vacation, I had learned to approach stray tourists on my own and give them private guided tours through the city all by myself, repeating what my history teacher had taught me about the area. I took my tourists to twice as many places as the licensed tour guides from the Capital did. Although they played big shots and pretended to know everything, they always came to me for help. They asked their questions in Arabic so that the tourists would not understand. But I always answered in English to stir up trouble and watch those guides blush and stutter. It pleased me to play this game, and in the process of playing it, many tourists began to approach me with questions. Consequently, my English improved as well as my repertoire of several other languages.

At school, the teacher bragged about my pronunciation and asked me to read aloud so that everybody could listen and learn. I read with a puffed chest like a peacock. Every once in a while, the teacher tried to correct me, just to humble me, and my chest would shrink, and I would behave like a human again. But I continued to fluff my wings each time I helped archeologists, historians, geologists, and history teachers find their way through the ruins. When I told my mother and brothers that I wanted to finish school and go to college and become an archeologist, my mother defended me with pride; my brothers called me a goofball. But I liked Lizard Boy better.

The old man hired me as an errand boy. Later, he promoted me to the position of administrative assistant. Of course, I never knew what the words meant until much later in life. At the time I thought it must have been something above errand boy and below professor. My first job, after he finally made it to the High Place, was to go back to his cave and fetch him the can-opener. He had carried his supper up the steep hill and then remembered he had forgotten to pack the can opener. I was back with his tool before he quit panting. He gave me that disgusted look again and followed it by a handful of coins and a smile. I took that as a good sign.

A few minutes later, he set his backpack on a flat rock and walked around as if to check out the place. I followed him from a distance trying not to disturb his peace. Not all tourists, especially old geezers, make it to the High Place of

Petra. There was a great deal of admiration, and disgust too, in my heart toward this man. After all, he made it all the way up and proved me fool.

The other curious feature about this man was his smile. It resembled that of my father in the picture. We had only one picture of my father at home. It was taken by a tourist, and my mother had framed and mounted it on the wall above her bed. I had spent hours staring at my father's face. I talked to him through the picture and sensed his presence in the room with me many times. His smile in the photo seemed real, just like this old stranger's. I stood stiff and stared at the man while his eyes roamed the hills.

The Nabateans had built several High Places. They were mostly shrines for their deities in the late centuries B.C., for they had honored the sun, and, Dushara, one of their two chief gods, was represented by a block of stone or obelisk that received the sun from the High Place. Dushara also means He of Shera (Thu Shera), referring to the Shera mountains that surrounded Petra. In the Old Testament, Shera is called Seer, and Jehovah is said to be "He of Seer" also, or, in other words, Dushara, and he also inhabited the House of God, which was represented in a block of stone, and his chief shrines were also built in high places.

The second chief Nabatean god was Allat, a spiritual power associated with springs and valleys. The flow of water in the springs and the valleys in and around Petra was a vital asset to the caravans that roamed the ancient world. And, to maintain a special god for such a necessity had become an asset to the ancients.

The High Place, on which the old man now stood, had a plateau that served as a natural observatory. A person could see the entire area all around; the Seeq, the only entrance to this hidden city stood inconspicuously between two monumental rocks; the ancient tombs with their carved facades and stairways decorated the hillside; the caves, in which the Nabateans had resided, now waited for hyenas in the foothills; the other monuments carved in rocks stood mysteriously and kept the archeologists busy until now trying to figure out their functions two thousand years ago; the water reservoirs, the dry river beds and all the objects down below gave the feeling of being on top of the world, the ancient world. There was nothing above, everything below, except the sky, the sun and a puff of cloud here and there.

"The High Place," murmured the old man, "just the High Place. That's what I would call it too." He seemed to acknowledge my existence behind him, yet he wasn't looking directly at me. His eyes still roamed the hills, near and far.

"We usually don't fool around with exotic names, Sir," I said. "We call things by what they are."

He laughed again. "You," he said and shook his head. I waited to hear the rest of the statement about me, but it ended right there. He walked over to his bag, pulled his supper out and began to prepare his meal. He made himself a small table out of a flat boulder and set on it some bread, a few leaves of lettuce, a tomato and two cans of sardines. I took one look at his meal and turned to go home.

"Lizard Boy," he called in a voice so strong; its echo bounced from hill to hill and came back after a long while. When he heard it come back, he lifted his eyebrows in surprise and smiled at his accomplishment. I was not that far away. He could have whispered, and I would have heard him well, but I gathered from his tone of voice that it was not time for me to leave yet. "Do you care to have a bite with me?" he asked. "I brought too much food up here." He must have realized we were the only two people in the old city and thought it would be only proper to have the other sole person over for supper.

"Thanks, but no – Thanks," I said. I hated sardines. The idea of eating a dozen of fish that had been crammed in a can for some time usually reduced my appetite a little; the smell took care of the rest, and I told the old man I'd rather go eat supper at home.

"What will you eat for supper?" he asked.

"Khmia," I said.

"Kkkhmi?" he repeated the word with much effort as if he wanted to learn it even if it choked him. "What's kkkhmi?"

"Plain yogurt cheese sauce with olive oil and bread."

"That's all?"

"Sometimes we have chunks of meat in it, mostly chickens. On special occasions, we would have lamb. We also have tomatoes and onions on the side." The man listened intently and tried to absorb everything I said. It made me feel like a waiter offering a mysterious dinner.

He sliced the tomato, mashed the sardines and made himself a three layer sandwich, tomatoes, sardines and lettuce. "Do you have kkk..."

"Khmia," I said, helping him out before he turned blue.

"Khamie. Do you have khamie every day for supper?"

"Almost every day. Sometimes we have lentils and rice. And when I make good money, I go eat at the restaurant in town."

"You're from Wadi Moussa, aren't you?" He asked. His eyes checked me out from head to toe, and I shrugged my shoulders. My face felt warm.

"Yes."

"What does your father do for a living?"

"My father is dead," I said. My throat croaked as I let the words out, and I cleared it.

His face sobered. "I'm sorry to hear that," he said.

CHAPTER 2

From his accent, I gathered he was American not British, because, to me, the British people spoke English with their lips gathered so tightly, you'd think they were growing snouts. And people of other nationalities usually spiced their English with their own languages. For example, I could tell the difference between Pakistani English and Greek English, German English and, worst of all, French English. I did not believe that the French spoke English at all. They just thought they did. This old man was definitely American, I concluded.

"What do they offer at the restaurant in town?" said the old man after he had nibbled on his sandwich. He wiped his mouth with a napkin that had the Guest House logo printed on one corner.

"Better food than sardines," I teased. He gave me the look again and took a big bite.

"Better than sardines, you say." He spoke with his mouth full, and a smile settled on his face as if it were painted. A reflection of a lonely cloud appeared in his glasses causing his eyes to diminish even more. He ate quietly while I walked to the edge of the cliff and watched the bright colors in the horizon slowly fade away and a full moon softly spread strings of light on the creeping darkness. It was time for me to go home. My mother would worry if I didn't, and then she would launch an argument with my brothers over me. But I was worried about the old man. I wanted to know whether he had planned to jump off the High Place, spend the night up there, or go back down to sleep in the cave he had claimed to be his. He would never make it back down in the dark, even with a flashlight. He would need a lizard to help him out, I decided. It was my fate, I thought as I walked back to him slowly. The last bite of his sandwich disappeared in his mouth, and he rubbed his hands together and then wiped them well with the napkin.

"Where do you plan to spend the night?" I asked.

He pointed to his big bulging backpack and then to the flat ground of the High Place. "Can you think of a better place?" he asked with pride. He deserved to be proud. At his age, I'd be proud too if I climbed that far.

"Then, have a good night, Sir," I said as I nodded and walked away.

"Good night Lizard Boy," he murmured. "Say," he added in a louder voice, and, patiently, I turned around and looked at him. His face glistened in the moonlight, and I felt like I had known this man for some time now. "Do you go to school?"

"Yes."

"Where?"

"Up at the village."

"What grade are you in?"

"I'll be in tenth grade next Fall."

"So school must be out for the summer."

I nodded and waited for him to dismiss me. But he didn't. The glow in the horizon dimmed some more as if someone had gently lowered the wick in an oil lamp. A trace of light marked the sky, and silence fell on the earth. Even the sounds of shepherds and their sheep and goats died away beyond the hills. "Can you find your way home in the dark?" he asked.

"Oh Yes. Besides, the moon is giving plenty of light tonight," I said pointing to the moon. He looked at the bright circle in the sky and then at the silence all around. The cool, desert, evening breeze continued to blow gently, quietly. The old man took a deep breath.

"Nice," he said. I nodded and tried to leave for the third time. But his voice stopped me again. "Are you coming back in the morning?" he asked.

"I could," I said impatiently.

"I might need your help again."

"Then I will, Mister...."

Chapter 2

"Jim. Just call me Jim."

"Jim."

On my way home, I saw a lizard in the moonlight staring at me as I passed between two rocks. I backed up and looked at him. "Hi Lizard Boy," I said quietly and tiptoed closer toward him. I had never watched lizards so closely before. There was no reason. Now, thanks to Jim, they shared my name, or I theirs. The lizard allowed me a closer look; my nose came within a few centimeters from his face. He neither moved nor panicked – just stared at me some more. His eyes focused on me like two beads, lifeless yet full of truth. I was tempted to feel them and check their reality. "Let's see how you slither," I whispered and tapped the rock softly below him, but still, he wouldn't move. "Hey," I finally said in a louder whisper. "Come on, let us see you go, my friend." I reached closer to nudge him, but he disappeared in a flash before I could reach him or see him go. The rock on which he froze a minute ago stood empty, and the beads, the eyes, were gone.

Chapter 3

Tourists, villagers, horses, sheep, goats, donkeys and all the other life forms of the village of Wadi Moussa began to stir around four o'clock in the morning. First, people had to do their chores before the scorching hot summer sun mounted the sky. Nature's melodies usually came in late. The roosters sang their morning song and then scampered for the shade between the vineyards. The hens followed the horses for a while and pecked behind them until they left the yards with their owners. Some women sat on the porches and kneaded bread; others hung clothes on the lines, and others sat cross legged on wicker chairs or small mats on the floor, pulled one of their enlarged breasts out through a slot in the front of their baggy dresses and nursed their babies.

Children played everywhere during the summer. Some clustered around the houses and built toy automobiles and airplanes from used wire. They built cars of all models with steering wheels and shafts, connected to the wire tires, and steered them all around the neighborhoods. The older children added fancy details and brand names to their wire cars. Tourists marveled at the home made toy cars and some even offered to buy them at times. Other children followed the tourists all the way down to Petra and either charmed them, pestered them, or made faces at them.

Our house lay at the edge of the village, less than half a kilometer away from the Guest House, where the tourists usually gathered to begin their journey through the Seeq. We had no sheep around our place, just a few chickens in the yard, and a large supply of pigeons that occupied our flat roof. For centuries, the abundance of fowl had supplied the poorer villagers with meat, and the pigeon had become a symbol of divine providence. On special occasions, especially during the Ramadan feast or the Adha holidays, my brothers would buy a lamb and have it butchered at the butcher shop, and my mother would fix it for us in yogurt sauce. I always looked forward to lamb treats. Chickens and pigeons usually satisfied the mouth and the stomach, but a hunk of lamb had enough meat to fill a person clear to the soul. It gave more wholesome satisfaction. But, fowl had to be the cheapest meat animals to raise in our part of the country, especially pigeons. We rarely had to feed them. They always flew away and fed themselves on different grains in the fields north of us and then came back at the end of the day to nestle in the special boxes we had built for them on the roof of our house. The flat roofs of the houses in this part of the world allowed people some extra space. Many used the roofs to hang laundry; others, mainly villagers, used them to raise pigeons for free meat.

Across the yard, stood the stables for the horses. They were built of mud walls and reinforced with straw. My brothers always reminded me that our house used to be a mud house too, but our father had saved enough money to build the concrete and stone tile house we lived in at that time. He also had had plans to upgrade the stalls but died before accomplishing all his projects. My brothers, boss 1, boss 2 and boss 3 took over the plans religiously. They also had intentions to expand and build a house for each of them somewhere in the village, but not for me, for, according to them, I was a pervert and, if I needed a house, I would have to build it myself. Mother said I could share her house. She cherished my individuality be it a goofball, a lizard, or a debaucher with donkey's ears, and I was grateful for that. I also liked the location of mother's house better than any other dream house in the village, because, from our front door, I could almost see the path to Petra, the path that continued to haunt the visitor, the passerby, and me.

I ate my breakfast in a hurry and rushed toward the Seeq, thinking of the adventurous old man. The morning was busy with small crowds here and there and pleasant village noises, the kind people took in like daily communion. It brought joy to the hearts, and I felt bursting with exhilaration for no particular reason. But then, I walked past the Guest House and saw Abu–Zeid, the owner, accosting me. He had been waiting for me to make an appearance, for he knew I could answer all his nosy questions just as efficiently as I could run his errands for him.

"I saw you follow the old man yesterday," he said gruffly. "Is he still alive?"

The son of a donkey was an espionage wizard, among other things. "As far as I know he is," I said and tried to resume my journey. But he took couple of long steps and cut in front of me and blocked my way.

"What is he up to anyway?"

"How would I know what he's up to."

"Knowing you, I don't think you would ever leave anybody roam around on this ground without making sure you knew everything." His right eyebrow went up simultaneously with the right side of his mouth, and the tip of his nose also moved slightly to the right, a personal expression to tell me he was positive about what he had said.

"Listen. All I know is that he spent the night up at the High Place, and he wanted me back today to help him."

"At the H... ." The aspirated letter lingered in his breathing pipe for a while. "Do you mean he climbed all the way up there last night?"

"He sure did."

"I'll be – I wonder what he's up to."

"Whatever it is can't be much. The man is slower than a snail."

"That doesn't matter. The way he roamed around yesterday gives me the feeling he's up to something."

"When did he get here anyway?"

"He arrived early yesterday morning with all kinds of luggage and spent the day roaming the area as if he were inspecting it. I believe he plans to stick around for a while."

"He won't be the first one."

"At his age? I'm afraid he will be," concluded Abu-Zeid.

Tourists usually came and went, but to arrive with long term intentions, especially in a small village like Wadi Moussa, a person would stick out like a red flag. Jim stuck out like a red flag with fluorescent brightness, because Petra used to be considered a place for the young, strong, and adventurous professionals. It was a rough and rugged place, where a simple mistake could take a life and add it to the ancients buried in the tombs. If a man should fall off a cliff, he would be received by a boulder; if he should get lost between the rocks, he may not be found for another two thousand years when his bones had settled in the chinks like those of ancient goats and other fellow adventurers, and, worst of all, if he should run out of water out there, he might die of thirst long before his feet could bring him all the way back to the village. Therefore, it was rare to see an adventurer roaming all alone in Petra, let alone, an old man like Jim. But the mystery of this hidden city drew in an entire range of people, and now, I dare say, people of all ages, thanks to Jim. And the Guest House, being the gateway to all paths resulted in creating an observation deck, or a gossip distribution center to be exact, within its walls. It was a check point, an information desk, and a place to help and hinder, depending on how sociable the visitor desired to be.

Some tourists walked the Seeq; others rode on horseback before it became a forbidden means of transportation, limited to only the elderly people and the handicapped. My three brothers always stood there, across the yard from the Guest House by the edge of the Seeq with our fifteen horses all lined up and ready to meet the first tourist to step out of a bus or out of the Guest House. Sometimes my older brother would make arrangements with the tour guides ahead of time and wait for them, especially when their groups included older or handicapped people who could not possibly walk the path. But, both man and beast always approached the rugged ground with caution and distrust. They all ambled at the same pace, for the road of crushed sand-stones of uneven sizes made it as difficult for the ankles as well as the hoofs to tread.

Visitors were already walking the path when I entered it. Those who walked steady could be heard around the bends of the Seeq; others took their time and studied the rocks and the water canals carved along each side of the cleft. The water canals were the first evidence of the Nabatean man in the path, and people marveled at their sight, ignorant of the unfathomed ancient city that awaited them ahead, just past the Seeq. They pulled magnifying glasses out of their bulging pouches to study the microcosm of the ancient place. Then they pulled out their binoculars and focused on the macrocosm that transferred them to a different world and time. They had papers, pencils, cameras, and contraptions that represented many of the human ways and means of learning to help them absorb and believe in the reality of their surroundings.

If only I had a camera, I often whined to myself. If only I had a way to capture and bring down the high and remote places I had discovered on my own, for the tracks of the ancient man had continued on, beyond the common tourist path, and only shepherds, goats, and lizard boys were able to visit such places. But at the time, I was but a peasant boy who could only greet the people he tried to pass politely, without upsetting their awe. I waived my hand up in the air and cheered those who looked up and smiled more warmly than others. This method normally served as a good way to initiate a conversation and perhaps even excite a guided tour of some sort. Most people responded kindly, unless they were engrossed in studying a certain spot or too cognizant of each step they took.

The canals on each side of the Seeq had supplied the Nabateans, the ancient inhabitants of Petra, with additional water from the hills outside the city. There were huge water reservoirs in the city, but apparently, at the time of the Nabateans, the springs within the city limits had been too small to meet the demands of the inhabitants and the passing caravans that crisscrossed the old world at a steady pace. Up by the village of Wadi Moussa and the surrounding hills, strong springs flowed, and they were abundant according to historians and archeologists. They kept the canals roaring down toward Petra. The canals were carved inconspicuously in the rock so that the enemy could not spot them and cut off the water supply. Now the man–made water paths lay there, dead, dry and disconnected from the rest of the world, just like the rest of the Nabatean city and its people. The modern man saw only ruins, monumental, secluded, and haunting.

CHAPTER 3

I sneaked up on a proper looking couple and greeted them like a gentleman. "Good morning," I said with a slight, humble bow.

"Good morning," answered the tall lady and the taller man beside her. They both had cameras hanging from their necks and water bottles that were strapped through their belts and seemed fastened to their hips. They wore identical clothes, bright colored T shirts with scribbles in a German-like language all over them, khaki shorts, white socks and heavy walking shoes that almost looked like army boots. When I saw their footwear I looked down at my cloth tennis shoes and poked my big toes through the two big holes at the top. The rough ground around here had a habit of eating up footwear, especially cheap cloth shoes like mine. The two holes on top of my shoes always marked and renewed my identity two days after I owned them. My family had figured that as long as the soles could still be traced, and the top of the shoes could still hide a major part of my feet, the shoes had to be in good shape.

The tall woman also had a pink scarf twisted like a rope and tied like a head band around her head, and the man had a pale blue sun hat pulled down his forehead. They both stared at my careless feet as I walked. Each of their steps was taken very carefully, even with the army–like boots they had on. If I had their shoes, I would walk with the confidence of a bulldozer, I thought.

"Could you please tell me what time it is?" I asked, trying to decide whether or not I had time to arouse someone's interest and give him a short tour before I went to see Jim at the High Place.

"It is five till six," said the man in a heavy German accent.

It had to be German; I knew it, for, like I said, I had been around tourists enough to gather up a repertoire of expressions in many languages, and German was one of them. It had been imperative that I learned these expressions. A person could never survive among German tourists if he did not speak their language. They never liked to speak English unless their life was at stake. I knew that from experience, just like I knew about their generosity. Germans had bountiful pockets, at least the few I had managed to meet in my life so far.

When the man told me the time in abused English, I slowed down, enough to follow his pace, and once I came in line with him and his lady, I said with a German gruff voice, "Danke schön," and followed it by, "Guten Morgen," and resumed to move ahead. But then there was light. Their faces lit up like torches and matched the sun rays that tried to penetrate through the cracks above the Seeq.

"Guten Morgen," they recited with such esprit de corps they almost lost their balance on the rocks. They grabbed each other's hands and balanced themselves again as they continued to look at me with admiration.

"Sprechen sie Deutsches?" asked the man.

"Not yet," I said in English. "But I try to learn a few sentences every time I meet German tourists."

"But you speak English very well," said the lady with a heavy accent and a hint of scolding.

"That's because I learn English at school, Madam" I said. "I wish they would teach us German too." She bought my excuse, and her face relaxed again.

"What other German sentences can you say?" asked the man with enthusiasm and high expectations. I recited most of the everyday expressions until I saw relief and satisfaction on his face too. And while I was still in my glory, practicing supreme diplomacy, I thought of something else that might even make him happier yet. I pulled a small piece of paper and pencil out of my pocket and asked him if he would kindly write a few more sentences, the ones I had not mentioned yet, so I could learn them. His laughter vibrated against the narrow walls of the Seeq and sent a tingle up my spine. He took the paper and pencil and walked over to the dry water canal at the edge of the path and used it as a table to write on. He filled the paper on both sides. I almost interrupted to remind him that I had asked for a few sentences - not an article for the national journal, but his enthusiasm constrained me, and I let him be. When he finally lifted his head up, he asked if I had more paper, and I firmly said no.

"Too bad," said the man in a pouting tone, "I could have written many more sentences for you."

"I know, but I can only learn a few at a time," I said as I scanned the words. "These are good for now. I'll have them memorized before I meet the next German. I promise."

"Yes, but the next German may not be a teacher," he said. The smile on his face and the look in his eyes belonged to a teacher all right. He spoke with patience, articulated and explained the sentences he had written, and then he went on to tell me how many more sentences he could have written me, and how they would have all been related and mnemonically listed for easy learning. He was also kind and gentle and had me repeat the words after him to make sure I pronounced them correctly and put each stress on the right syllable.

That made me tired before the day started. By the time we arrived to the end of the Seeq, I almost had most of the expressions memorized, and I felt light headed from exertion. Pronouncing German for a long time could cause a person to hyperventilate if he were not careful. A person should take a breath or two in his own language every once in a while to maintain equilibrium. But the German tourist looked mighty proud of me. His chest puffed like a peacock, ready to spread its feathers.

When we finally arrived at the end of the path and resumed to cross the wide smooth road that met the Seeq perpendicularly and led to the rest of the city, I tried to leave the couple to their bewilderment, for they had faced the first hidden building in Petra, the Treasury. But the man stopped me.

"Wait. What is your name?" he asked.

I hesitated for a moment, and he waited patiently. The look on his face made me wonder whether he thought I had forgotten my name or gone crazy. The problem was that I had too many names. "Lizard Boy," I finally remembered. "You can call me Lizard Boy," I said. He frowned until a tangled up knot was formed between his eyebrows, and his wife opened her mouth and gasped. "It's a long story," I explained. "If I tell you my real name, you'll never be able to say it anyway. So I try to make it easy on everybody."

"But I'd like to know your real name," he insisted, looking toward his wife. A faint smile appeared on his face, and he waited with staring gray eyes.

"Well. You asked for it," I said. "It's Raji, short for Rajaiiddeen Mansour AlMohtadi."

"Does it mean Lizard Boy?" asked the woman.

"Actually, no. It means Hope, Faith, Victory, and Guidance from God."

The man shook his head in confusion. He threw his hands up in the air and spread his palms to indicate he had given up. "Okay, Lizard Boy," he said quickly as if it were a curse. "Can you tell us how far we'd have to walk in order to see the main highlights of this place? We need to be back in Wadi Moussa before sunset."

I pointed out to them some of the most accessible caves, tombs and old dwellings on the right side and told them to follow the dry river bed all the way to the cluster of poplar trees where a small booth offered some sandwiches and refreshments till mid–afternoon. That was how I used to receive my free pop from the owner of the booth. I did not tell the tourists that. The man shook my hand tightly and jolted my arm vehemently, as if he were trying to yank it out of its socket. He thanked me several times in English and in German, and when he finally let go of my squashed fingers, I felt him leave a piece of paper in my hand.

Germans were good people, except for the handshake, I thought as I walked toward the High Place, rubbing my sore shoulder. At the bottom of the hill, I looked at the paper the man had left in my hand. It was a five dinar bill. I let out a scream of joy, loud enough to shake the ancient tombs and awaken their dead. Then I went to see Jim.

Chapter 4

To the onlooker, there was always very little contrast in the picture that exposed parts of Petra, the outskirts of Wadi Moussa, and the sandstone hills and valleys that surrounded them. The only deep green patches were confined to the vineyards that dressed up the yards around the houses of the village. The few gardens were carefully terraced to hold the maximum amount of moisture, for, to the villagers, water was gold.

The rest of this semi-arid zone had been overgrazed, for, according to old history, the reason people called the land semi arid was because it used to provide richer, natural pasture ground, sufficient to raise a good variety of animals such as sheep, goats, and occasionally, a few cows here and there. These animals supplied the entire southern towns and villages with ample meat. But desertification had crept up like a padded foot monster over the years and stripped most of the land to its basic elements. The elders of our community complained that the Saudi Arabian camels used to be herded from the south into the heart of the semi arid zones of Jordan and over-graze them, forcing the desert to expand further and further north into the good farmland. However, agriculture had never been the main equity of this place. The treasure, rather, lay hidden in its monumental sandstones, which sustained an aura that never allowed a passerby to breeze through the place without leaving a queasy feeling inside him, a feeling of being surrounded by hidden secrets, all tucked in, somewhere, between the high and the low cliffs.

Archeologists came from different parts of the world with their maps, ropes, chisels and other necessary paraphernalia. They crawled and climbed each and every cliff in search of the unknown. They breathed, smelled and tasted the abrasive sand and watched it rub against their skin and dry it up like cheap leather, leaving it all wrinkled and pale, earth tone pale, just like the hills and the rocks and the lizards that watched from a distance. Some of these people died somewhere in the holes they had dug and the sand covered them gently and the land allowed them to become part of its history. Goats and sheep tripped over these natural graves every once in a while, and the shepherds followed and uncovered bones of lost explorers and reported them to the authorities so they would be recorded somewhere in the books of the unknown, over–dedicated scholars. But the rest remained buried, waiting for more people to come with their maps, ropes and chisels or more goats and sheep to graze over their graves and discover them.

People kept coming. Some, like Jim, most likely younger, tried to tackle the place all alone; others came in groups. Universities and colleges from many countries sent their students of history, archeology, anthropology, and all the related disciplines, to study and dig, until Petra revealed many of its secrets to the world and exposed hidden colors that had expanded the spectrum beyond its gamut. A civilization had been unveiled and added to the books of history of ancient civilizations, and then the tourists came. They arrived every single day of the year and brought progress, tour business, and profit.

I tucked the five dinar bill deep down in my pocket, feeling it over and over again as if it were made of velvet. Then I hopped over the boulders of the High Place. The sun was warming up the crust of the earth fast, but the soft morning breeze still maintained a pleasant weather. The colors of the carved rocks looked brighter than they did at sunset. I stopped about half way up and sat on a rock for a while. It was still early, perhaps too early for an old man to be out of bed yet, unless, of course, a scorpion or a desert snake had bit him during the night. But then, I thought, that would be too unlikely, because those critters usually lived under the rocks and hardly ever bothered the dwellers above. Occasionally, the inhabitants would surprise each other, and one of them would initiate an unpleasant attack. However, if each rested quietly and kept to his/its own side of the boulder, peace usually prevailed.

The paper money crackled in my pocket as I sat, and I remembered how rich I was. I need to make another deposit in my olive oil can before the day is over, I thought. I had kept my dough safe in an olive oil tin can up in a special cave, a great hiding place, all mine, beyond and above the common path of people. My brothers never learned about it. Nobody could climb up there and loot it. The rodents tried, but they were unable to penetrate the tin can. It was well sealed, and I had kept its original round tin lid on, which fit very tightly in the five centimeter hole and made it hard even for me to pry open. I had to use a pocket knife to lift it each time I needed to make a deposit.

The breeze eased off and the sun began to beat down with all its might. I stood up to continue my journey to the top, but something caught my eye on the trail. I walked over to one of the "stair" boulders and saw a wallet resting on one end, half opened like a book. When I picked it up, the first thing I noticed was Jim's picture in it, and the smile, my father's smile. I stared at the grinning old man for a while. This time the picture was in my hand, not on the wall like a rarity I dared not touch. It was close and clear in the bright sun, and I could talk to it, but then I noticed other pictures in the wallet, a stack of them, profiles of strangers that invaded my privacy. I counted two boys and two girls. The youngest boy seemed to be about seven years old in the picture. He had a huge bubble from a piece of bubble gum sticking out of his mouth. I had tried numerous times to blow a bubble this big but it always ended up collapsing all over my mouth and nose. The girls in the pictures were dressed in fancy dresses with ruffles layered on their chests. We called the ruffles kashkash in Arabic. Little girls in my village wore them on their dresses for weddings and during the Ramadan feast. To me, girls looked silly in kashkash. I preferred the shepherdesses traditional, simple dresses, long and wide; they blew in the wind and outlined their slim bodies.

The last picture in the wallet was of a woman. She had soft lines and an easy smile. Her brown eyes had a broad almond shape. They rested deep above the cheek bones, and her mouth had a subtle hint of a red color. She wore no ruffles, but her dress had a rather low cut and revealed a small charm at the end of a golden chain on her breast. I could not make out the figure on the charm although it seemed to be raised; however, it was clearly a profile but not of a modern man. The head resembled that of an ancient god. I wondered if Jim had given her that charm, and if she and the children were Jim's family, and how come he was here all alone, on the other side of the world, taking all kinds of risks. But the family looked too young to be Jim's, much too young.

CHAPTER 4

The last space in the wallet had an international driver's license. "Jim Johnson," I read – long ways from Ahmed AlMohtadi, my father. It confirmed the lack of relationship between us, although his smile still puzzled me. A piece of paper slipped out of the large compartment. It was an emergency card; "In case of emergency, please call," and then there was a list of numbers and names. They included the American Embassy in Amman and some other numbers in the Capital, and the rest had USA addresses.

The heat continued to rise from the earth. I looked up into the sky. It was impeccable, no hint of a cloud, not even the white string I sometimes see, left by a jet plane coming or going somewhere. The leather of Jim's wallet felt warm and soft in my hand. I flipped the pictures back to Jim's and sat down with my day dream again, asking questions that had no answer, wondering who is who. Meanwhile, the sound of people and animals echoed in the valley. The noise grew louder as the hour progressed. My reverie slowly diminished and dissipated in the heat and the noise and the brightness of the sky. I folded the wallet carefully, secured it in my pocket, and moved on.

Jim was looking through the lenses of large binoculars. He had on a green short sleeve Tee shirt and brown shorts. For some reason, he looked younger than he did the night before. It must have been the light, I thought. I walked up closer and stood beside him for a while and waited for him to acknowledge my presence, but he must not have heard me. His breakfast mess still covered his boulder table; orange peel, bread crumbs and a piece of paper that had once covered a small triangle of yellow soft cheese were scattered all over. I recognized the brand name of the cheese on the paper, La Vache Qui Ris, the laughing cow, imported, French. They sold it at the small grocery store up by the Guest House.

"Good morning," I said politely with a slight feeling of guilt, for he looked entranced.

He jerked the binoculars away from his face and turned around. "You startled me, young man," he said. "When did you get here?"

"About an hour ago."

"I bet."

"How much."

"You," he said with a grin. He shook his head and pointed to me. "I should have known better than asking a lizard. It slithers all over." He tucked the binoculars in their pouch and walked over to his mess and began to tidy up the place.

"Need a hand?" I asked.

"Not yet, Lizard. Not yet."

I stood there patiently and watched him work. He slaved carefully over his scattered possessions and secured each piece in its proper place. His pack had more pockets and zippers than I had ever seen on one piece of luggage.

"Jim," I said quietly. He turned and looked at me. "This is yours, I believe." I pulled out the wallet and showed it to him. "I found it on the trail this morning."

He stared at me until a gush of blood rose into my face and increased my body heat to the level of discomfort. Then, without moving his eyes, his hand slowly reached the wallet in my hand and took it. "Thank you," he said emphatically.

"It shouldn't be missing anything, Jim," I said. "Nobody had been up the Place yet, and it looks like I beat the rodents to it."

He nodded with a smile and didn't seem worried. "Did you have breakfast?" he asked.

"Yes, and I suppose you'd like to know what I had for breakfast too."

CHAPTER 4

"It would be interesting."

"I had white cheese and hummos with bread and slices of tomatoes."

A wide range smile covered his entire face. He put the wallet in his pocket without looking inside it and continued to study me from head to toe. "Now, you have to tell me what in the world is hummos?"

"I knew that was coming," I said. "It's a bean dip, a breakfast dip which my mother makes. She also makes the white cheese herself at home. I hate imported yellow mushy cheeses just as much as I hate sardines."

"Picky young man, aren't you?"

"Picky and rich," I added. "Here, look at this." I reached inside my pocket and pulled out my early morning wages. "Five dinars - earned them just this morning – German tourists. Good people and very generous too."

"What did you do - take them to the moon?" He checked to make sure all the items were safely packed, zipped and buttoned all the holes shut and set the big monster on the rock table. Then he sat in front of it and centered it well on his back as he wore the shoulder straps one at a time and stood up.

"They liked my German," I said.

"Do you speak German too?"

"No."

He laughed and nudged me with his fist on the shoulder. "Let's go down and look at the Treasury," he said.

"You brought me all the way up here so we go back down?"

"What difference does it make to you, salamander."

"Lizard."

He giggled. "You make any ground seem flat and nullify the distance between any two points on my map."

"What kind of a map do you carry?"

"The accurate one that fits my calculations."

"And speed."

"You ...." He shook his head.

"You ain't seen nothing yet."

His eyebrows shot up. "You've even picked up American slang."

"I pick up anything that gets dropped around here, Jim," I said. He nodded happily, turned around, and began to climb down, one easy boulder at a time.

On the way down, I asked him what he needed me for, and he said that he had come to do some excavations in Petra and planned to stay for an entire year. He said he had hopes to discover something very exclusive.

"Nobody leaves here disappointed," I said. This made his eyes shine and match his greasy forehead. He said he was looking for a particular place that was mentioned in an old notebook that belonged to a wealthy French explorer who had worked his way through the Middle East in the early 1800's. "Actually," he said, "it is an ancient god I am seeking."

"Not to let you down, Jim, but the Nabatean deities are already discovered." I said.

"Not this one Lizard."

"How do you know he exists?"

"According to that explorer, there was a cave inside a cave. It was described as being in the bosom of a hill in a hidden city that exactly matched the description of Petra, and inside that cave, a spring once flowed on one side, and an obelisk rested in the middle of it. To the Nabateans, according to the explorer, this was the place where the deity of the sun, namely Dushara, and the deity of the rivers and springs, namely Allat, had met, and they were both worshiped as one, because, according to the old explorer's notebook, the place was one shrine, full of fine pottery and wonders, and it gave a sense of unity and oneness. The explorer also said that the god in the obelisk had stared at him with ancient eyes, and he had to back up and pay reverence before he could approach him again. To him it was just as much a religious experience as it was archeological. Then the explorer decided to seal both caves, the inner one and the outer one so that they would be inconspicuous to the eyes of intruders, for he had left the place intact. He had wanted to go home and return later with more equipment and man help to finish his exploration; however, there was no evidence of his return whatsoever."

I had seen archeologists and explorers look for all sorts of weird things, but to look for a god had to be the weirdest of all. I told Jim that, and he thanked me as if I were complimenting him for his weirdness. Then he said, "As soon as I settle down, I will start looking for the right place to excavate. How would you like to be my assistant, Lizard?"

"I would like that," I said. "The excavations this year seemed to have moved up north to the hills around Madaba, closer to Amman, the Capital. The Byzantine ruins are all over in that part of the country. My cousin went to work up there for the summer. He says there are German excavators, British, Americans, you name it. Everybody has his spot on those hills."

"I'm not looking for Byzantine ruins," said Jim. "We will have our own excavations right here in the bosom of the Nabatean land."

My stomach shrank from excitement, and my mouth jabbered like a broken faucet. "One thing you should watch for, Jim," I said as I skipped over the rocks and annoyed Jim some more with my careless steps. However, I could tell he was excited too. My speech matched my step, and I spoke to Jim's elongated smile and glistening forehead that shimmered in the sun. "The authorities are getting very strict these days," I said. "Too many foreigners have looted valuables from the ground and sold them to the museums in their own countries and became rich. The government is now very fussy about the exact reporting of all findings. Rarities are usually kept here in the local museums, and only common pieces are permitted to licensed archeologists to keep and take abroad."

"I'm all squared away with the authorities," said Jim. "I have my permit, and I signed my agreement about what I could keep and what I should turn in."

The man was legal, a bit crazy, but legitimate, and he offered me a summer job. What more would a person need, I thought. So what if we were looking for a god, an obelisk, or an orangutan. I couldn't wait to tell Aisheh, my friend, the shepherdess.

The monument, named the Treasury, towered above our heads. Its antae were plain and silent, yet in their quietness, they exhibited strength, the kind that held the ancient man and his victory over rock and sand. Two antae rested against the sides at the bottom of the carved cliff and supported the two lateral columns. The other pillars had decorated bases. All the capitals were carved with similar designs, but the parts that had been exposed to the elements were not as crisp and clear. The weather had worked on their carved tips and rounded the edges of each bulging tip, leaving enough of the design to tell rather than to show. The real intricate and well preserved designs were usually found tucked under a protecting cliff or surrounded by protecting walls that had sheltered them from the weather.

The capitals of the Treasury also carried an architrave, straight and plain. It received direct sunlight, which reflected the bright colors of sand rock above the pillars. Designs and arrangements of wreaths of laurel leaves and berries intertwined with flowers, suns and moons and rings of eternity decorated the frieze and the cornice. But the human images were mostly distorted. The bodies were readable in the rocks, but the faces had faded like the years, leaving their owners unknown, securing their mortality in the heavy boulders.

The monument continued up and up toward the sun. Its cornice did not mark the top of the building. Rather, it continued on, mounting the monolith with another set of pilasters, smaller in size than the bottom ones. Three sets of two pilasters rested against the cliff. Each set had its own entablature, an architrave, a frieze, and a cornice, and between each set, there was a base that carried another human figure, a small one, maimed by the years, and again, to the point that it had lost its identity. What was left of each figure reflected a jumble of light and shade, an abstract and a theme for each tourist to meditate upon and try to decide what was, is and will be of the human track two thousand years from now.

A group of tourists and their guide walked out of the Seeq and faced the Treasury. They were all on foot, so I did not fear the danger of facing my brothers and having to put up with a few words of insult. When the tourists finished their oohs and aahs, their tour guide resumed his jabbering. Jim and I quickly walked inside the Treasury so that Jim could see it before the crowds moved in.

"The first building of Petra is called the Treasury, because early discoverers thought it was full of gold," the tour guide rattled behind us. I looked at Jim and mimicked the guide as I finished his words for him, "Once, the archeologists managed to open the front door, they found out that the place was empty, and after debating between a temple and a tomb, most of them decided it must have been a temple."

"A lizard and a monkey," said Jim, "a monkey with a language."

"I told you; I pick up anything that gets dropped."

"Why don't you go get yourself a tour guide license too."

"No, thank you, Sir," I said firmly, making sure of a serious expression on my face. "I want to be more than that. I want to be an archeologist."

Jim studied my face for a moment as if to check the seriousness of my statement. Then he nodded, turned his face away and moved on. He fell silent again and made me wonder about what I said. We stepped into the large central room of the Treasury. This main room had three narrow steps in the center. They led to another small room which led to two others, one on each side. The side rooms were smaller yet big enough for three or four people to stand in them side by side.

"That's it," I said to Jim. "The place is vacant, and the Nabateans are gone."

"No, Lizard," he whispered. His eyes drifted off in a reverie as he talked. "It is not empty. It has colors. Look at all these colors." He touched the wall gently with the tips of his fingers as if it were a sacred shrine. "The weathered rock on the outside does not show this variety of bright sand colors."

"Jim," I said impatiently. "You want colors? I'll show you colors."

"Where?"

"I have a cave, a hiding place, which I discovered a while back. I use it as a second home whenever I want to be away from everybody. No one else had set foot in it yet since the Nabateans, except for my friend Aisheh, of course. She's a shepherdess. The cave has more colors than you can name. It's been well protected from the weather. I'll take you up there some day, and you'll see for yourself."

Jim did not seem interested in my jabbering anymore. I don't think he heard much of my last proclamation. He continued to live his dream until the voices of the crowds outside came in louder and indicated that these people were on their way in. We stepped outside the Treasury and listened to the tour guide for a moment as he and his tourists crowded themselves between the pillars. "The Nabatean Civilization had confused the archeologists, because it was centered between the biggest powers of the ancient world, the Persian Empire and the Roman Empire, and later, the Byzantine Empire, yet it belonged to none of them," the tour guide went on. "The information most archeologists had agreed upon resulted in a compound culture that had its own distinctive characteristics which separated the Nabatean civilization from the other ancient civilizations. These unique characteristics were especially reflected in the matchless Nabatean pottery." The lecture went on and on. I wanted to slip by and move away, but Jim stood there and listened. "For communication," the guide continued, "the Nabateans had used the Aramaic language, a very close relative of the Arabic language. They practiced a Semitic religion, and its architecture had combined the Greek, Roman art and added to it the Nabatean art, a distinctive characteristic, as you can see." He pointed to the facade of the Treasury. "The Nabatean kings and their subjects had Semitic names like Hareth, Malek, Obada and Jamila..."

Jim finally lost interest, and the guide's voice faded away as we headed down the road toward the dry river bed.

"Do you know that every one of the Nabatean names mentioned by the guide has a meaning in the Arabic language?" I asked Jim.

"Like what?"

"Like Obada," I said. "It means adoration; Hareth means the man who plows the land; Malek means owner, and Jamila," I paused and smiled at Jim. "Jamila is a woman's name. It means pretty." Then I waited for the old man to make a guess. But, after a moment of silence, I added, "Jamila is my mother's name."

"Jamila," he murmured.

The dry river bed interrupted our path, and before we turned to go left, I pointed out to Jim the location of my cave, way up near the top of the hill on the right side of the city with no hint of hope for a path or any passage way whatsoever. Jim said the cave looked worse than a crow's nest, and that only lizards could climb up there.

"There's a way, Jim," I said emphatically. "Easier than you think."

"For a lizard, there is a way everywhere," said Jim without looking at me. He shook his head and continued down the road watching the ground in front of him. When we arrived at the refreshment booth, he bought us each a bottle of orange soda, and we sat down under the shade of a poplar tree and drank quietly for a while.

"Jim," I said finally, breaking the silence and disturbing his day dream again.

"What?"

"I've got to tell you this true story. It's short; don't worry. It helps me prove to you that most of the domestic creatures know how to find their way around here easily enough, not only lizards, and if you live here long enough, you'll discover these easy ways too. You'll be able to climb all the way up to my cave like a salamander."

"I thought it was a lizard."

"Glad you caught on."

Jim nudged me. "I believe you, Lizard," he mumbled, maintaining his dream. His eyes focused on a boulder in front of us, and his limbs were still. He looked as if he had joined the statues of Petra, like a freshly positioned statue that had no chance to weather yet like the rest of them. I thought he had meant for me to be quiet again, so I did. But then he turned his sweaty head toward me and said, "Go ahead. Tell your true story."

"I don't have to."

Chapter 4

"Go ahead. I'm going to hear it anyway, at one point or another."

"It's about the engineers who came to build the main road that connected the desert highway with Wadi Moussa. They had come to eat at the Guest House. It was much smaller back then." Jim noticed that I spoke with my hands, and he seemed amused. "On their way there, these engineers met with one of the villagers who happened to be walking his donkey home," I continued, "The peasant noticed the big commotion the professionals were making, and he saw them holding their maps, tools and all sorts of equipment. So he stopped to asked them what the fuss was all about, and they told him that they were engineers and that they were looking for the best place to build a road through this rocky ground. 'Easy,' said the villager.' Why, you schooled people, you always make a big commotion over nothing.' When the engineers asked him what he meant, he said, 'Just send the donkey ahead of you. He'll show you where the best road is, and then all you'll have to do is pave it.' But the engineers asked him what they should do if they had no donkey. The villager scratched his head for a moment and said, 'I guess, in that case, you'd just have to call the engineers.'"

Jim laughed until he was wet all over. He pulled his handkerchief and wiped the sweat and tears that streamed down his face and blew his nose several times. Then he tucked his handkerchief in his pocket and stood up.

"Let's go," he said. "I need to get this load off my shoulders."

We ambled alongside the dry river bed until we stood below Jim's cave. Then we swung around toward the small hill and climbed a few easy steps to his new home. He had rented the cave from the booth owner who also had a huge room with shower facilities located between Jim's cave and the booth on the side of the hill. The large room and showers were used by those who wanted to camp within the ancient city limits, and they were the only facilities available in Petra, past the Seeq.

When we walked in, Jim unloaded his back and straightened up his bones with a few stretching exercises. His hands reached for the roof, and his upper body twisted and turned, first to the right and then to the left. Then he reached his toes with the tips of his fingers and stayed there for a while as if he were locked in that position. Just before I opened my mouth to ask if he were okay, he eased himself up again. "I have a few more loads to bring from the Guest House," he said. "Then I'll have all my belongings down here in this cave, my home sweet home," he sang the home sweet home portion of his sentence.

"I'll help you," I said.

"Thank you. I believe I'm going to need all the help I can get."

We went back to the booth again and had lunch. Then we walked back down the road and up the Seeq to get the rest of his possessions. Tourists walked by at a steady pace. We met three organized groups with their tour guides. Many stray couples and smaller groups of three or four were also sauntering up and down the path. Two of my brothers appeared like ghosts before me. They were walking the horses and their riders through the path. To my relief, they ignored me and focused their attention on their company, and, at that point, I believed, they had given up on me, which was the best thing to do for all parties concerned.

It felt good in the shade of the Seeq, and the rock walls that towered and bulged here and there on each side provided enough humidity to ease the dryness in the air. Jim stopped and rested in the shade while I drew circles around him. Two men cleared the bend and became visible to us.

Chapter 4

We had heard them coming, long before we saw them. They spoke steadily with frivolity and zest. They spoke with their hands and waved them in the air as far as they could reach. I recognized their language.

"Those are Italians," I said to Jim.

"How do you know," he snorted. "Now I suppose you're going to tell me you speak Italian."

"Watch this," I whispered and leaned against the water canal. "Vide 'o mare quant'é bello," I sang as nicely and as loud as my voice could project, "Spira tantu sentimento. Comme tu a chi tiene mente." The two men dropped silent. Their hands froze in mid air, and the two heads turned around and looked at me. I thought their necks were going to squeak or click, for they looked as stiff as rusty door hinges. Their mouths were dropped open and their chins hung down like filled pouches. They were both handsome looking chaps in khaki shorts and plaid shirts. The fronts of their shirts were half unbuttoned, and they exposed a mass of dark hair on each chest. One of them had a funny hat on, a hybrid, somewhere between an American cowboy hat and a French casquette. I guess that must have made it Italian.

"Parlate italiano?" asked the one with the funny hat.

"No," I said. "An Italian friend of mine taught me some old folk songs."

"You pronounce the words well and sing well too."

"Thank you."

"Are you from here?"

"I'm from the village, up by the the Guest House."

"Do you, by any chance, know if a person can get something to drink in Petra?" He pointed to the end of the Seeq. "We forgot to bring something to drink, and we were debating whether to go back and get some or not."

"There's a booth about two kilometers past the path," I said. "When you clear the Seeq, turn right on the main road and go straight until you get to the dry riverbed and then turn left. You'll find the booth straight ahead. You cannot miss it. It will have all the drinks you need. It stays open till late afternoon."

"Thank you."

"Who was your Italian friend?" asked the other man as they began to walk again. They expected me to walk with them, so I left Jim resting with the same wide range grin on his face and walked with the Italians for a while. They talked steadily, spoke with their hands and rolled their R's worse than I did. My head rattled by the time I managed to escape from them. They asked questions and had me sing more Italian songs and sang with me until I felt embarrassed. People stared at us as if we had just finished a carafe of Arak, the rather powerful Jordanian alcoholic drink, straight, undiluted. By the time I got back to Jim, he was already walking up the Seeq again.

"You provide ample entertainment in this place," said Jim. "I shall need no television."

"Hey. Look at this," I said and waved a new dinar bill in front of him. "Italian generosity this time. Not too bad – heh?"

"That is worth three dollars. What did you do this time?"

"Gave a few directions here and there."

"Gave a few directions here and there," he mimicked. "That's all?"

"And charmed them to death."

"That, I believe, Lizard Boy," he said. "That I believe."

Chapter 5

The Guest House, being located at the mouth of the historical, Nabatean home, served as a comfortable orientation place for those who sought to experience the ancient city of Petra. The term hotel or motel or guest house or any other modern expression of such a place would not quite fit. It was rather a facility that combined the lifestyle of the cave-man with the modern man. The building, or so to speak, occupied the east side of an entire rocky cliff that towered above the village, just before the Seeq. The cave-man, or the guests who chose to be cave people, experienced the lower layers of the facility while the modern man delighted in the comfort of the top portion of the building. The cave-man, below, had nothing; the modern man, above, had everything, electricity, water, bathrooms, heat in winter, air conditioning in summer, room service and even, sometimes, live night entertainment. The hierarchy came in natural rather than intentional, for the back walls of the entire facility belonged to the hill. The caves below and the modern rooms above were terraced on the side of the hill like a series of daylight basements, one above the other. The cliff had been carved in easy stair–like steps, so that the guests could roam up and down and in between the terraces and the restaurant which was on the main street level.

The lower layers of the facility had a set of caverns which the owners used to rent out for hitchhikers, back packers, and those who intended to experience the life of a caveman. These caverns had no modern conveniences whatsoever, and the rent never exceeded half a dinar per night, adequately cheap for an empty cave. Each renter had to supply his/her own needs, including a sleeping bag, a pillow and perhaps a fairly sizable stick to kill a snake or a rat, just in case. Although the restaurant workers cleaned up the caves and drove out all the intruding pests every day, "one never knows," the owner used to say. Since the caves had no doors, they continued to welcome any critter looking for a place to spend the night.

Jim had kept his possessions temporarily in one of the caverns. He had two huge bundles wrapped in heavy plastic. I told him I knew someone in the village who might lend us a mule for the rest of the day , so we could carry everything to Petra in one load. "That's how the owner of the booth carries his stock every day through the path," I said to Jim. "He even has his own mule."

"He carries all the supplies on a mule?" asked Jim. His eyes shrank as he frowned. I frowned too at his dullness.

"What do you think, Jim? Cars can't go through the Seeq very easily, and who's going to carry all the pop and sandwiches all the way to the booth on his back?"

He was silent for a moment, and I could tell he had never had a mule experience in his life before. "How much do you think your friend would charge for the mule?" he finally asked.

"Much less than a taxi driver would charge you."

"He'd better. Taxi drivers ripped me off in the Capital."

Chapter 5

"I'll bargain for you. Don't worry. Besides, if a mule owner ripped you off in the village, it would be more like a fair deal. Villagers are usually happy with much less. But I'll bargain for you. I promise. I'll find you a good deal."

"I guess I just have to trust you, lizard."

"You'd better. If you want me to work for you."

He smiled, shook his head and shooed me off with his hands. "Off with you," he said. "Go get the darn mule. I'll wait for you up at the restaurant. I'm due for a cup of coffee anyway."

Fifteen minutes later, I came back with the mule and its owner, Omar, who convinced me that the mule just might not cooperate over the rocks without him.

At the restaurant, Jim bought us each a bottle of soda pop to drink while he finished his small cup of Turkish coffee. The restaurant occupied the center of the Guest House facility. However, its was not a modern, built–in room, added on to the lower caves like the boarding rooms above. It was just another natural but huge cave, much bigger than the caves below, and it occupied a good portion of the east side of the hill. The Department of Tourism had cleverly converted it into a unique restaurant.

All around the main restaurant–cave, there were little openings that led to smaller caves and were used as side rooms with more tables and chairs. In the center of the back wall, a large opening faced the guests. It led to a larger cave that was converted into a modern kitchen. A large bar separated the kitchen from the eating area. The furniture was made of wood, carved in the old Mid-Eastern style. The entire restaurant maintained a traditional Mid-Eastern atmosphere with its decor. There were shelves with dolls dressed up in traditional clothes; brass coffee pots with long spouts decorated each table, and above the tables there were chandeliers with multi-colored glass that threw abstract reflections on the cave walls.

"Is this the place you told me you eat at when you make money?" asked Jim. He drank his coffee wrong, and I began to feel sorry for him. He had consumed the Turkish coffee clear to the bottom of the cup, grounds and all. His lips gathered to collect the sediments from the sides of his mouth, and then he didn't know what to do with them. His lips were stuck in a quacking position. He looked like a duck in pain, perhaps ready to lay an egg or two.

"Jim," I said. "Not to change the subject, but the Turkish coffee, being finely ground like flour and boiled, it leaves dregs at the bottom of the cup, and you're supposed to drink it only till you see the grounds at the bottom of the cup and stop."

"Now you're telling me," he said as he struggled to swallow the last of the silty grounds. He squeezed the last portion down his throat, while his lips and his tongue kept busy coming and going, cleaning all the sediments out of the corners of his mouth and shoving them down his throat. Then he opened his tight lips with a thud of relief. I handed him my glass of water and watched him drink it all down. "Thank God the water has no grounds at the bottom," he said.

"About the restaurant," I continued, ignoring his comment. "No. This is not where I eat when I make money. This place belongs to tourists and those who do not know any better, like the wealthy snobs of our village. I can't afford it, Jim. But, up in the village, there is Abu-Mustafa's, not nearly as fancy, in fact, not fancy at all. Americans would call it a hole in the wall, which is equivalent to the villagers' expression, a scorpion's bladder." Jim's laughter interrupted me. The man could laugh and make everybody laugh at his laughter and forget the joke. He would start out with a low pitch, just loud enough for everybody to hear, and then he would gradually change it into a high pitch, and if he couldn't control it by then, it would go back to the low pitch again and keep making the round until he would finally settle down.

"But the food is great," I continued. "You ought to go there sometime. And the price is right too. He serves all local foods, nothing imported."

Omar writhed in his seat. He was not used to strangers, nor was he comfortable in fancy restaurants. "We'd better get the mule on the road," he said. "It is going to take us a good share of the afternoon to get him there and back."

The mule had two huge pouches on each side of the saddle. But Jim's bundles were still much too big to fit in the pouches, so we just hooked them on the edges the best we could and balanced them so that the weight was dispersed evenly, and then we tied them around the mule's belly with a rope. The mule tried to rebel, but Omar kept talking to him and bribing him with treats from the large pockets on the sides of his baggy jacket. Jim was impressed, until we got to the Seeq.

We ambled down the road toward the Seeq, first Omar, then the mule, then Jim on one side, toward the rear end of the mule, and I on the other. The spirits were in harmony and the objects in balance. An ethereal atmosphere surrounded the scene, and I felt like the prophet ascending to heaven with good company, even though we were descending at the moment toward the path. Jim hummed a familiar tune. I had heard it from many tourists. Some of them even had words to go with it, something like, "She'll be coming round the mountain when she comes." I never knew who in the heck she was. Nobody told me. It could have been the mule for all I cared.

Omar led the way in silence until we arrived at the mouth of the Seeq. Then, suddenly, a very strange happening surfaced ominously. At the sight of the rocky path, the mule made a one hundred eighty degree turn. Jim and I made ample room for him. And then he stopped; the mule did. His rear end faced the path, and his face motioned to the village in perpendicular actions.

"Has this mule ever been through the path before?" asked Jim. I translated the question to Omar, and he said no. The mule had strictly been used to haul supplies from the fields to the village. It had never experienced the rocky roads before.

The look on Jim's face demanded to be recorded in history. He simply became expressionless, not mad, not happy, not anything that I could tell. His eyebrows froze in place; his lips tightened up again but left no particular expression on the face; his glasses slid down his greasy nose so that his distorted eyes became more so, and I couldn't see the pupils at all. Omar was horrified. He tried to talk things over with the mule to see if he would at least turn around and face the right direction, but the mule wouldn't respond. Neither would Jim. Then I took a turn and tried to reason with the beast and told him to behave himself and save my face in front of the guest, just this once, but my attempts also failed. After debating over the odds, Omar and I decided to work on the mule, and if, after a while, we convinced him to budge, Jim might even follow.

Omar talked as he pushed and pulled and shoved. I wasn't used to mule talk that much, but I mimicked Omar carefully so as not to upset the animal and have him take off with the possessions of the already angry old man.

"Hirrrrr ta' Hirrrr ta'," said Omar nicely as he patted the beast.

CHAPTER 5

"Hirrr ta' – Hirrr ta'," I repeated. These sounds meant something like, "come on now, roll it – please." I discovered that the rolled R's had some input in the forward movement. We rolled R's for that stubborn mule until my tongue tingled.

Omar slipped some treats in the mule's mouth between hirrr ta's and switched to baby talk every once in a while. "Now this one is for Omar," he begged and pulled. "And this one is for Raji. Hirrr ta' now–Hirrr ta' now." He tried to pull again. It didn't work. "And this one is for that old man who's as angry as you are." The mule nodded, and we both laughed.

"Let me try one," I said. Omar gave me a lump of crushed carob, glued together with a sweet syrup made of wild apples called Dibbiss. I reached the mule's mouth and begged and pleaded and cursed his sister's honor in a very nice tone. He grunted and closed his eyes.

We gave treats and begged for all the relatives, friends and foes until the mule finally turned around and faced the blessed path, but he wouldn't take one step. His hoofs rested in peace between the rocks as if they were part of the road. So we started all over again. Omar talked, and I talked, and we pulled and tugged and even cleared some of the sharp looking rocks out of the mule's way. Then Omar began to mumble some prayers from the Koran, and then we both prayed and cussed in a nice tone so that the mule would think it were a word of praise, until we finally convinced him to give it a try and move forward, carefully, one step at a time.

Half an hour later, Omar, the mule, Jim, and I were slowly walking down the Seeq in somewhat harmony and balance. However, the equilibrium we once sensed between all four of us had disappeared to no return. The atmosphere lost its ethereal aura. My hands and my shoulders were aching from pushing and pulling. Omar's tongue was still confused between sweet talk and cussing. But I had to hand it to him. The man did everything but kiss the mule's hoofs to make him go again. Jim said nothing the rest of the way. I couldn't tell whether he was praying or humming a war song in his mind. Every once in a while the mule would let out a strange sound that would scare the devil out of Omar and me. We would look at each other and get ready to work again. But the mule kept his pace, and we finally decided that the noise that came out of him every now and then meant a curse in mule language.

"Suppose he is cursing you, Jim, or his fate," I asked Omar. But he was in no mood for a joke. He must have been praying. I had known him as a very pious man. He feared God and the Prophet and believed in their miracles.

The mule grunted again. "You can work on cleaning up his language after you get back," I said, trying to change the mood, but Omar didn't laugh. His face never relaxed until he saw the light at the end of the Seeq.

We made it. We all made it, even Jim.

Once we cleared the Seeq and turned on the wide, cleared road that crossed the middle of Petra, we switched to a nimble step to match the mule's. We all pranced happily on the easy road. But by the time we arrived at Jim's cave, we had spent three hours on the road. Jim paid Omar and sent him and his mule back to the village, and then he turned to me.

"Unless you have a gun," I said to Jim. "I can outrun you." His serious look began to give way to a faint smile, then a giggle, and then he burst into laughter – low pitch, high pitch again. He pulled his wallet from his back pocket again and opened it. The picture of the child with the bubble gum inflated on his mouth peeked between Jim's fingers. I was tempted to ask him the who, what, why, and where questions, but then I decided to wait for better times. Also, although I had sensed a comfortable camaraderie between us, I thought he still knew nothing about me, and therefore, there was no reason for me to inquire about him at that point.

He handed me two bills of one dinar each. "Here," he said. "This is an advance on your salary. I'll pay you ten dinars a month for your help."

"Thanks Jim," I said as I took the money. "I really didn't expect to have a regular salary." My spine tingled. I never worked for a salary before. The first person that came to my mind was my mother. I would share the money with her. She would be proud. But I wondered what would my brothers say, now that I could prove to them that I was able to earn money – my own way.

"If you plan to go to college some day, you'd better start saving your dimes and nickels, young man," said Jim. He lifted his chin up and looked at me with pride. "You don't have to come in the morning," he said. "I'll be doing some housekeeping around here. But you can come in the afternoon, and maybe we'll get some plans going."

When I reached the foot of the hill, I looked back at Jim's cave and noticed a huge wooden door resting on the left side of his cave. It had large hinges and a matching bolt. In the center of the door, toward the top half, there was a small window with a screen. The booth owner had had it nicely fixed so that it would be livable, unlike the caves below the Guest House, up by the village. There, the caves had no doors or any hint of development.

There was noise coming from the showers and the bathrooms on the hill above Jim's cave. Campers were spending the night there, and Jim would have to share the facilities with them.

A few minutes later, I saw Jim reaching for the door and closing it. I sat down on a boulder by the side of the road and watched the tiny screen on Jim's door for a while. When a lamp light flickered through the window, I stood up and left.

On my way home, I saw Omar and the mule, still walking up the Seeq. They hadn't progressed much yet, and this time, Omar's face sagged and matched the mule's. I asked my friend what was the matter with him, and he said he had never been embarrassed by his mule before, and he would never bring that beast down the Seeq ever again. I told him not to worry.

"Jim is fine," I said. "Really, he's not mad at you or anything."

"I will never bring that mule down the Seeq again," he repeated.

"Give him another chance with a lighter cargo," I said. "He might even appreciate that. The poor thing had a killer load today."

"I will never bring that mule down the Seeq again."

Omar walked silently in melancholy. He had been humiliated by the mule which he considered a faithful companion. There was nothing I could do to cheer him up. He just continued to follow the same rhythm which the mule's hoofs produced over the rocks. I walked with him for a while to reassure him that things were okay. I even tried to talk to him again, but he was in no mood to talk. Every once in a while, the mule's hoofs would send a small rock flying off ahead of us or to the side, and Omar would kick one to match it. Soon I gave up on the man and his monster, zoomed past them, and ran home, past the horses, the Guest House, the returning tourists, their jabbering tour guides and the whole commotion that marked the end of the day. Tomorrow, I will be an archeologist, I mumbled excitedly.

Abu-Zeid, the owner of the Guest House waited for me up the road. I saw his silhouette in the distance and quickly hid in the middle of a returning crowd, slipped sideways and disappeared in the village.

Chapter 6

Throughout the centuries, the uniformed figures continued to march down the colonnade of Petra, entering and exiting the monumental gate in step. Nabatean army men had once paraded through to honor the visit of an emperor or a king. Two thousand years later, herds of fat-tail sheep, called Awassi sheep, paraded through the ruins, all in uniform, off-white in color, monotonous in tone. They followed a bellwether for a captain. Their fat, round tails wobbled back and forth and bounced off their hind legs as they marched. Each had its head tucked in below the tail of the sheep in front for protection from the beating sun and for easy following.

Every once in a while, a herd of black goats would replace the sheep and provide contrast to the pale sandy colors of cobblestone roads and towering ruins. The goats, however, were more adventurous. They wouldn't just follow and keep their heads low. Rather, they would go astray every once in a while and check out the scattered caves all around and lead the shepherds to hidden human secrets from centuries behind. Sometimes, the secrets hid in pieces of pottery which the ancients had used once upon a time to drink or eat out of and entertain their guests. Other times, the secrets lay in dug out coins that once had purchased spices from Yemen, silk from China, ivory from India, Henna from Damascus, glass and fragrance from Lebanon, pearl from the Arabian Gulf, porcelain from Rome, and gold, silver, bay leaves and sesame oil from the surroundings of Petra. But after two thousand years, these coins had grown to purchase more than food and silks and kitchenware from exotic places - much more. That money had brought forward high interest from the earth and the history it had recorded over the years.

When the pieces of pottery, clay, sculpture and coins were identified and read, they told stories about the times when the caravans crossed the ancient world all the way from China to Europe. They would pass through the Middle East and make loops around the Arabian desert to avoid its scorching hot core and to trade with the inhabitants of its rich surroundings.

One of these loops penetrated Petra and then continued on north to the Syrian ports on the Mediterranean. The dry river beds and reservoirs in Petra proved that the land had possessed an abundance of water at the time to quench the thirst of merchants and their camels. It also provided a safe shelter, good food and kind people to trade goods and mingle with. These people would also order valuables from far away places to enhance their standards of living, and the merchants would bring the ordered merchandise with them on their next trip. Roman, Persian, local Nabatean and many other coins had been identified, labeled and displayed in the local museums. Unfortunately, many coins as well as other pieces of antiquity were smuggled out of the country and were displayed in many museums around the world.

"Dishes from China, coffee from Ceylon, Turkish coffee cups made in France, and Swiss cheese, purchased at the local grocery store in Wadi Moussa," said Jim when I stopped by to see him the next morning. He had finished his breakfast and read all the labels on his table service and studied the origin of his food and the containers it had come in. "Funny we're still doing the same thing the Nabateans did two thousand years ago," he declared.

"Except for the camels, Jim; they all retired some time ago. Cars, semi trucks and airplanes took their place."

"That's right. How come I haven't seen any camels yet?"

"You can ride one at the tourist resort down by the beach in Aqaba if you wish. But I wouldn't do it if I were you."

"Why not?"

"I'd feel stupid riding a camel around a resort. It seems so worthless. The poor beast just lost its true value; it has this helpless look on its face, just like the city tour guides."

"Is that all they do with camels anymore - have them give rides to tourists?"

"They also raise them for races. They race them just like horses at the Royal Racing Club."

"Interesting."

"Here - I brought you something more interesting," I said. "Actually, I brought it for your lunch, but it is best to try it when it is still warm." I pulled two loaves of bread out of my bag and handed them to him. They were round and had indentations where the dough had lain on the hot rocks. "Fresh village bread, baked this morning in the taboon."

"Taboo?" he asked. The knot between his eyebrows aimed straight at my face.

"No, Jim. It's Taboonnnn," I scolded and stressed the consonant at the end of the word so that he could hear it well. "It's a hot rock oven we, uncivilized villagers, use to bake everything. I felt sorry for you when I saw you eat the bread that came to the Guest House from Amman."

"What's wrong with it?"

"You can't even chew it like you ought to do with bread. It dissolves in your mouth like tasteless mush."

Jim broke a piece of the bread and took a bite. "Good bread," he said and chewed well to my satisfaction. "What else do you have to show me?" He looked at the notebook that rested under my arm.

The man had become dependent on me, just like the Guest House owner. These people expected me to produce news and challenges to make their life in the middle of nowhere more exciting. I have to admit, I enjoyed playing this game with them to a certain extent. After all, I was only Lizard Boy who sought just as much entertainment out of them as they did out of me.

"This is for you," I said and handed him the notebook. It is my translations of some of the shepherds' songs you've been hearing around you every day. I thought you might be interested."

Jim opened the notebook and read the first stanza of the first song. He read with sincerity and passion, and I could tell he liked poetry, for even my crude translations sounded good out of his mouth. He read nicely, almost like chanting:

"Mother, I saw the moon under our roof,
while its place in the sky stood vacant.
O Lord, forgive me, for I have strayed;
it must be love - too much love."

"It's supposed to rhyme, Jim, but I couldn't make it and keep the meaning straight."

"That's okay, Lizard. Good poetry is not supposed to rhyme, anymore."

"But the shepherds' songs have to. Otherwise, the melody will die. The melody is just as important as the words; it is set for a rhyming verse."

"Then I promise you I won't sing it in English. I'll try to learn the Arabic words for it."

Chapter 6

"You won't sing it in Arabic either, Jim."

"Why not?"

"You'll kill the language. You can't even pronounce *good morning* without diluting the sounds silly. The shepherds will be humiliated."

"You know, Lizard, you make my life so difficult sometimes. You just have absolutely no confidence in me."

"In you, yes. In your Arabic, no, and I can't let you intimidate the shepherds. They're my best friends, and if you stick around long enough, they'll be yours too. Their company is comforting and essential for the well being of Petra and Wadi Moussa."

Jim listened while I told him about the shepherds. He read my notebook faithfully and recited from memory some English verses that, to him, expressed the same feelings and portrayed them in different but compatible images. He said the shepherds now meant something to him, more than peasants who crossed his path every day on their way to the hills.

The shepherds, some with the help of their goats, had gathered items, like pieces of pottery and weapons that dated as far back as the early iron age and, in the past, they sold them to tourists for trifles, enough to buy them plastic shoes to cover their bare feet and thin silver jewelry to rattle around their wrists and dangle down their ears. But the shepherds were happy, as long as they had their hills and valleys to roam with their sheep and goats and reed pipes that brought music to the stillness of the ruins and inspired a special kind of poetry that belonged only to shepherds and villagers of the semi arid zones.

There was a time, however, when city poets paid visits to the shepherds and recorded poetry from their mouths. Then the city poets published these poems under their own names and became famous. They won national and international prizes, until more city poets discovered those who had beat them to the rich poetry that had no roof to confine it nor pressure to smear up its images. The scandals grew until the shepherds' names finally found their way to the books. But the shepherds didn't care one way or the other. They were happy to give, as long as they continued to have their hills and valleys to roam.

Then the government used the shepherds to help its employees seize those who came to loot the land. They were reported to the police and government representatives. And the shepherds learned the value of their antique findings and began to turn these valuables in to the government and get paid for their services. With that, they enriched the local museums and the Department of Archeology at the local university. So the shepherds became invaluable assets, simple, uncorrupted beings. Jim called them "the last of the human dignity," but he also said that life was changing fast in this part of the world. He said the day would soon come, and the hills and the valleys would have no shepherds and all the caves would be converted to condominiums. His talk frightened me, and I prayed not to live to see that day, for it was to Aisheh, the shepherdess, that I owed my good fortune.

I used to follow Aisheh up the hill so I could listen to her sing. Then she would tell me about places she had discovered with her goats - places, no man had burdened for thousands of years. And one day, Aisheh led me to my cave. That was the year before I met Jim.

One of the goats had continued to climb up the steep rocky hill, ignoring the hollering of the shepherdess. It marched on with a steady, determined foot, until it reached a few weeds that had grown around the mouth of a cave, mostly buried in dirt and dry brush. Aisheh scolded the goat and ordered it back again, but the goat gave its owner a haughty look and a pouting sound. It kicked and snorted and continued to munch on weeds.

"Halimeh has a mind of her own," said Aisheh.

"Halimeh?" I asked.

"Yes. That goat up there. She's Halimeh."

"Halimeh," I muttered. It meant patience, and it was a strange name for a goat.

"She taught me how to be patient," said Aisheh, "and there is something about that goat's eyes I still have to figure out. I don't know what it could be, but it makes her give you such a peculiar look as if she knows more than you do. Sometimes I think of it as the gleam of wisdom; other times, I get the feeling it is just a sign of eccentricity."

Each of the goats knew its name and responded immediately when called by their shepherdess, all but Halimeh, of course. Most shepherds I knew, however, gave their sheep and goats names more suitable for animals like Shaggy, Greasy, Bony, Cross-eyed, etc. Sometimes, the animals were given humorous, meaningless names with funny sounds like Fannouneh, Hannouneh, and Daloanah, etc. But Aisheh gave her goats names that carried the characteristics of God–like Wisdom, Patience, Justice Compassion, etc. She said all the she had to do was look at the goat's eyes, and the name would come to her, for, to Aisheh, the eyes of man and beast had the power to reveal the secrets of the hidden soul and were better tools of communication than sound. She looked the animals straight in the eyes when she talked to them, and they obeyed, except for Halimeh, of course.

"Halimeh is a goat with piercing eyes," Aisheh continued. "She must be an archeologist in a second life, because all she does is separate herself from the herd to excavate around remote weeds and dig up clumps of small rocks and dirt as if searching for more beneath the surface of the earth."

"Perhaps an archeologist who had never been able to discover anything in his first life," I said. "Don't let her miss a chance now. She might lead to hidden treasures."

"Oh, I won't. Even if I try, she won't miss a chance to endeavor. In fact, she may have accomplished her mission already." She giggled and shook her head like a happy mother whose child had just taken a few steps for the first time on his own.

"She did?" I asked. The woman never had to say much to wake up my curiosity. She always laid out half statements and waited to entice the devil inside me.

Aisheh laughed happily and sat on a small boulder. She supported her chin with the heels of her hand. Her elbows rested just above the knees, and her long black dress flared and dropped carelessly on the ground all around. She let the goats roam the hill while her eyes gazed at the distance. I sat down on a lower rock and faced her.

"There is a cave up where Halimeh is grazing right now," she said. "We ought to check it out. I could hardly see its mouth, for it is mostly covered with small rocks, dirt, and grass, but it shouldn't be difficult to dig open. Loose dirt must have slid and covered it at one time, and the grass hid it completely until Halimeh munched on enough weeds, pulled their roots out with clumps of dirt and exposed a little hole, just enough for me to peek through and see the cave."

"Was there anything in it?" I asked. She looked at me with dark penetrating eyes like broad almonds, and eyelashes, so long, isolated and as scarce as the rarest piece of antiquity ever found. I knew what she had meant when she accused her goat of having piercing eyes.

Chapter 6

"I don't know," she said. "I couldn't see much. It is too dark. We'd have to dig out much more dirt to uncover the mouth enough to see the inside. We might even need a flashlight or two."

"Did you leave the hole uncovered?"

"No. I rolled a rock and pushed it tightly against it. I was afraid to leave it open. You know, in case there is something inside - after all these years. The thing is," she continued after a short pause, "I am not interested in this kind of work anymore. If you wish to pursue this cave, it is all yours, Raji." She spoke with remote eyes that went far beyond comprehension. There was sudden sadness in her voice as if she had discovered antiquities in her own heart - long buried antiques. Her face sobered, and she was quiet. Then she took a deep breath, closed her eyes and let silence take over for a while. The goats made some noise every now and then, but their sound became part of the silence she seemed to be seeking.

I left her to her dream and followed the goat up the cliff where she was munching. The tall weeds around the boulder indicated a thick layer of soil underneath. A mud slide must have covered the mouth of the cave. I stood within two meters of the goat and hoped it would retreat enough so I could get close to the hole and check it out. But the goat ignored my existence and continued to enjoy her meal.

"Hirrrrr," I shooed and motioned to the goat to move down. But she gave me the same look her owner did a few minutes ago and continued on with her endeavor. She ate leisurely and gazed at the sky every now and then. Aisheh's laughter behind me filled the air. She had followed me up the cliff, lifting her dress enough to expose bright orange plastic shoes and skinny ankles. When the goat saw Aisheh coming, she snorted and moved down toward the herd. I stood there, humiliated, but Aisheh continued on toward the boulder and began to pull the weeds and throw them down to the goats.

We spent the entire afternoon pulling weeds to loosen the dirt beneath it. We dug with our hands, with sticks, with some sharp rocks and whatever else we could find and identify as a helping tool. Suddenly, Aisheh looked at the horizon and hurried to collect her goats.

"I've got to leave," she said frantically. "My father will be waiting for me. I'm late. Perhaps we can finish tomorrow." Her plastic soles tapped the boulders like loose rock, sliding down the hill.

"Blame it on Halimeh," I shouted after her. "Tell your father his stubborn goat finally put her hoof down."

"I'll see you tomorrow." Her voice echoed. She was already half way to the valley.

"I'll bring some tools," I yelled again, but she didn't hear me. She scampered with her herd all the way down the hill. She hollered, and the goats responded like a chorus and gathered up around her. They crossed the ruins in the valley and disappeared around the bend. I watched Aisheh until she was gone. Then I looked at my hands, still full of weeds and dirt clumps. I threw everything on the ground, shook some of the dirt off my hands and clothes and walked down to where we were sitting and sat down again, watching her dust. It lingered like the cloud of a jet plane on a still day.

She had finished sixth grade - compulsory education, but she too had a boss at home to impede her aspirations. This time it was not a big brother but an old father. Being a peasant woman, she could not rebel like I did; however, being Aisheh, she had let everybody know of her true wishes and never cared about the gossip of the village. I used to bring my books up the hill for her to read every chance I had, and she would dive at them ferociously and make me envious. The woman had more brains than I and all my classmates put together. It reached the point where she would figure out math problems long before I did and even explain them to me and make me piss vinegar from jealousy. She would talk about history and remember dates and events and names I hated to study. In times like these, I wanted her to be a shepherdess and nothing more, but I knew she was more whether I liked it or not; she was much more, and I liked it, the same way I liked my freedom and the ruins and the sunset and the quietness of the old city at dusk.

What made Petra a unique place, very different from the rest of the world was not only its ruins but the fact that the old city filled up with people every day and emptied out every evening. People came with all their modern conveniences - all except wheels. They crossed the only path to this place on foot or horseback and hauled in everything they needed for the day every morning at dawn, and they hauled everything back out to the real world at dusk, and the city became abandoned, and the spirits of its ancients were set free. Darkness mixed with silence and bulging, monumental rocks and towering pillars and pilasters and statues of people, maimed by the years, carved in sand rocks and colors: reds, yellows, blues, greens blended with a touch of moonlight and a mass of darkness had always left shadows: small shadows, tall shadows, shapeless shadows everywhere.

We too came to the city every morning, Aisheh and I. It took us four days to uncover the mouth of the cave. Every day, we would carry a load of tools, wood, food, flashlights and whatever we could gather up there to help facilitate the excavations. I had weaseled some freight lumber and nails out of the Guest House manager. He used to have me run errands for him every once in a while, and then he would pay me in goods, food and whatever I happened to need at the time.

I nailed the pieces of wood together and made a door for the cave. We still had to roll a rock behind it to secure it shut and camouflage it, for we were worried about it getting exposed to weather and beast, mostly the latter one, the one with binoculars and a gluttonous ambition.

When the cave's mouth stood open before us, I aimed the flashlight at the hollow darkness. Aisheh shivered, and I could feel the goosebumps grow on my skin. We stood there for a moment, not knowing what to do. There were things in there - things we weren't sure anybody deserved to see. I felt as if we were trespassing on history. Aisheh retreated a little, but I motioned toward the gap with the palm of my hand and said, "After you, Ma'am."

"You've been around tourists too much," she said, "either that or you're just too chicken to be the first to go in." She was right, and she knew it and giggled about it as she talked and bravely walked in. I followed closely with the flashlight in my hand, aiming it at the wall of the cave and slowly moving it from one end of the grotto to the other. The cold damp air made me shiver too, and the smell of the old, closed earth filled my nostrils; I sneezed.

Aisheh and I toured the cave in silence. I could not touch anything for fear of awakening some protecting spirit. Aisheh reached with her skinny fingers and caressed a large clay jug against the wall. There were Nabatean water jugs of many sizes, but they were all large - large, larger and huge. I remembered an archeologist who had told me once that Nabatean pottery was finer than porcelain. It was made with a high degree of technical and artistic mastery. Its thinness and finesse matched only the best porcelain; however, what made it exceed the porcelain in quality was the fact that it was all thrown on the wheel and turned; either that, or it was smoothed down afterwards, whereas porcelain was only cast in a mold. The archeologist also told me that the Nabatean pottery included many open bowl type containers, and this was "notoriously one of the most difficult forms to throw on a wheel, even when it was made very thick."

We counted thirty-two big pieces of pottery, scattered all around the cave, all intact, last touched by a Nabatean hand, over two thousand years ago.

"Do you know that ancient Egyptians believed that the spirit of a dog-like animal can protect the tombs from intruders like us?" I whispered.

"This is not a tomb," she said. "Neither are we in Egypt."

"This place is not all a natural cave either."

"It's been carved, some," she whispered and motioned to the wall that had a grated surface and right angles. And then there were colors. I called them reds, but Aisheh said they weren't, although she did not know what to call them. They were neither red nor brown nor pink nor anything I had learnt at school.

Halimeh stood at the door and made noise. Aisheh shooed her off, dared her take another step. The goat snorted and retreated a few steps, but she wouldn't go away.

"That stubborn animal should have been a mule," said Aisheh.

I chuckled. "One minute she's a spirit of an archeologist, and the next she's demoted to mule."

"Maybe she's on her third life already," said Aisheh. "She stood by the door to keep an eye on the animals. "What are you going to do with all this, now?" she asked.

"I don't know. What are you going to do?"

"I asked you first."

"I asked you second."

Our childish argument ended, and we ran out of speech as we stood there, in awe, nervous and numb.

"This cave is a museum," she said after a while. "It is a big responsibility, beyond our capacity."

"It is also too high and difficult to reach - too far for anybody but you, me and the goats, Aisheh. What are we to do?"

"What are *you* to do, Raji. The place is all yours, not ours. I don't wish to get involved anymore." Her cheeks sagged as she spoke, and she frowned at the ground.

"Why?"

"Because."

"Because is an incomplete sentence. Out with it."

She hesitated and looked at me as if to beg me off, but I faced her with a stubborn look and tried to make it as piercing as possible without looking like a moron. "My father would take the money away from me anyway," she said finally. "I would have no way to hide it, nor would I have the chance to spend it the way I want. It might as well be all yours."

"This place is yours too, Aisheh."

"And I'm giving my share to you, Raji. You'll need the money to go to college, and I know you will go."

"What about you."

"Since I can't do what I want with my earnings, I do not want them anymore."

"Let's keep it undisturbed for now. I'm scared of it."

"It is a monster, and it shouldn't be misused."

"Let's not tell anybody about it for now. We'll close it up and keep it hidden. It's our cave, our own place. If one of us needs it in the future, we'll reveal it then. What do you say?"

"Good deal," she mumbled.

Chapter 6

When we stepped out in the sun, I spread my arms up high, turned in a full circle and shouted with excitement, "Welcome to Raji and Aisheh's Nabatean Museum. Admissions: Free." But Aisheh had already turned away and left. She disappeared like a ghost.

I could never figure out this woman. Jim told me much later that all women were supposed to be that way, and I just needed to be patient. I felt I might as well be Halimeh, the goat, subject of this shepherdess who, some days, would prance all over the country, singing and jabbering without a worry in the world, and other days her mind would seem shackled to a rock, that would not respond anymore, neither to wind nor rain.

Chapter 7

Very few eyes turned to the sky in Petra, for the sky was barren most of the year. But, the fertility of the ground helped maintain a constant influx of human beings who came to cultivate its rocks and harvest its dried fruit. The fertility of this soil lay in the layers of dead civilizations and the chapters of history they had folded in their ruins. Men and women came and searched with all their senses like hungry hogs. They filled their snouts with dust and allowed the fine rocks and sand to cover their bodies. Each person wanted to uncover a secret inherent deep down in his or her own soul. And then there was Jim.

His profile became one of the daily sights in Petra. A small shoulder bag rested on his hip and contained his tools, maps, notebooks, food and drink. A hat that fit tightly on his head had left a permanent looking circle that sharply marked the line between the tanned and white areas on his forehead. It took me a long time to convince him to get rid of the worthless hat and put on a decent, cotton, white, desert head cover, the kind that draped loosely on the head and provided ample shade and allowed some air to reach around the neck and keep a person cool and comfortable. The man resisted proper clothing until discomfort almost injured him.

He had left his synthetic hat on his bleached head for too long in the heat of the day, and when he tried to take it off, he discovered that his flesh had simmered inside it to a medium rare state, and his skin, slightly scorched, was stuck to the brim. When he finally peeled the hat off, his forehead looked like the rear end of a monkey, shiny, slick and red. That afternoon, I took him up to the village, introduced him to the general store manager and told him to fit the wretch with a decent head cover.

"I look silly in this white rag," objected Jim. "It feels as if I'm wearing a table cloth on my head."

"Jim," I said. "You look sillier in that absurd hat you wear, and when you take it off, you look like the missing link in the human race."

"Lizard. You're the most crude and uncivilized creature that ever slithered on rocks." He stopped sharply and then quickly added in a reversed tone. "Actually, the table cloth does feel good. Thank you."

"You're welcome, I think."

The store keeper, who couldn't understand the conversation but realized it had included an argument, thought that there was something wrong in the quality of his product, so he quickly began to defend his merchandise, "Tell the Mister this is the finest cotton hatta he will find in the country," he said.

"It's not the hatta, my friend. It's the alien who's wearing it," I said. "Just be patient with us here."

"Just tell me what his problem is," said the storekeeper. He stared at Jim as he fiddled with the head cover and rearranged it in front of the small mirror that rested on the counter.

"I think I have him convinced now. Don't worry," I said.

Chapter 7

Jim bought the head dress and wore it faithfully from then on. As for the hat, he gave it to me after he made sure of its futility. I, in turn, gave it to Aisheh and watched her fit it nicely on one of her goats. She called it Jim. With a little imagination, anything could look like Jim, I thought. Aisheh's laughter echoed in the valley as she watched her goat take off with the hat. It sauntered up the side of the colonnade where Jim had been working. I stared at the site until I spotted him. He was there alright. His nose, followed by the rest of his body, was down in the dirt fumbling through a maze of rocks and man–made treasures. The white head cover he had on moved up and down in a regular motion. It peeked above the ruins like a head of a mummy, trying to come back to life. I told Aisheh she could see Jim's white head pop up if she looked long enough, but she said she would rather look at the goat. Jim never saw his impersonator go by.

All the uncovered ruins around the colonnade were sections of a major thoroughfare, disconnected and missing essential parts, according to Jim. But, he had no interest in uncovering these parts. He said he would leave that job for the students of archeology who come to this part of the world eager to uncover anything. He and I began to inspect the hills far and near for a potentially hidden shrine where he believed the unity had taken place between the Nabatean gods, Dushara and Allat, the god that descended from the sun, and the one that dwelled in the springs and the valleys.

Jim kept reminding himself that the French explorer had indicated in his notes that the shrine would be in the bosom of the hill. "In the bosom of the hill," he mumbled all day long. But the metaphor was so obscure that it forced us to search the hills (the feasible ones for Jim to excavate) from head to toe, calling each part a possible bosom. We would comb one hill at a time, and he would have me climb up what he called the lizard tracks to identify certain spots which he had located with his binoculars but was unable to reach with his clumsy feet.

In the process, we gathered many shards of old pottery and revealed many stones that had been carved for Dushara and his shrines. Some of these blocks of stones were decorated with inlaid marble and hard, painted plaster, just like the ones found in the major temple of Dushara, the one the villagers had named Quasr Bint Far'un (The Castle of Pharaoh's daughter). But we found no tracks of a spring or dried streams that could provide hope for our mission, and there was a day or two when I wondered about the validity of what we were looking for anyway.

According to Jim, the problem lay in the fact that the discovery of the cave within a cave he was seeking had taken place long before Petra was fully discovered.

"There were no roads back then, nor were there known names for the sites to compare the location of the cave to in order to facilitate its discovery again," he said to me one day. He was exhausted, and I was crabby.

"When we find the place, I'm going to call it Halimeh's cave," I said. The sun had been beating down on me as I worked, and the heat began to broil the cells in my brain.

"Who the heck is Halimeh?" Jim asked. He tried to pronounce the name Halimeh like I did, with the Arabic (only half aspirated) H. But then he began to choke. That man would never learn how to speak Arabic, I decided. He still couldn't say good morning in a half decent way without taking two cough drops to clear his throat.

"Halimeh is Patience," I said. "And she has piercing eyes that could spot caves without much effort."

"Maybe she should be helping us," said Jim seriously.

Chapter 7

"Oh no. You don't need Halimeh's help," I answered quickly, realizing that I had put my foot in my mouth. I thought it wouldn't be proper to tell him that Halimeh was a goat, nor would it be polite to indicate that she wore his hat on hot scorching days like that day.

"Why can't she help us?"

"Because...because you're stuck with me," I said, "for I come of a line of princes ruling by divine right, since no bad stock would produce men like me," I recited proudly without looking at him. I pretended to be indulged in my work and focused my eyes on my own hands.

"You're a pain in the neck, Lizard."

"Thank you."

"Where did you learn your heroic speech, anyway?"

"Didn't I tell you I read Homer? My teacher had a translation of the Iliad, and he let me borrow it. He lets me borrow his books all the time."

"You like to read?"

"That's all I do when I'm not excavating gods with you." I threw a small piece of pottery toward him and he caught it. "Now this piece," I recited again, "could tell the story of a man, one who was never at a loss. He had traveled far in the world... ."

"Shut–up, Lizard," he whined and turned around and began to climb down.

It took all five senses to determine the excavation site. Actually, it took ten senses between Jim and me, for his eye sight was different from mine. He couldn't spot a bush without looking at it through the binoculars and wasting half an hour or so adjusting and focusing, and his sense of smell was always blocked by strange perfumes, worse than the kind the pilgrims wore when they went to Mecca. And his hearing – who would want to hear about his hearing anyway? He would hear certain sounds and miss the main pitch.

Then he would get all confused and try to mix and match what he had heard and try to make an intelligent guess, and when that failed, he would look at me with wondering eyes, and I would straighten him out. But he was a strong son of a gun. When it came to digging in the ground, his muscles would bulge twice as big as mine, and he would dig with the power of a miniature bulldozer. It embarrassed me to see him so strong. He made me look like a subordinate creature, and I had to ask him how he came to be this strong.

"A person has to have something good about him you know, Lizard," he said teasingly and realizing my shame. "You're fast; I'm strong. You slither; I dig." He pushed the shovel in the ground and began to stand up and straighten his back. About half way up, he pressed on the middle of his spine with his fingers and eased himself up. "The muscles are still in good shape, but the bones are getting ancient," he complained. "I'm not nearly as strong as I used to be when I was your age. I used to lift weights every day to keep in shape, and my bones where all there, no corrosion." That embarrassed me even more. If the old geezer thought he wasn't very strong then, I hated to think of how strong he used to be forty years ago.

At the end of the day, Jim looked down into the valley, and his face sobered. "What we really need is a sixth sense, Lizard," he said. By then, the sun had worked on his brain cells too.

"What for?"

"So we can sense our way to the cave rather than dig it out."

"If we find the cave so easily, I'd be out of job, Jim. Now take it easy. I am enjoying this."

He shook his head and handed me a bottle of Pepsi. I got the hint and quit talking. By that time, we were both bored, tired, and cranky. When we reached the bottom of the hill, Jim eased himself down on a large boulder. I sat beside him, and we sipped our pop, and rested for a while. "Isn't it weird," I started again, "that archeologists spend their life cleaning up the debris that had been buried deep down in the ground for thousands of years?" I asked.

"It's good for them, Lizard, better than cleaning chimneys." He licked his lips clean and wiped them with his sleeve.

"It's good if they get lucky and find something worth a bottle of Arak."

He laughed. "I'll buy you a bottle of Arak if that's all you're worried about."

"Thanks, Jim. I don't drink. I just like to use the metaphor."

"Does your family drink?"

"No. Mother is too conservative, and my brothers are anti."

"Anti what?"

"Everything." Jim hated it when I dropped my sentences just like that, and I loved to drive him crazy. "What are you going to do when you find the cave anyway?" I asked.

"Go home."

"That's what I thought."

That became a typical day for a while. We would work until the heat reaches the zenith of tolerance and our bones ache from constant digging and our eyes droop and water and burn from the hot sand. Then we would sit down to have a good drink and talk nonsense for a few minutes. The next morning, we would begin our laborious job early and watch the sun rise quietly and illuminate the ruins and take away the ghostly shapelessness of the rocks. We would work until our mouths begin to utter nonsense again. Then we would stop for a drink. Some days our senseless discussion would reach its peak, and we would begin to philosophize or recite poetry. This went on for a while, and Jim and I continued to tolerate each other, just like we tolerated the heat and the sardine breath.

When all the potential hills were checked and the word from the gods remained secret, we finally decided to go for the most likely place to do our excavations. Since the degree of positiveness had been lowered down to fifty-fifty by the time we were done surveying the feasible hills, we took the one that offered the most hope. Besides, it was a close one, and Jim could easily walk to it every day from his cave. He could also see the site from his home cave.

Jim said that the excavations on the chosen site should be of medium difficulty, because its layers had been results of minor rock slides and earthquakes, typical causes of the natural land formation, for Jordan had lately received only traces of earthquakes which usually took place in Eastern Turkey. According to Jim, these minor rock slides could have easily buried the mouth of a cave or two.

The more he thought of the site, the more excited he became and the more supplies he bought. He filled his cave with tools and archeological paraphernalia until there was hardly place for him to live. It was ludicrous. Finally, he declared readiness. He danced around in ecstasy and drifted off into deep day dreams and looked like the prey of a hyena, all hypnotized and ready to be swallowed by ghosts of ancient civilizations.

I had to consult with Aisheh first. After all, the hills belonged to her. Jim and I were only intruders with special permission given by outsiders. She had the right to give these permissions just as much as the officials, I thought. Besides, she always helped me make wise decisions which caused me to become dependent on her opinion in taking every step in my life. The girl could see through and beyond me, and I trusted her judgment. When my brothers let me down, she was the only person outside of home I could talk to without feeling manipulated or low.

The sun still lingered high in the sky when I spotted Aisheh near my/our cave. I hurried up the hill and let her goats grumble and scurry out of my way. Jim had gone to his cave to dream about his project for the last time before the digging took place. The sounds of tourists from the valley below were heard with uneven intervals. Aisheh was sitting on a boulder next to the cave. Her back rested on the hill, and her face soaked the sun. I thought she was asleep, for her eyes were closed, but she opened them as soon as I stood in front of her, like she had been waiting for me to shade them from the sun.

"Now what are you up to," she said.

"Tomorrow, Jim and I will start the project."

"Are you going to tell him about this project?" She pointed to our cave.

"I tried, but he thinks it's beyond his reach. Besides, he's only interested in one particular discovery, and that involves more than one cave. It's supposed to be a cave within a cave with a dry spring and a whole bunch of fiddlesticks. All the other rarities don't seem too important to him."

"I hope he doesn't get disappointed."

"That's the trouble. I told him nobody leaves here disappointed, but that was before I knew what he was up to."

"Well, you said he pays well. At least it won't be all a waste of your time."

I was silent. Somehow, the money didn't matter much when I worked with Jim. The stubborn old man wasn't just like any other tourist or excavator. He was Jim. I sensed a reason for his being there, for my being his helper, for the nonsense we babbled every day as we sipped our Cola.

"The old geezer is a good – what should I say..., " I said to Aisheh. I wanted to say father but then remembered Aisheh's father meant nothing but a tyrant to her, "family," I finally declared. "He's becoming like a good family to me."

She laughed. "It takes an alien from the end of the world to make a good relative," she said. "Isn't it funny? The close ones seem to use you, even when you think they're being nice to you, but the aliens seem to inspire and delight you, even when you think they're using you." She hid a faint smile, and then she continued, "I'd say enjoy him while he's here, Raji. There's nothing you can do about the success of the project, and I'm sure he knows his chances too. He's not a young kid."

"Between the two of us, there is a young kid, Aisheh."

Her silence stipulated the truth of my statement. She leaned back against the hill and closed her eyes again. The goats were scattered all around. They munched on half dried grass and made noise in the sun. I stared at the sleeping shepherdess, her black goats, the green and yellow weeds that poked through the crushed sandstones, and the pale rocks of soft pink, brown, tan, and red tones. The sun was bright orange. I didn't look up, just felt it through the colors down below.

Chapter 8

Jim and I dug and cleared rocks every day, five days a week and sometimes six and even seven, depending on whether Jim decided to go to the Capital for the week-end or not. He went to Amman to buy supplies and clothes and to get out of the ruins for a while and, I suppose, to socialize with city folks, for I had heard archeologists say that spending too much time in a secluded area out in the middle of nowhere could drive a person mad. We, peasants didn't know any better, so it never bothered us being left alone at the far edge of civilization and away from city crowds. We were home. Sometimes, Jim would take trips to different parts of the country with his friends in Amman. He would tour other archeological sites and more ancient ruins as if he could never have enough of them in Petra. One day, he came back and told me how much he had missed his hole, and I knew then that the old man was home, safe. He wouldn't go mad on me out here anymore, for he had gone past the danger zone.

"There's no place like home," he said, first thing after he stepped out of the car.

Home! I thought. His home lay over the ocean, beyond my imagination, for the only water I had ever seen in my life was the Red Sea down south at the tip of the desert. I had learned about oceans at school and was able to identify them on the map; huge chunks of blue that separated the brown, the yellow, and the green. "Do you call your cave home, Jim?" I inquired. His eye balls danced and glittered, and I might as well say he had arrived late that day and was full of merriment and Arak. I could smell it on his breath.

"Home is where you make a comfortable bed." He hummed and danced and chirped like a silly bird putting on a show.

"You're full of Arak, Jim."

"True," he admitted gaily. "Do you know that in Southern France, your Arak is called Water of Life, Lizard? Eau de Vie," he enunciated the French words as he formed a snout with his lips. "That's what I am now, full of life."

"I just hope you don't drop dead because you're too full."

"Nah." He shooed me off with his hand as if I had uttered nonsense.

"Do you know that the prophet forbids this stuff, and the Nabateans never allowed the making of alcohol on their grounds."

"Yeah. The prophets always liked to forbid things, and the Nabateans managed to destroy themselves just as bad as those who drank their life away, Lizard. Don't worry. I only do it once in a blonde moon." He turned his head around to search for the moon and couldn't find it. The Guest House had blocked it from us completely.

"What happened to blue moon?"

"That's right. I thought the color was too strong."

The Arak was too strong, I thought, and Jim wouldn't admit it. I walked him to his cave and told him to go to bed if he wanted to get to work in the morning.

CHAPTER 8

I worked with Jim in the mornings most of the days. In the afternoons, I chased tourists and helped them find places, gave them tours, explained unexplainable phenomena, local cultural behaviors and so on. My olive oil tin can treasury continued to fill up at a steady pace; Jim's hole grew progressively wider and deeper against the hill. We uncovered piles of shattered pottery, most of which were fine chips, too tiny, lost and disconnected. They were scattered between fine rocks and sand. The hill began to look sore with our torn up site, presumably on its bosom. All these ancient man–made chips encouraged Jim to keep going though. To him, the cave was just a layer or two away. We worked diligently, and our friendship continued to grow until finally, my family came to know Jim and welcome him with the traditional hospitality.

Like Jim would say, it all happened on a full moon. Abu–Zeid, the restaurant manager at the Guest House had calculated wrong again. He always calculated wrong. His math was worse than my Chinese. There was this big calendar mounted on the wall in his office that told him all about those who were coming from the Capital to visit Petra, when they were coming, how many were supposed to come and so on and so forth. Every once in a while, he would forget to add a zero to the right side of his figures and end up with ten times as many tourists as he had accounted for. This time, he messed up big time, and was I glad he did! His figures said fifty, and the facts came up to five hundred, and it happened during the peak of the season.

When the buses pulled into his driveway, Abu–Zeid's lower jaw dropped suddenly as if there was nothing there to catch it, and when it stopped, his eyes bulged like the lizard that had sensed danger. So, there he stood, in the middle of warm bodies, all huffing and puffing and asking for something to drink– all at the same time. The pop in his refrigerator was enough for about half of the guests, and the rest of the pop was still in boxes, stacked, warm as urine. He and his men crushed the little ice they had had into powder and spooned a teaspoon of ice in each glass to satisfy the customers enough so they would spare his life. But once he made the first round, he was out of ice, and the customers were asking for more so they could fill their canteens before they went on their tour to Petra. They waved their plastic bottles in the air and asked for ice.

"We need more ice, please," said a sweet old lady.

"More ice please," said a man with a long beard. He looked like a prophet in modern clothing.

"Ice please," recited several people.

"Ice." The word became a chorus word.

"In a minute. In a minute, please," said Abu-Zeid. He tried to stay calm as he kindly moved the swarming bodies away from him.

"Ice?"

"Ice is on its way. In a minute please." His eyes were ready to pop, and he began to perspire rivers, streams and waterfalls.

Then the word please disappeared, and the requests became demands and then turned into nasty speeches.

"We were told this place has everything we would need."

"Where's the ice?"

"Ice?"

"What kind of a place is this?"

"What a rotten service."

"I should have known better," said the prophet–like man.

"Ice?"

"Yes. Yes. Ice is coming."

"I should have known better," repeated the prophet.

"Ice?"

"Coming. Coming."

Chapter 8

"When?"

"After we die?"

"No. No. You won't die. Just relax. Ice is on the way."

"Where is the ice?"

"Don't you have cold Coke? This bottle is warm."

"Cold Coke is coming too."

"Ice please?"

Abu–Zeid came begging on his hands and knees. He sent me off with one of the bus drivers to fetch more ice and cold pop. We went to Abu-Mustafa's restaurant in the village. The humble village restaurant always had a large supply of ice and pop for the pilgrims who came from Turkey and crossed the Jordanian desert to go south to Saudi Arabia, on their way to Mecca. Abu-Mustafa happened to have enough ice and cold pop to settle a war. We hauled it all to the Guest House and helped distribute it. Soon, the people began to calm down, and everybody was happy and ready for the tour.

"How can I pay you," said Abu–Zeid when he saw the last of the tourists leave the yard. The wrinkles on his face softened. He took a deep breath and relaxed as if he had missed a gunshot by two millimeters. He pulled his soggy handkerchief out of his pocket and wiped his face again.

"I want a lamb," I said. "All butchered and cleaned up."

"You don't waste any breath," he said sharply. He had known me well for a long time, yet he always made the same comment every time I told him what I wanted from him for a payment. "You know. Sometimes I hate you, Raji," he said.

"I know."

"What do you need a lamb for – tired of chicken and pigeons?"

"No. My mother agreed to cook Mansaf for Jim and me, but I have to bring her the lamb. Jim hasn't had Mansaf yet. It's a shame; don't you think? To be here for so long and not to have the traditional guest meal? It's a shame."

"Didn't he ever have Mansaf here at the Guest House?"

Abu–Zeid seemed surprised, because he fixed Mansaf quite often for the tourists, and Jim ate there every once in a while.

"Never. Besides, your Mansaf does not count," I snorted. "I want him to try the real, home–made, whole lamb, layered with all its condiments on the round pans and everything."

Abu–Zeid nudged me with one hand and pulled out a stack of bills from his pocket with the other.

"Here," he said. His fingers fumbled between the green papers for a moment. Then he pulled out two–ten dinar bills and handed them to me. "This ought to cover two lambs with all the condiments that come with the meal."

"Thanks," I said. "I'll tell Jim you're also in on this treat." I appreciated his generosity, although I realized how much he knew he would need me again.

A sudden smile appeared on his face. "I don't really hate you that much, Raji," he said.

"I know."

The next day, Jim came over to our house for a Mansaf/ welcome to the village meal. Just before he and I left the project, the wild sunset colors had highlighted the colored sandstone monoliths of Petra and blended the heaven and the earth with streaks of shadows and beams of light. Jim and I stood on a boulder and looked around in the quiet hue. There were these moments when he and I knew we had a revelation coming through colors and light. We paused, and the entire surroundings seemed to pause with us. Then, slowly, we sat down, each to his own line of thought, undisturbed; each to his silent conversation with the gods.

Chapter 8

I had neglected to remind Jim that my family would be waiting for us soon. Mother would be cooking up a storm, while my brothers sat around in a circle and fidgeted, because they never trusted my endeavors and accepted them earnestly, and this whole party had been well labeled as my own. What bothered them the most was the fact that Mother always complied to my requests and treated me as an independent member of the family. To them, I was just a foolish boy with unrealistic dreams.

When I finally woke up from my trance, I told Jim we'd better start walking toward the village.

"I hope you did not put your mother through a lot of trouble," he said. His leg had gone to sleep, and he tried to pump the blood through it again.

"My mother likes to go through a lot of trouble, Jim. She likes cooking for company."

"How do you know that?"

"She told me so. My brothers never invite anybody home like my father used to do. They don't do anything to make her life interesting. All they do is lead a rigorous and monotonous life, which makes them no different than the animals they saddle every morning, and, by the way, I told them that."

"Oh, Lizard, you just don't know how to be..."

"Civilized?"

"Let's say, diplomatic."

"I can be diplomatic when I want to be, Jim – only when I want to be."

Jim remained silent the rest of the way. At the edge of the village, we could smell the cooked lamb and yogurt and the frying of almonds, pine nuts, and garlic. The smell had permeated the air clear to Seeq. To my surprise, my brothers welcomed Jim like gentlemen. They waited for him at the front door and shook hands with him and asked him to come in. Boss one even asked me to translate the traditional Arabic saying which states that "He who lives forty days in a community becomes a legal member." I told Jim that he was officially initiated.

My older brother also suggested that we recline on the wicker chairs on the front porch and visit for a while. The cool evening desert air had brought comfort to the lungs, and there was no point in breathing the restricted warm air inside the house. We listened to mother's clattering in the kitchen and visited in peace. Jim talked, and I translated, and my brothers talked, and I translated. Jim told my brothers how much he admired their hard work and patience, and how much the tourists appreciated their efforts in relieving them from taking the rough path on foot. My brothers talked about their horses, their names and behaviors.

The visiting continued on until an unexpected guest showed up at our front door. It was the government employee from the extension office at the Capital. He had come to vaccinate our chickens, because Mother had put in a request for that. There were no appointments made, for most of the villagers had no telephones. They just waited their turn to be served whenever the service people got around to it.

"It's kind of late to vaccinate the chickens. Isn't it?" asked my older brother.

"It's been a long day for me out here," begged the extension man. His eyes wilted as he spoke; his shoulders sagged, and he looked hot, miserable, and desperate. "I have sprayed trees, delivered supplies to seven farmers, and drank a bucket of bitter coffee. All I have left is your chickens to vaccinate. I really would like to finish tonight so I don't have to come all the way back tomorrow."

"But it is already five o'clock," said my brother, "and it is a four hour drive to Amman, which means you will arrive there real late if you vaccinate the chickens yet tonight.

Why don't you spend the night here in the village and finish your work early tomorrow morning." He tried desperately to discourage the man and get him out of our way, so we could eat in peace, but his attempts failed.

"I can't spend the night out here," said the man. He looked around with condescending eyes. "I never did. Besides, my family expects me back home tonight."

"Well then. Here they are – all yours, I guess," said my brother. He pointed to the chickens all over the yard, the fence, and clear down into the street. The man's eyes moved from one end of the yard to the other. Then he stood still and stiff as a rock. Jim wondered what the problem was, and I explained it to him.

"I'll help him catch the chickens if that's all he's worried about."

"No, Jim," I said. "Just watch and enjoy. Like we say in Arabic, these city folks don't know their tops from their bottoms."

"Oh, Lizard, Lizard."

"Just watch."

"What's the problem?" my brother asked the extension man. A facetious smile covered his face.

"Those chickens are scattered everywhere," said the man desperately. "It would take hours just to catch them." His face expressed pathetic depression.

"Wait just a second," said my brother. He went into the house and called my mother. A minute later, Mother came out into the yard and pulled two large boxes from the shed. Then she stood in the middle of the yard and called her chickens.

"Tei'a, tei'a, tei'a," she hollered and didn't have to wait, for as soon as the chickens heard her voice, they all gathered up and jumped in the boxes in front of her. She gave them a few grains to eat and told the extension man to get busy. From then on, the man's job was easy. He vaccinated the chickens and sighed in relief and thanked the woman and praised the Almighty for his support. My brother felt sorry for him and invited him for dinner too.

"We're having Mansaf," said my brother. "There's never enough people to eat it all, so why don't you stick around for dinner since you're late anyway."

Jim was amused. Within minutes the man's job was done, and the chickens were tucked in and the noise diminished, leaving room for the silence of the evening to take over. When mother called for dinner, my stomach growled. I hadn't had Mansaf for a long time. We walked into the house, and Jim's eyes grew big, for he had experienced our true hospitality for the first time. The large round pan (Jim called it a huge round, heavy duty pizza pan) rested in the middle of the table, heaped with layers of food.

"The first layer is a thin round sheet of bread, baked specially to fit the pan," I explained to Jim. "We call this kind of bread Shrak. It is unleavened. The second layer is a huge heap of rice. You cannot cook just a little bit of rice for this meal," I said. "Because it has to hold the lamb on top, the whole lamb."

"I see that. I see that," repeated Jim.

"The whole lamb is cooked with spices in plain yogurt sauce," I continued, "and it is centered on top of the heaped rice. Then an abundance of roasted pine nuts and almonds is spread on the very top."

"Does it have to be a whole lamb?" asked Jim. "This food is enough to feed the whole village."

"Whether you're hosting one guest or fifty," I said. "Strict traditions call for a whole lamb to honor the guest fully. The lamb is to be carved in front of the guest. Now city folks don't do that, of course. This is strictly the hospitality of us, peasants. In the city you'll eat Mansaf already dished up in a china plate with one small hunk of meat on top, and you eat it with a fork and a knife. Now, we don't call that Mansaf.

"Come to think of it," said Jim. "I think I had that at the Guest House one time, all dished up like you said."

"Today you get to eat the real stuff," I said. "With your hands, just like the desert people do."

Jim's eyes widened. He giggled and rubbed his hands together with excitement. He was ready to eat.

"Now," I continued. "Hold it. Hold it." Jim obediently put his hands behind his back. "Whether you washed your hands or not; that's beside the point. You still have to wash them in the basin that is passed around." I put the basin in front of Jim, and mother poured water from a large pitcher and watched him wash his hands and pass the basin on.

"Now you take a small piece of the lamb like this," I said as I tore a small piece of meat. "And you say, in the name of God the merciful and compassionate. Then you combine the meat with a small lump of rice and a small piece of bread from the bottom and mold the whole thing into one big bite in the palm of your hand." I watched Jim imitate me like a child, afraid to make a mistake. "Then you flick the bite in your mouth by giving it a push with your thumb like a marble. That way your hand will not touch your mouth, because it has to go back into the pan for more bites."

The extension man watched patiently. He looked disgusted and wondered if I would ever get the show on the road.

"This is worse than excavating," said Jim. "I never thought even rice has to be excavated before it is eaten around here."

"Don't worry," I said to Jim. "We don't follow traditions that strictly anymore either."

My mother stood behind Jim with a stack of china plates and silverware in her hands. She laughed and shook her head at me. Jim heard her and turned around. She handed him a plate and some silverware and asked him to help himself. "Don't mind this boy," she said. "Sometimes he's just a pain."

I had to translate her words to Jim, and he nodded in agreement. He ate and ate until he declared that he began to look pregnant.

"Now I have to fast for a week," he said, feeling his belly.

"No, Jim," I said. "Tomorrow, I'll bring you leftovers. Someone has to eat them."

Chapter 9

There had been a cry of help from the government, and it received a favorable response from several large corporations and institutions around the world. The massive number of historical sites in the country were being uncovered at an alarming rate, and the exposure of these treasures, especially the Byzantine mosaic floors, discovered in the area of Madaba, a suburb of the Capital, had caused them to crumble fast. It had also attracted thieves, both local and foreign to come in and loot; other people simply destroyed carelessly. The local government budget was limited, and to maintain and preserve such an abundance of valuable lands would cost more than what a small government could provide.

There were Byzantine church floors covered with tiny mosaic stones, perfectly cubed, in all colors, both bright and dull to provide contrast and to highlight the pictures which they had intricately formed. They depicted life in the Byzantine era. Wildlife, hunters, fruit press, people of all professions, kings and Biblical images and designs that were created during that epoch of history covered the floors. They were scattered all around the area of Madaba – hundreds of ancient church floors, buried, half buried, intact, dilapidated or part ruined by weather, man, and animal. Wherever people disturbed the ground, they found and continued to find historical treasures until the thrill of excavating and discovering the secrets of history in that area had died down, but the thieves continued to come from everywhere, and the cry of help was finally heard and answered.

The Mercedes Company responded immediately. German experts were sent to save the most critical places discovered. Dr. Donor came with his wife and toured and studied and went back home and came again with Dr. Schneller, Dr. Brener, and Mr. Hans. I forgot Hans's last name, but he was the fat man who smiled all the time. The rest of them were tall and slim. They all came with their wives and toured around and decided to work on one of the mosaic floors in Madaba. Their object was to preserve and seal the tiny cubes together before they ran off like corn on the cob and lost and distorted the images they had portrayed for hundreds of years.

The Franciscans also had a similar project in Mount Nebo, near Madaba, and several other institutions established restoration projects in the same area. But nobody seemed interested in Petra, because it had no fragile mosaic floors for one thing, and its temperature in the summer continued to challenge the limit line of tolerance at times, for it had bordered the real desert. Madaba, on the other hand, being further north and a suburb of the Capital, its weather maintained mild and gentle temperatures and attracted more archeologists. The temperature in the Madaba area never exceeded ninety five degrees Fahrenheit, not even at the peak of the season, and it always provided a gentle breeze which helped ease the heat.

Most archeologists came to know Jim, however, because, even though the focus of their interest remained up north, they all took the chance, at least once during their stay in the country, to visit the Nabatean land and Jim's project. The old man became admired like a Nabatean god. "It takes courage and a bit of idiosyncrasy to work so close to the desert," visitors would say to Jim whenever they visited the site, and he would thank them, answer their questions and go back to work. Sometimes he would take a break and visit and socialize, especially with archeologists like himself. But his ancient Nabatean god always awaited him in his ditch. To him, his god was much older and more powerful than the Byzantine flamboyant mosaic figures.

When Dr. Donor, Dr. Schneller, Dr. Brener and Mr. Hans and their wives came to visit us in Petra, they chose to spend the night down in the lower caves of the Guest House, and that puzzled me, because usually ritzy people, especially those sent by rich companies, stayed in the upper rooms where they had electricity, air conditioning, and comfortable furniture. They never rented the caves down below the restaurant. But Jim said that these friends were archeologists; real people, he called them, which meant they were the kind who preferred to be close to the earth – as close as possible so they could hear, see and feel history first hand.

We had spent the morning and most of the afternoon with the German archeologists. They checked our excavation site, and then Jim and I took them on a professional tour of Petra, an inclusive and tiresome tour, mostly because the pace was too slow for me. I had the urge to give each of them a push every now and then, but then I feared they might fall and slow down the pace even more. They talked and talked as they ambled until their jabbering turned to incessant, monotonous ringing in my ear. I also discovered that whenever a person visits in a foreign language or even listens to a foreign tongue for some time, he gets tired much faster, even if he were fluent in that foreign language. A headache settled in my skull, and I felt the urge to change everything, the pace, the tongue, and the scenery.

That was a good idea – change the scenery, I thought. "How would you like to see a spectacular cave?" I asked our company. "I have a cave up there." I pointed to the boulder that stood in front my cave way up on the peak of the hill. "It is well covered so nobody can see it, but it's a great place for archeologists to see. Anybody interested in climbing with me? I'll show you an easy way up there, and I'll show you some Nabatean wonders. Something you have never seen before."

They looked up and squinted at the cave site as if it were a visiting star, and then they looked at me.

"Nice hiding place," said Donor.

"Wait until you see the inside. It's stupendous and very exotic," I bragged with all the pedantic words I could think of.

"What a good place to have especially up there where no one can get to but you," said Hans.

Jim read the disappointment on my face. "I don't think they'll climb up there, Raji," he said. "We're running out of time. They need to be back at the Guest House for dinner very shortly."

"We don't have your fast shoes," said Schneller. He must have sensed my disappointment too. "You are very lucky to have such skill."

"I wish I were twenty years younger and fifty pounds lighter," said Hans. "I would give it a try."

I scanned their faces and nodded. They were all up there in age, not particularly young and not too old either, but the fact that they were not young remained an impeding factor in their risk taking to my cave. "Some day I'd like to invite an archeologist up there," I said.

"I'm sure you'll find someone," said Hans. "There are many young people out there looking for challenges like this."

CHAPTER 9

Hans would have come with me up there had he been younger and thinner like he said, I thought. He was the hard worker of the bunch and the nosy one too. At every site we stopped, we had to wait for him a bit longer so he would finish his scrupulous view of the place. I just hoped that by the time I found a young Hans, I wouldn't be too old to make the trip up there myself. But, at that moment, I was stuck with old geezers, seeking easy discoveries. What bothered me most was the fact that they too believed in Jim's god. They looked in his book and studied all the sketches of the god and his shrine and his stream and thought we were up for a great discovery.

They were all looking at me, by the time I finished day dreaming. Each had a faint smile on his face. I felt embarrassed and alone. I had hoped for someone to check out my cave and tell me what to do with it, but not this time. I watched them all stomp around in their bulky boots, believing they had seen it all.

When we came back to our site, Donor invited Jim and me to have dinner with his group at the Guest House, and we accepted the invitation. Jim said we'd better spend the night up there too so he didn't have to cross the Seeq back in the dark. The moon was just a crescent, and its skimpy light would never make it around the bulging rocks that towered above the path. Jim said he'd rent a cave for the two of us right next to the German guests if I wanted to join them for the rest of the night.

My body could barely keep up with my feet when I dashed home to get my bedding. We had no sleeping bags like the tourists did, but my mother gave me an old thin mattress (we called it Jodal in Arabic), which was just a large throw rug, used for throwing on porches to nap on during the day. I also picked up a pillow, a blanket, and my book, because I couldn't sleep without reading by a flashlight every night. I read under my covers so nobody could catch me, and it was nice and cozy. Jim brought his sleeping bag and a change of clothes for the morning.

Abu–Zeid had prepared baked chicken and rice heaped with roasted pine nuts and almonds for dinner. He fixed a different main meal every night for those who craved a good hearty hot meal at the end of the day. When he saw me sitting with the guests, talking, eating and laughing, he commented that next I'd be sitting with the Queen of England. I told him I just might.

"Somehow, you don't surprise me, Raji," whispered Abu–Zeid to me in Arabic. "You stick your nose in everything and always manage to get out of it clean. Some day, I'd like to see that nose of yours pinched, just because. Someone needs to teach you a tough lesson in life. You can't just go on living it the easy way like this."

He sounded just like my brothers, and I hated him again. But the food was good. I had to admit. When Jim asked me what I thought of it, I said it was passable.

Donor picked on the pine nuts all evening until he made sure none was left in the rice. Jim and the others noticed his fondness of the little brown nuts, and they all helped him pick them with their forks and uncover the ones half buried in the rice. Each person excavated the large serving dish of rice until it looked as if the chickens had been through it several times. Some of the rice even spilled on the table, but nobody cared. They ate and visited and listened to Majid, the musician, who came to entertain the late guests before the end of the day.

Majid played the reed pipe, a common desert instrument, easy to carry around and play, and it was as ancient as the ruins and the human existence in this part of the world. It was also the shepherds' specialty instrument. Its tunes were light and catchy, yet they were monotonous to help man and beast fall in step when roaming the hills all day long. People chanted and swayed as they listened, each making up his or her own words.

"That's an easy tune to follow," said Hans as he swayed with the music. "Are there any words to go with it?"

"Yes," I said. "But you can make up your own words if you wish. There are as many verses to this tune as there are people who know it."

"Does it have a common title?" asked Brener.

"Mother, I saw the moon at night," I said. "That's the first line of the most popular verse."

Jim smiled. "It's the desert's Moonlight Sonata," he said, and they all laughed and followed the melody with their heads going up and down and up again.

"That's almost like the camel's step," said Hans.

"It is," I said. "When the caravans used to cross the desert, the only thing that helped them maintain a steady pace for a long distance was the monotony or the rhythm. Now, the shepherds use it to herd their sheep and keep them going at a steady pace, and the villagers use it as they work in the sun, and the lovers use it as they meditate in the moonlight. Each makes up his own verse, based on the type of work and the mood he's in."

Hans tried to make up some German words for it, but the language did not quite lend itself to the tune, or at least, I didn't think so. The fat man made it sound like a war song, and it lost its romance. My ears resisted it, but the rest of the company hummed and sang with Hans and continued to follow the tune with their heads until they almost fell in a trance. Then I found myself picking up the words and singing with them – something about rice and pine nuts and indigestion.

When the musician was done, Donor got up, walked up to him and thanked him, shaking his hand and shoulder with the normal German passion. Donor also left a bill in Majid's hand, tapped him on the shoulder and walked back to the table. Majid looked at the bill, and then his eyes followed the professor to his seat. A big smile appeared on the musician's face. He thanked Donor with a nod of his head. Then he turned around and left the restaurant, rich, happy, and with a sore shoulder, I thought.

Hans stood up and stretched his muscles and pushed his hands up in the air as if he were carrying heavy weight.

"I'm ready to play caveman," he announced. His belly puffed like a balloon, and he caressed it gently with the palm of his hand. The men got up, and the women looked at each other and hesitated. Abu–Zeid came in with two large flashlights.

"We usually don't provide light down at the caves," said Abu–Zeid. "We don't have enough of them, but since nobody is using these right now, you may have them for the night. Take one for each cave."

Two of the women extended their hands and took the flashlights. Then one of them tried to hand hers to Jim.

"You may have them both," said Jim. "I brought a couple of mine along, and that ought to do for Lizard and me."

"Do the facilities stay open at night?" asked a woman.

"No," I said. "Abu–Zeid is very fussy about his treasures, especially in the restaurant. But you can use the restrooms now before he closes for the night."

"And if we need to go at night," said Hans, "we just have to step into the desert."

"Join the Hyenas," said Jim.

"Hyenas," recited the women.

Jim and I laughed and took off toward the lower caves.

We spread our bedding against the inner wall and crawled in. Jim put a flashlight by my pillow and one by his.

"There, now we're all set," he said.

Chapter 9

Before long, Jim was snoring aloud – loud enough to keep all the wildlife safely far away from the facility. Although it was late, I couldn't sleep, and I didn't see any danger in waking Jim up if I read. So, I gently stole his flashlight from the side of his pillow and turned on both lights, mine and his. I anchored them and aimed them at my book. They provided ample light for me to read in the silence of the night. Jim's snoring didn't count once I began to read Kahlil Gibran. My teacher had given me Gibran's collection of poems and short writings. I had read several pieces of his work and was fascinated by the abundance of ideas that man had produced and the images his mind had woven together, especially in his *Creation*, *Slavery*, and *The Day of My Birth*. I thought the man couldn't have left many ideas for other writers to write about. I read until I came upon a poem called *A Lover's Call*. After I read it once silently, I found myself reading it out loud a second time. I read in an audible whisper.

I called this poem, *A Call for Aisheh*. The book slipped out of my hand. I let it drop and allowed my eyelids to fall as I drifted into sleep. Meanwhile, the flashlights remained on, and the snoring continued to warn the intruders and keep the peace in the camp.

It couldn't have been much later when I woke up to a scratching sound in the cave, for the flashlights were still beaming strongly, and their batteries did not seem to have died down much. I quickly grabbed one of them and aimed it at the noise. It was then when I came face to face with the largest rodent I had ever seen in my life, for I had seen rats in caves and in many places before, but I had never seen anything like this one, ever. Abu–Zeid must have kept this monster for a pet, feeding him all the grease and the guts of the Awassi fat–tail sheep and chicken scum.

When the rodent found himself in the spot light, he froze. So did I. He looked at me just like the lizard did on the rock down in Petra. But, this time, there was no common relationship or any pleasant feelings toward this fat living blob. The only mutual expression that could be extrapolated from the looks of all four eyes, mine and his, was that of hatred and fear. His round belly dragged on the ground like the stomach of a pregnant cat. A long gray mustache hung on each side of his face beginning from the side of his upper lip and ending on the floor. He looked old, prudent, patient and stubborn.

"Hi there," I whispered. The rat took two steps and then froze again, as if to change directions, but then he couldn't decide which direction would be best for his well being. I was scared stiff. Rats had been known to munch on campers' ears at night, but this beast could go for a whole limb if I left him. "See," I continued. "This cave is taken tonight. You'd have to go someplace else or find a better host." His eyes watched mine and waited. We each waited patiently for the other to take the next step. But neither one of us had the courage to attack, at least not I, and he seemed to be in no mood for violence.

"Listen, you, now," I finally said. "One of us has to do something, so why don't you go first, and why am I talking to a fat rat in the middle of the night, I don't know. All I know is that one of us has to do something," I insisted. His stubborn eyes focused on mine and waited. He acted as if he had all the patience in the world, and I was slowly running out of it. I was tired and sleepy, and the more I waited, the more stubborn the rat appeared to be. I stared at his big belly until it started to look like Hans's. "Please friend, enemy, whoever you are," I pleaded. "Do something." But the rat wouldn't do anything. He scratched under his mustache with his front legs and cleaned up his face as if to make himself more presentable, and he was satisfied. He looked up again and waited. I began to say a prayer to God, Lord of the Moslems, Christians, and Jews – to the united gods of the Nabateans and all the natural and supernatural powers. I wanted this ominous creature out this cave.

Finally, I gathered my strength and jumped off to one side of the intruder. He darted off across the cave, past Jim's feet and disappeared through a hole in the wall. I flashed my light in his direction and saw the hole for the first time. It was big and deep, and it seemed to me that it led to the cave adjacent to ours. I quickly grabbed my pillow and shoved it in the hole and pushed Jim's back pack against it to secure it shut. Then I went back to my bed and slept till morning.

I never said anything to Jim. Before he woke up, I quickly put his back pack where it lay the night before and pulled my pillow out of the hole and packed my belongings. When we walked into the restaurant, Hans told us this long story about a mythical Ratte that had visited them in their cave last night, and how he chased him all over the place, trying not to wake up anybody and how he finally killed him with Donor's hard cover book, the one he had purchased at the Guest House the night before. Hans held up the book to show off the tool of the crime. It was entitled, *The Antiquities of Jordan*.

I continued to pretend not to know anything about the rat. Jim asked me if I had ever seen a rat as big as the one Hans was describing over and over again like a fragment in a broken record, using all the powerful adjectives in the language, and I said yes, I had seen one that big, but I never told him where or when, and he never bothered to ask.

On my way home, I thought of Hans and the rat chasing one another, each dragging his big belly on the ground and trying to outwit the other. I wondered what would have happened had the rat nibbled on somebody's ear before he was discovered. But then, I also wondered about many other things that would make more interesting stories.

Chapter 10

The mixture of sweat, grease melting off the bodies, fine sand and dirt gradually found its way to the eyes, mouths and noses and then continued on to the lungs of the people who dug in the ground. Excavators inhaled and then stopped about half way to make sure of the capability of their systems to refine the air, at least to a breathable level. Then they exhaled while their heads were still up, just before they bent over again, and their heads disappeared in the holes. Jim and I followed this ritual all summer long, day in and day out.

At the end of each day, the ritual required going over the body and cleaning it with solutions, soaps and plenty of water. Thanks to the springs of Wadi Moussa. They allowed this necessity, and without them, the excavations would have been beyond the human tolerance. Archeologists were used to this life because of their faith in the mysterious adventures of history and in the hope that accompanied this faith and provided impetus and patience. There was hope in a revelation, and it always paid off for all the work. It paid, not in monetary form but, rather, in a feeling of satisfaction that could never be expressed in a physical matter, nor could it ever be appreciated and comprehended unless it was fully experienced, that is, unless the eyes, mouths and noses were plugged up with pasty mixtures of sweat and dirt, and the level of discomfort raised up so high and bordered desperation at certain points.

Jim and I used our hands, shovels of different sizes, and wheelbarrows for the first few layers of rock and sand. Then, when we reached the finer dirt, we had to use matching equipment, small tools, then smaller and smallest. They scratched the fine dirt lightly and dropped it loose on the ground and stopped whenever they touched a solid body without causing any damage to it. Then, with a finer tool yet, we scratched around the solid body until we uncovered it, only to find out it was but a solid rock trapped in a mass of fine sand. We continued to haul dirt and rock from the site and dump it in a nearby pile of rubble.

Jim continued to travel to the Capital on weekends whenever he felt the need for more supplies and moral support. Although he never struck me as being too religious, he did go to Amman on the Christian weekends so he could socialize with his friends there at the International Church. This schedule worked out very well, because when school started, early in September, I was able to put in full days with him on government weekends – Islamic weekends, Thursdays and Fridays. He would leave Saturday, early in the morning, and come back either Sunday evening or Monday early in the morning. I tried to put in some hours after school on Mondays through Wednesdays, but they never added to much, because my teacher, Mr. Rami, had been known for his generosity in giving killer homework, especially to those who proved competent. He would push every student to the limit and then some. I complained to Jim, but he made sure I had my homework done before I could touch his tools. He said if I started to weasel out of school work, I'd have to go work for my brothers instead, not him – heaven forbid.

"If you are planning on becoming an archeologist, young man, better keep that brain working," he said. "You have what it takes; now, take what you have and use it well. Otherwise you'll spend the rest of your life chanting to the mules through the Seeq." He gave me a disparaging look and began to chant the desert moonlight song in a heavy, clumsy accent, "Ya yumma shuftal gamarrrr balbeit, U matrahhu mnassama Khali." He rolled his r's and stressed his h's and kh's and made them sound like mule grunts.

"O, please, Jim," I said. "You certainly don't have what it takes, neither to sing nor to speak a foreign language."

"I know that, Lizard," he said with the most facetious look on his face. "I just love to see your mad expression."

Sometimes, Jim would bring his friends with him from Amman, and they would visit the site and the ruins and spend the night in Jim's cave. Some of them would even help us dig and clear the area, and others would just watch and admire without allowing their hands to get dirty. I learned to tell the difference between those who loved the earth for all its worth and those who just walked on it. The latter ones watched but never saw, for the earth rewarded only those with rough hands and soiled clothes. Most of Jim's friends, however, belonged to this latter group, although, a few expressed their fascination in weirder ways than others.

An old lady had come to visit Jim's project once, and she spotted a fragment of broken pottery at the edge of the road. She picked it up and brushed it gently with her handkerchief and exposed the edge of a design. Then her face flushed and her speech staggered. The tips of her fingers weakened from her shaky hands and she dropped the piece of pottery on the ground. She picked it up again and cradled it this time in the palm of her hand and rushed it to Jim.

"This is typical Nabatean pottery," said Jim calmly.

The woman's face turned from peach to watermelon. "You mean this is old?"

Jim's lower lip pushed against his upper one as he tried to make a guess. "About two thousand years old," he said.

"You...you mean." By this time, the woman had bordered insanity. The few words that came out of her mouth were strident. Her face turned into a loud torch. She had metamorphosed from a proper looking English lady to a hyper frog. I had never seen a scene like that before. It scared me. Jim felt obligated. He had to do something to calm her down.

"There are millions of these fragments around here," he said. "The trick is to find a whole one." There was challenge in his voice, but the woman ignored it. She was still caressing the fragment with the tips of her fingers as if it were a newly born pet. It was disgusting.

"Can...Can you imagine?" she repeated over and over again. "Can you imagine? Someone made this two thousand years ago."

"I am sure they'd let you keep it if you want to," continued Jim. "It's just a tiny fragment," and by that he added fuel to the fire, and the woman went wild. She pulled a tissue paper from her purse and carefully wrapped the sliver of pottery and laid it gently in her purse.

"Can you imagine that?" This time she looked at me, and I tried to smile.

"Yes, Ma'am," I whispered.

Chapter 10

"This, this is my porte–bonheur," she cooed. "Can you imagine that?" Nothing would shut her up, and was I glad when Jim finally led her and her silent husband away from the project. Yes, she did have a husband. He followed her around, the entire way, in extreme silence.

Every once in a while we would move a rock and uncover a lizard, a mouse, or a snake and disturb its peace or the other way around. The mouse would scurry between our feet and out of site; the lizard would do the same after staring at us for a moment or two as if to study our intentions, and the snake would create a problem between Jim and me.

He liked snakes; I feared them. He wanted to save them; I wanted to smash their heads with the nearest rock. I tried to tell Jim that all snakes in this part of the world were poisonous, and most people, if not all, feared them; therefore, the first reaction of a local person toward a snake would be destruction. Jim thought that snakes were beautiful creatures and should be left alone. Our most bitter argument took place when we found the first snake. After that, I could no longer trust Jim nor the site, because I was not allowed to kill the dumb critters; neither was I allowed to call them "dumb critters", at least not in front of Jim. I called them "Them things", trying to utilize my American slang word and mute it so it would almost sound like "Dumb things" and satisfy myself.

I made up my mind that if Jim could not find his god, I would give him some live snakes for a token. But I wasn't sure I could ever convince myself to keep "Dem things" alive long enough for him to take them away. The idea of a snake existing on the same premises that held me, usually, stripped all the peace out of my soul and left me scared and stiff as a mummy.

I would never forget Jim's and my first confrontation with the snake. I had just dumped a load of fine dirt and come back for another when Jim motioned for me to be quiet.

"There is a snake," he whispered.

"Where?"

"Under this rock right here."

The rock had been balanced on a few smaller rocks and I could see something hiding underneath, a design in the shades of brown coiled against a mass of colored sand, not much different in color but seemed enough different in texture. The sand looked coarse against the leather of the hidden creature. Jim slowly reached with the shovel, used it as a crowbar, and raised the rock. The snake slipped out and headed for the hill, but by then, I was there, ready, waiting for it with my shovel, and I lowered it on its head, using all the power in my muscles. The snake tried to coil its tail and lift its head, but I hit it again and again until it collapsed. I continued to pound the beast with all my might until I was sure it was good and dead. Then I chopped the head off and scooped it with the shovel.

"There," I said and headed for the wheelbarrow.

"What the hell do you think you're doing?" shouted Jim. He had been shouting the same words over and over while I was killing the snake, but I never heard them exactly. I had never seen him so angry and shocked before. His lips fluttered, and his speech turned hoarse, and his words were tangled up with each other, you'd think he was chewing on a rubber ball. I could hardly understand him. His voice matched the sound of the goats down by the road, except they were much calmer than he. "What'd you do that for? He was jus' resting, poor thing, an' you ruined his day and mine and yours." He spoke so fast; his mouth slobbered and foamed. I didn't know what to say. I couldn't even understand why he was angry. What I did was a natural and a very normal reaction; what I said next made him explode.

"I killed the snake for you," I said.

"Fo' me," he shouted. "Fo' me. Well, you." For a moment I thought he was going to lower the shovel on me, but then he threw it on the ground and kicked his feet like a child throwing tantrum. Then he controlled himself by digging his dirty fingernails into the heels of his own hands. I stood there and watched nervously as if I were waiting for my punishment from an angry god at doomsday. He took a deep breath and went to the nearest rock and sat down. I looked around for an escape, and Majid's music suddenly filled the air.

The musician had come to play his reed pipe for the tourists and the excavators. But this time, the music came in at the wrong time for Jim. He looked irritated – shook his head and covered his ears with his hands while his elbows stuck out like small wings. I assumed he didn't want to have anything to do with anybody for a while, so I headed down for safety, toward the broken pillar, where Majid was sitting, and took refuge.

The musician always located himself on one of the broken pillars and entertained. The pillars were low enough to make perfect stools to sit on and be seen by the passers by. The local people sang with him, and the foreigners hummed, and everybody went about, looking, testing, studying, digging, and shoveling and moving their heads with the beat. The music always smothered the jabbering of the tour guides and blended all the noises in a comfortable monotony, so the neighing of horses and beating of hoofs against rocks and all the human rattling would fall in step.

When I arrived at Majid's site, I was so shaken, and all my being had fallen out of step. I collapsed on the rock next to him and kicked a small rock out of my way. It went soaring down the road and hit nobody. He put his instrument down and frowned at me.

"What did you do – kill a man?" said Majid.

"No." I covered my face with the palms of my hands and rested my elbows on my knees.

"You sure look like it."

"I think the old man has lost it," I said.

"Well. We're all going to lose it some day," said Majid disparagingly in a voice that expressed condolences.

"He found a snake," I said, "and I killed it for him, and he got all mad as if I had killed his mother."

"You know. I heard that some foreigners actually like snakes. It is weird, but they do. Did you tell Jim he'd be facing the Almighty by now had you not killed the dumb thing?"

"No," I said. "You should have seen the look on his face, and the words he was spitting at a hundred and fifty kilometers an hour. He never gave me a chance to speak."

"You go tell him the facts about snakes in this country. I've heard of nonpoisonous snakes before, Raji. They do exist in other places, you know. And people play with them as if they were cats. Maybe Jim thinks snakes are nonpoisonous around here too," said Majid. "You go tell him the facts. Tell him if he finds a nonpoisonous snake in the ground here, I'll come and charm it for him. Maybe I'll make more money as a snake charmer. I'll put on a turban like an Indian and charm snakes with my music." He fell in a reverie and kept on talking and talking until I got tired of his daydream and went back to Jim. Majid's voice followed me until he realized I was no longer there. Then I heard his music starting all over again.

When I got back to the site, Jim was skinning the snake.

"What the hell do you think you're doing?" I asked.

Chapter 10

"I'm skinning the snake for you," he said. His wide range smile covered his face, and he looked at me with vindictive eyes. He looked calm and composed. It scared me half to death to see him like that.

"Fo' me?" I said.

"Yes for you. I'm going to dry its skin, and you're going to hang it on the wall in your room. It will remind you of an innocent life you have taken so brutally."

"Innocent my foot," I said. "Jim, the snakes here are extremely deadly."

"I know that," he said calmly. "But they'll leave you alone if you leave them alone."

"Well, you tell the snakes that," I snorted. "And if I get the snake skin anywhere near my house, I'd join that innocent life you claim. My family would think I'm nuts."

"Then hang it in your cave. I want you to look at it and admire its beauty. Focus your eyes on the wonderful design that decorates it. Forget about the poison. Just admire the beauty of the creature."

"I'd rather admire Aisheh's goat," I said and stared at Aisheh who, at that very moment, was heading with her goats toward the hill. Jim watched me quietly. When the shepherdess heard the music of the reed pipe, she began to sing and swing her body with the step. She was beautiful. I followed her with my eyes and forgot about the snake, the poison, Jim, and the whole world of dirt and excavations.

"She has a beautiful voice," said Jim, trying to stir up trouble. He had this cynical look on his face again. I could read that man like a first grade book. His eyes always told what he had in mind, all crisp and clear. I looked down at him and watched him operate on his poor innocent snake and laughed. Then I wheeled my wheelbarrow and began to fill it up with dirt. We worked in silence for the rest of the day.

Just before quitting time, Jim felt something solid in the dirt. Gently, he began to loosen the fine dirt around it and brush it off.

"We'd better find out what this is, right here, before we quit," he said.

My stomach was growling, and I had really had enough for one day. I still couldn't get over his snake episode, and now he wanted to hold my hunger for a while yet.

"I'm hungry," I said. I had never admitted my needs to him before, but the aberration of this day had caused all my manners to diminish. They dissipated in all the confusion of the anomalous happenings.

"Why don't you wait, and I'll feed you today," he said. "We'll eat up in the village. I'm going to spend the night at the Guest house, because tomorrow I have to head for the big city, bright and early."

I couldn't argue with that statement. He knew how to pull my leg. I liked eating out. I liked eating anywhere.

His brush began to expose a round shape, too perfect to be a rock.

"Come. Look at this," he said. His eyes bulged, and he looked all excited like a kid.

A dome surface with a radius of about ten centimeters, all smooth and perfect, bulged out of the dirt. Jim brushed carefully on one side and I on the other. The bulging dome continued to get larger and larger. Gradually, Jim and I grew more excited and silent. Our lips and our teeth tightened as we worked. I couldn't even hear or feel his breath in my face anymore. We worked for a long time without looking at each other. Then, I glimpsed at Jim's glasses and caught the reflection of the dome in them. He turned to me and smiled, and then we turned back and worked some more. We crouched in the hole like two rodents. Our noses, not too far behind our fine tools, inhaled the damp earth. Our faces moved closer to the bulging shape as we worked. We were so close. I had to say something.

"Jim," I finally whispered.

"Yes, son."

I wondered if the closeness made him call me son, and I wanted to call him yaba, or father, but I didn't. "You know. Some lucky people found pots full of ancient gold in the ground in several different parts of the country. Burying valuables is a very ancient tradition. Do you suppose we hit one of those?"

"Raji," he said softly, "an ancient, complete, intact piece of antiquity is worth a pot of gold."

I thought of the many pieces that sat in my cave, all well preserved. Then I decided they wouldn't be worth much for Jim, for he was determined to discover his own, the hard way, and I had to let him be and quit nagging him about my cave.

Half an hour later, we pulled a Nabatean cooking clay pot out of the dirt. It was empty, but the feeling of pulling something so wholesome and complete out of the ground was like helping the earth give birth or, rather, a rebirth to one of its ancient people.

"Just knowing that a man had helped himself out of this pot two thousand years ago gives me enough satisfaction," said Jim. "Who cares about gold."

"Heck, I do."

His smile disappeared sharply, and I read disappointment all over his face. "I guess, that's the difference between a fifteen year old kid and an old geezer," he mumbled.

"No, Jim," I said. "I know what you meant. I just love to see your mad expression."

He shook his head and gently lifted the pot up toward the light. "Look at her," he whispered. "Isn't she beautiful!"

My stomach growled again, and this time, Jim heard it.

"Now we can go eat," he said. "We can eat all night long if you wish." He set the pot on the fine dirt and scurried to collect all the tools and close down for the day. He hopped around like a happy child, all excited as if someone had just given him a lollipop.

He had me wheel the tools to his cave while he wrapped the clay pot with his head dress and carried it like a baby, all bundled up nicely. He even hummed and sang for it on the way home. I had never seen him so happy before. In the morning the man had expressed extreme anger, and now, he beamed with happiness. I hoped his heart could take it all.

We went to Abu–Mustafa's restaurant in town instead of the Guest House. I told Jim I wanted to eat a decent meal not a polished dish, and he complied. The restaurant had no menu. The waiter told us the meals available for that particular evening. Of course, the condiments were available all the time, and there was no need for listing them each time. Jim trusted me with the order, and I told him he wouldn't regret it.

A few minutes later, the waiter came with two dishes of hot rice and two bowls of steaming vegetable sauce with chunks of lamb sticking through. Then he left and came back with a stack of pocket bread, a dish of olives and a dish of sliced onions. And, finally, on his last trip to our table, he brought two cups of hot tea.

"Enjoy your meal," said the waiter. "Tomorrow will be a long day."

I had forgotten all about it. The next day was the first day of the Islamic Lent. I explained to Jim that the next day was the first day of the month of Ramadan, during which all restaurants (except the ones in the tourist areas) would close all day during the day and open only in the evenings.

Chapter 10

"Why would they do that?"

"Because most people fast, and it doesn't pay for the restaurants to stay open all day. Besides, people who do not fast are not supposed to eat publicly, courtesy to the majority that does."

"What do they do, starve all day?"

"Yes, Jim," I said. I never thought it would be so hard to explain all the nitty gritty details about our culture and religion to a stranger. I did not want him to misunderstand anything, yet I was getting tired of explaining things all the time. I could feel the pressure on my brain. It nagged. "The idea of fasting, I suppose, is to let people experience hunger so they would feel with the hungry," I continued. "At least, that's what the Sheik told us in religious studies. Not everybody fasts, but many do. Some do it faithfully and joyfully, others, only for fear of going to hell. They labor on hungry stomachs all day – supposed to. Some of them grumble about it; others do it with passion, and when they hear the call for prayer from the minaret at sunset, they eat. Everybody eats. That's the best part about it."

"Do you fast?"

"I fast whenever I feel like it. The discipline is too much for me, Jim. I know I am a sinful man, but spending thirty days in fasting and penitence is more than my sins would call for. I'm not that bad."

Jim laughed. "Does your family fast?"

He was full of questions. I tried to eat just enough to satisfy my stomach while I answered his interrogations. It was hard. I made an effort to swallow quickly between questions, but I couldn't always make it in time. They kept coming at me faster than I could think. I was still chewing on the first piece of bread and hadn't touched the rice yet.

"My mother does. I try not to disappoint her, and I don't know about my brothers. All I know is that we all eat the evening and the early morning meals with Mother. What we do during the day is out of her sight."

"You lie to her?"

"A white lie on a full stomach can't hurt anybody, Jim."

"You sinful wretch."

"Yes, God," I grumbled and put a spoonful of vegetable sauce on top of my rice and took a bite. "Now that's what I would call food, Jim."

He must have agreed, because he ate silently with a silly smile on his face. He cleaned up his rice and vegetables and ate two pieces of the pocket bread, plain. I ate my rice and two pieces of pocket bread with olives and onions. There were two pieces left in the dish.

"You may eat the rest if you wish," said Jim. "I'm full."

I cleaned up all the dishes, the bread, the olives, and the onions, and I wiped the last of the vegetable sauce with the last bite of the bread. Jim watched me and grinned the entire time. When I was done, I pushed the dishes aside and began to sip my tea.

"There," I said with a sigh of satisfaction. "Now I'm not hungry anymore."

Jim folded his hands and closed his eyes. "Thank God," he said. "I began to wonder whether you have a real stomach or a bottomless pit."

"I get hungry when I'm overworked, Jim."

"I'll never overwork you again, Lizard. Honest to God."

"See to it that you don't get any of Dem snakes near me either. I can't promise a peaceful confrontation with Dem things."

"That, I can't assure you of, Lizard. The snakes and the lizards are akin, and you just might have a family reunion one of these days."

"I'd rather keep a family feud in this case; thank you."

"Raji, you're a pain in the neck."

"I know," I said sweetly as if it were a compliment.

The tea was getting cold. We gulped it fast, and I asked for a refill. Jim frowned and shook his head.

"Refill is free, Jim. Don't worry," I said. "It is just that I like my tea hot. The first cup didn't count. It didn't cut it." Jim shook his head again and covered his cup with his hand. The waiter understood the gesture and filled only my cup. Both Jim and I watched him fill it clear to the very top. He poured slowly, carefully, maliciously, for he too had had it with me. In our culture, filling someone's cup too full was an expression of acrimony. I told Jim that, and he laughed.

There was no way I could pick up that cup without spilling hot tea either on the table or on my fingers, so I bent over the table and slowly slurped the first few sips so loud, made it clear to everybody that I was having so much fun and just couldn't let these moments of my life slip away too fast. Jim giggled, deeply; the waiter grunted and went away mumbling all sorts of colorful words.

Jim paid the bill and headed toward the Guest House to spend the night. I ambled home in the dark, kicking dirt and thinking of snakes, antiquities, fasting people, God, and man digging in the desert. Tomorrow, the fasting month of Ramadan would start, and we would have to adjust our lives; all of us would have to do that – Jim, Aisheh, and I.

Chapter 11

Traditions held that many spooky but benevolent deeds take place during the month of Ramadan, especially to those who fast and mean it. They deprive themselves, feed the hungry and do many good deeds. But I had already excused myself from this rather difficult task, since I could never get myself to fast and barely kept up with my own forever growling stomach, and since the only good deeds I was able to perform at the time were to keep Jim from getting himself in trouble. He paid me for that, so it did not even count. Mother had also told us once that fasting teaches the person how to discipline himself so he doesn't turn into an animal. Oh well, I thought. Since nobody in the family thought of me as the disciplined sibling anyway, there was no point in disappointing them during Ramadan. I had work to do. I needed to go see Jim and tell him my Ramadan schedule. School would let us out an hour early, and I would have more chances to work with him on weekdays too.

He had spent a quiet night at the Guest house, and when he woke up the next day, he experienced the first day of the holy month. Nobody shared the breakfast meal with him at the restaurant. He ate alone and had the entire place to himself. There was nobody to talk to, no local people to visit with, except Abu–Zeid who waited on him and finally set an entire pot of Turkish coffee in front of him and wished him a good Ramadan day.

Jim refilled his cup of coffee and took a sip.

"Good coffee," he said.

"In Ramadan, everything seems to taste better," said Abu–Zeid. "Even to those who do not fast. You just wait and see. People make extra special food and treats for others as well as themselves to feast on at the end of each day. Everybody suffers during the day and waits patiently for the evening prayer. Then everybody becomes relieved – stuffed and relieved."

"Do you make any of the special Ramadan foods?"

"I wouldn't dare not to. Come this evening and you'll have Katayef." Abu–Zeid gathered his fingers together and kissed their tips to express how delicious the Katayef could be. "Top delicious, and they're made only during Ramadan."

"You sound worse than Raji. Kata... whatever they are do not mean much to me."

"I'm sorry, Jim. I forgot. You know, it gets to be tiring sometimes to have to explain every nitty gritty word to the tourists."

"It gets more tiring being left in the dark."

"I know. I just keep forgetting, and to me, you are one of us now, and I keep forgetting. Anyway, Katayef is pastry filled with a meat mix and roasted pine nuts and then baked to golden brown." He licked his lips as he talked and swallowed his saliva at the thought of food. Fasting had started to work on him already. "And for dessert," he continued, "we'll have the same pastry filled with a cheese mix, baked to golden brown and then dipped in a honey syrup."

"Sounds good to me. I won't be able to come tonight, however," said Jim. "Perhaps I will try it some other night."

Chapter 11

"I'm sure you will, Jim. We cannot run out of Katayef during Ramadan, not even for one day. We wouldn't dare. People would consider it a blasphemy, and they would pray for God and the Prophet's mercy."

Abu–Zeid left Jim reading the pictures in the newspaper and headed back toward the kitchen. The Arabic characters in the journal were good as Chinese to Jim, so it never took him long to go through the entire paper. Customers usually visited with him and translated some of the articles to him, but not today. Ramadan was going to be a long boring month, he thought, but not for long.

When I walked into the restaurant to catch Jim before he left for the Capital, I was horrified the minute I walked through the door. I stretched my eyebrows up so high and opened my eyes as wide as a wild cat that had seen its prey and tried not to blink to make sure that I was fully awake and that the sight before my very eyes was actual, real, not a fantasy. It was all true. I had witnessed a legend in the making. The old archeologist was sitting on the floor in the clearing by the entrance of the restaurant, facing Um–Sleiman, the fortuneteller who was squatting in front of him, studying the coffee grounds in his coffee cup and, occasionally, looking into his eyes and studying his face and uttering words of luck and misfortune.

Um–Sleiman walked crooked, spoke funny and did strange things. Her voice was too low for a woman, although she had some shrill pitches every once in a while. But her speech had power and confidence like a policeman's. According to the villagers, she was a strange woman, barren like a dry stump. People knew her as the cursed wretch, because her womb bore no blessings. She and her husband had moved to Wadi Moussa many years ago, when the Guest House was first being built. Her husband had been one of the builders. The villagers talk about him as a good man. He worked diligently and feared God. But, by the time the construction of the Guest House was completed, he had developed a chronic disease and died shortly after. So, Um–Sleiman was left all alone, stuck in the village, abandoned, with no children, no pillars to lean on. She just remained there, like the empty tombs and the ruins of Petra.

She owned a small house surrounded by a spacious piece of land at the far side of town. The property had ample room for a large garden and a huge hot rock oven, a taboon, which she also owned, just beyond the garden fence.

The reason people called her Um–Sleiman, or mother of Solomon was because each person must have a nickname or a title in our culture, and this title normally comes from the first born child to the family. The parents then would be called, father of so and so or mother of so and so. And if the parents had no children, the community would give them a child's name (usually a grandfather's name) in anticipation or hope for children to come to that family in the future. Therefore, this woman was called Um–Sleiman, although no children had come to her family, and her husband's illness and then his death had eliminated every hope. She had to make it on her own.

Her garden was surrounded by a rock fence and lined with grape vines, a copious number of grape vines that twisted and grew up above and over the fence. Another wooden fence ran parallel to the rock fence and helped the vines spread out and open up a tunnel–like cavity underneath. It looked like an eerie path, full of shadows that reflected unfamiliar shapes, formed by thick branches, leaves and clusters of grapes. Um–Sleiman sold the sweet grapes that ripened on her vines and grape leaves, soft and flavorful, perfect for making grape leaf rolls, stuffed with rice and meat, and she made vinegar with the extra or over ripe grapes and sold it to the villagers.

She managed a cornucopia of fresh produce, and she owned an abundance of chickens, mostly layers, for she also sold eggs and garden produce to the villagers. A few sheep, kept in a small fenced area outside the garden, supplied her with milk, and she sold milk and cheese, fresh white cheese that she made. When Jim saw that kind of cheese, he called it blocks of cottage cheese. People would buy the blocks of fresh white cheese and cure them by boiling them in brine and then keep them in the brine. They would keep for an entire season.

Um–Sleiman was also known for her ethnic bread which she baked in her taboon. She had introduced it to the tourists at the Guest House. When Abu–Zeid saw how much his customers had admired it, he proceeded to buy it from her and brag about it as his restaurant's special ethnic bread. He also allowed Um–Sleiman to read the grounds of the Turkish coffee cups to his tourists. Reading the grounds had been an old fortune-telling device to those duped enough to believe in it. Abu–Zeid's convincing vernacular had lured most people to believe that Um–Sleiman was the best fortuneteller in the northern hemisphere. He had adopted her as a needy widow and allowed her to earn some money on his premises. I suppose that was his good deed – perhaps his only one. This had also enhanced his public relations with the tourist agencies and counted as a unique attraction.

Some say that he even convinced Um–Sleiman to raise the price to ten piasters for every cup she read, not a bad sum of money at the time for squatting in front of people and reciting to them what they wanted to hear about themselves anyway. People constantly dropped the coins in the sack that lay open at her side and listened ecstatically to her broken English words that conveyed potent information about the future.

People believed Um–Sleiman. Someone swore once that she had told him the story of his life, and it scared him how much she knew about him.

"How does she do that?" he asked. "How could she know so much about people?"

"It's the secret of the profession," said Abu–Zeid.

"Don't worry," said Um–Sleiman. "The secret would be taken away from me if I betrayed a customer. Your secret will never leave my chest." She pounded her chest with the palm of her hand.

The secret lay in the fact that the woman happened to be a good psychologist, a natural, superior to the professionals. She took from the people as much as she gave them, and the more they responded to her, the more she gave. She knew people, their behavior and response or reaction to every action; she knew the nature of man and was able to figure out the nature of every individual a few minutes after she had visited with him or her. She knew what people needed and gave it to them. They took it and believed in her. Many were scared of her.

The villagers preferred to avoid her most of the time. They bought her produce and let her go. Some feared her and regarded her as a witch, especially since, in their eyes, she was the cursed woman who bore no children. The distance, however, between her and the rest of the villagers never seemed to bother her. She always looked happy and contented to be alone. I thought of her as the ancient city of Petra, isolated yet full of deep secrets from the roots of man. I too feared her, some.

Chapter 11

"There is a large hyena in your cup," she was saying to Jim as I approached them with a wide open mouth and bulging eyes, "a huge monster, monumental, bigger than any hyena I had ever seen, and it is standing very closely between you and your dream, towering up there."

"Now, what does the hyena represent," asked Jim calmly and respectfully. His eyes focused on the words as they came out of her mouth, and he seemed happy and amused.

"Hyenas are known for having the power to stun their prey, just by staring at it. This would, in a way, paralyze the prey and weaken it. Some old folks even tell stories about hyenas stunning little children. However, the validity of these stories is questionable, mostly because the old folks used these stories to warn the little children against wandering alone away from home."

"But what does the hyena have to do with me; what is it doing in my cup?" asked Jim with trusting eyes.

"Oh, Mister Jim, this hyena is haunting you. It is tall as a mountain, but its head is lowered down. Her mouth is close to you as if she's ready to talk to you, but you're not talking, nor are you listening to her. You try to turn your back to her. Sometimes you feel as if the beast is sitting on your chest with her weight pressing against you, and her eyes staring down at you. You need to talk and listen, Mister. You need to talk and listen. All beasts are friendly when you talk to them with good intentions. They know your intentions, sometimes better than you do. Talk, listen, and she will let you through. Meanwhile, she's waiting."

Jim's face changed all of a sudden. It turned serious, gloomy and silent like the old walls of the restaurant, dark and full of odd shadows. He let his lips sag and parallel the wrinkles on his cheeks, and his eyes stared at the floor in front of the woman. It scared her. When she looked up at his face, she retreated and reached the table with her hand and laid his coffee cup down gently so it wouldn't make any noise. Then, with a soft whisper, she wished him peace and anchored her feet so she could stand up, but when she stood half way off the floor, she tightened the palms of her hands around her waist toward her back, and her face shriveled in pain.

"Young man," she said to me as she eased herself to a full posture.

"I don't have a cup of coffee," I said quickly. "I don't drink any coffee."

"I know that, silly. I just need some help. You're a good young man. I've been watching you, and I believe you might be able to help me a little today. What do you say?"

Now, I was really scared. She'd been watching me. What had she been doing that for? What did she want from me? I had an urge to turn around and run, but then I became curious and tried to control my fear. "What do you want?" I asked and stumbled over the words as if they were foreign.

"There is some stuff I need to carry to town this afternoon before the evening prayer. Suppose I could convince you to lend me a hand about an hour before the prayer?"

I had always jumped in to help people without hesitation and before I was even asked, but I wasn't sure about helping this woman. What kind of stuff did she wish to carry to town? I had never been anywhere near her side of town. It had been proclaimed as the venturesome part by the villagers, especially the little children. I wondered how safe it would be to try to walk up there.

"Sure," I said reflexively, although I was no way near sure at all, and she sensed it. She sensed my fears and somehow conveyed to me that she had sensed them. I never knew how. It could have been the eyes. Her eyes spoke with power. "Don't worry, young man," she scolded. "I just need two more hands to help me carry some food to town. Stop by my taboon. I'll be baking there."

Chapter 11

Her voice conveyed ample reassurance, and her words duped me to promise her to come and help her, and I promised myself I would never let anybody in town know or see me help her. I had no idea how I was going to do that. Omnipotent eyes quite frequently roamed the village. Sometimes the eyes were attached to many ears, noses and other inexplicable senses.

Jim woke up from his day dream all shook up by Um–Sleiman's words. They bothered Jim. He dropped the coin in her pouch and left. I tried to talk to him, but he wouldn't talk.

CHAPTER 12

I couldn't wait to arrive at Um–Sleiman's place, partly because I wanted to have a hand in revealing a mystery, and partly because I wanted to get it over with. A slight fear had settled in my chest. It reduced my appetite and caused the hours to slow down to a creeping pace. I watched every second tick while my heartbeat raced with excitement and worry. At school, I half-way listened to the teachers' lectures and half-way dreamed about what Um–Sleiman's place would look like. But my mind failed to picture anything of a credible quality.

I had no idea what the woman was up to; nobody in the village ever did, yet everybody believed that she had to be up to something no good most likely. Although nothing ever happened, the expectations were always there, especially among the children of the village. Today, I knew she was up to something, and she had planned for me to be a part of it.

The school boys called her Black Elephant because of her big size and tried to steal produce from her cart every once in a while, and the girls ran away at the sight of her. They hid in the street corners, pointed to each other and giggled and whispered aloud words like "She's going to get you. She's after you this time." And Um–Sleiman would make a sudden shift with her cart toward their corner, laugh aloud and say, "Next time. I'll get you next time. You just wait and see." Her words would increase their anxieties and add more stories and speculations to the mysteries related to the Black Elephant.

Today she got me. What she would do with a creature like me developed into another hypothesis. I pondered over it off and on. I had never tried to steal anything from her cart and wondered whether she knew that or not. When I asked one of the school mates who had a history of pestering her what it would be like to go to her place, he said, "You don't talk about this woman during Ramadan. You don't even think of her. She's a one way ticket to the devil's domain."

"Why?" I asked, hoping he would tell me some facts to lean on.

"Why? Well, I'll tell you why when you tell me why she lives all by herself all closed up like that. She has nobody but the spirits, the evil ones to call upon for company."

"How do you know that? Have you ever been in her place."

"I came as close as the fence once and then condemned the devil and ran home, faster than lightning. The place looked haunted. I condemned the devil all the way home. I felt him following me too. I tell you. It was scary."

"Did you actually see anything scary in particular?"

"I didn't have to. The looks of that place is enough to give you the hint."

"I don't know. It would be nice to find out for sure what all is hidden there."

"Nice! Are you nuts or what? You want something nice you go down to the beach of Aqaba and look at the half naked city ladies."

Chapter 12

"I meant challenging."

"I'd condemn the devil, Raji."

Normally, I would condemn the devil. Today, however, it felt as if I had a contract with him, especially since my classmate had nothing but imagined nightmares to tell about the unmentionable. I repeatedly tried to convince myself that there had been no solid facts about the woman's ill deeds. There were ample speculations but not one actual fact to prove the woman guilty of any of the accusations. As the hour drew nearer, my courage seemed to rise to a higher level. I finally became determined to discover the woman, once and for all. I could condemn the devil all the way there and all the way back and hope that God would have an escape for me somewhere if I needed it.

The smell of good food permeated the area all around her property, and it was strong enough to break anybody's fasting vows. I drooled and swallowed several times. Thick smoke twirled above the hot rock oven hut. The plumes dissipated in a ghostly dance as they traveled toward the ancient city. She must be preparing the oven for a good one, I thought and prayed it would not be me. The villagers who still cooked in the taboon had to prepare it the night before. It took all night for the rocks to get hot and ready for baking. The women usually lit it late in the evening and did all the baking and the cooking early next morning.

The entire place, the garden, the small house and the taboon looked ghostly all right – different, I should say. She had too many items crammed in her space, made use of every spot on the property, no waste, no vacancy. Her grape vines rested heavily on the thick wooden fence. Each vine took the shape of a small hut, yet it also formed one section of a long green tunnel, for the vines were connected, one with the next. Vine huts arched all around and opened up entrances and exits here and there that made them look spooky and haunted. I hated my speculations and tried to get rid of the scary thoughts, but they wouldn't go away. My legs felt weak, and I just wanted out of that place.

"There you are."

The voice was sharp, and it came out of the taboon area. I looked at the smoke, and it looked back at me as if it were doing the talking. Then Um–Sleiman came wobbling around the corner of the hut. "Come here, son. We have work to do," she said. "I hope you are a strong boy. It doesn't look like your mother feeds you enough."

She was large, tall and wide, and she walked crooked and always felt around her waist with the palms of her hands as she walked and twisted and turned as if to loosen up painful muscles. Her black dress engulfed her big body and seemed to have ample room left. She wore a sash and used it to pull the dress up so she wouldn't step on it. Multiple layers of the dress hung over her belly and all around her waist. But the garment was pulled crooked, and it exposed her ankle on one side. It stuck out as she walked crooked. The other ankle was still covered with the dress. The pink plastic shoes she had on also stuck out sorely. She looked like a black bear wearing the shoes of a small princess. So far, going to her place had been both a fantasy and a nightmare, but still, I found no sound proof of ill deeds anywhere on the site.

I followed her toward the house. It took more minutes than I had wished for to get there. When she finally arrived at the porch, she turned around and motioned for me to sit down on one of the small wicker chairs that were lined up by the wall. I obeyed. Then she slowly walked over to the chair next to mine and sat down. She sat next to me and looked at me with soft eyes, full of pain, harmless, almost pleading. My fears diminished in the few silent moments that followed.

CHAPTER 12

"Before we get busy, young man," she finally said. "You have to promise me you would never let anybody know of what you will be doing here." Her eyes looked determined now. "Not a soul," she said emphatically.

"I promise. I promise," I said. My legs felt weak again and began to shake. She sensed them through my clothes.

"Don't worry. It's nothing bad," she said and let her voice drop, almost to a whisper. "It's just that I'm getting old, and my bones can't take the work anymore. You see. I need help during the month of Ramadan. Just a few minutes every day until the month is over. Now, go take a look inside the kitchen and come back and tell me what you see." She motioned to the kitchen door. It was closed.

I walked over, turned the nob, and shrieked as the old door squeaked loudly. Then I closed my eyes and pushed it open with all my might, expecting a horrid beast beyond imagination to jump at me or chase me clear to the High Places of Petra. Nothing happened. Then I poked my head inside and allowed my eyes and my mind to adjust to the lack of light. The kitchen counters were full, and I mean, clear to the ceiling in certain places. Five large, heavy pots of steaming food that had been cooking in the taboon all day, stacks of taboon bread that smelled like heaven – at least fifty round plump loaves of dark bread covered one side of the kitchen. In the far corner stood stacks of cheap and used aluminum containers. They towered all the way up to the ceiling. I stood there for a moment admiring the abundance and then turned around and told her that I saw enough food to satisfy a large crowd and then some. She smiled and nodded with satisfaction.

"My husband died during the month of Ramadan," she said in a soft voice that belonged to a small, delicate person, "and I've been doing this every year, ever since he died. I do it for his soul and mine and some other lost souls I come upon each day. Every poor family and every lonely person I know in this village gets at least one turn, one portion of rice and lamb, and two turns of taboon bread. I keep track of that, so you don't have to worry about it.

"I always used to distribute the food myself without ever being caught doing it. Of course, it helped to be healthy and nimble in those days. I hid well, and nobody ever discovered me. I never let it happen, for you know what the good Books say, even your left hand should never learn about your right hand's offerings. Never do that. I was never caught. People never knew who gave them the food. I heard rumors about who they thought it was." She laughed and shook her head happily. "They still don't know, and I intend to keep them that way." Her last statement was declared with a serious frown, and she looked at me straight in the eye. "Do you understand?"

I nodded. "Who do they think is the food giver?"

"At first they thought it was some charitable organization but then decided that most organizations brag about their donations and don't keep it secret, so they finally decided that it had to be only one person, a wealthy man, trying to give generously as a repentance for his sins. That's what they believe, and I intend to keep it that way," she repeated firmly. "My blessings will be taken away from me if people knew. They would start bragging about my donations, and they would no longer be good. Do you understand?"

I nodded again, and she continued, "I've been watching you, Raji. You're the kid I need just now. You have a fast, nimble foot and know how to steal away from trouble when you see it. I've watched you sneak away from that old weasel, Abu–Zeid, and some other school kids on many occasions. You're good – my kind of guy, and I believe you could help me deliver my secret meals. Would you do it for me?"

CHAPTER 12

Never before had I felt ready for a job like I did at that moment. Whether the reason was her bragging about me so much or the revelation and the relief that eased its way through my head and chest, I couldn't tell, but I was ready to go.

"When do we begin?" I asked in a ready and obedient tone of voice.

"Right now. Each day I leave at a different time. That way, people cannot expect me at a certain time. Sometimes I go as early as noon. I watch and take my chances when the villagers are busy and not watching their door step. You can dash here from school during the noon hour and deliver some if you wish. I'll give you lunch."

"But how do you carry it all?"

"On my produce cart, of course. I cover it with blankets and top them with a layer of produce." I remembered her produce cart. It was a huge, a custom built wooden cart that held mountains of produce. She rolled it to town every day like a store on wheels. "The pain in my back and all my muscles is more than I can handle anymore, and I need help," she repeated.

"Why don't you go to the government clinic. They should be able to give you something to ease your pain."

"Oh, I did. I've got my pills, but they don't always work very well. I'm just getting too old. People get old, you know. They're lucky, though. The ones who get old are lucky. They get to know more fine people like you and old Mister Jim." She pronounced his name as if she had known him for a while. She must have been watching him too, I thought. "But when people get old, they also get pain; it's the price they pay for living so long."

I pushed the cart as far as the first house in town. Um–Sleiman followed slowly yet closely behind. Then she took over behind the cart. The people were busy getting ready for the prayer and the evening meal. Their gates were shut and one could hear the clattering of dishes and the jabbering of adults and the screaming of children behind the doors. We kept our eyes opened on the roads, and whenever I spotted a moving shadow, I pretended to be walking down the street all alone, while the ugly cart of the old witch rolled all alone, disavowed. It strolled heavily down the road, lonely and rejected like a bad omen.

I ran the meals to the first assigned door, knocked and disappeared, while Um–Sleiman pushed the cart slowly down the main street of the village. Then I met her again at the next destination after we made sure it was safe for me to accomplish my second mission.

The first meal went to Abu–Hamdoon's house. The father had disappeared and left an emaciating woman with eight children. Some people said that the man had gone to Syria or Lebanon, but nobody really knew where he had gone. His three older boys had had to quit school and join the army so they could be fed and to provide some income for the rest of the family. Um–Sleiman had a large bundle ready for them. There was a large bowl of rice, a pot of lamb and vegetables cooked in the juice, and a stack of taboon bread, enough to feed the family and then some. She had used the cheap, used aluminum pots to dish up and deliver the meals in. That way she did not have to have her containers back. When I was ready to dash with the bundle, she reached down in her front pouch, deep inside her baggy dress and pulled out a bag of sugar candy.

"Here," she said. "Give them this bag too. One of the tourists gave it to me. I can't eat this stuff anymore – can't eat anything anymore. Let the kids enjoy it."

The deserted village streets, the roaring cart, Um–Sleiman, and I became a conspiracy, a clandestine plot, more exciting than Jim's project, my cave, or any endeavor I had ever indulged myself in. We tiptoed beyond gossip, although it didn't matter much to me anymore. Suddenly, the mystery turned into a scheme well planned, and the gossip, a useful tool to keep the people busy, away from the blessings of the old woman. Only the silence of the streets, the light footsteps, and the squeaking of the wooden cart could tell Um–Sleiman's tale. She was well protected, and I intended to keep her that way.

On the first day, we stopped at several places, some of which I never knew that well, but my biggest surprise came when I had to deliver a portion to the doorstep of my history teacher.

"Do you know this man?" I asked Um–Sleiman.

"Of course I do. Poor lonely soul. He's a good man, but he's living in bad times. I told him his good times are coming yet. I read his coffee cup for him once and told him that God is on his side. He said that he was stuck in a rut, and it would take a miracle for his life to change, and I told him God has all the miracles at his fingertips. He didn't believe me. I could tell. He thought I was reading the stupid coffee grounds."

"You mean you don't really read the coffee grounds?"

"What do you think, young man. You're supposed to be a learned man too. Is there a language in the dregs?"

"No … Not that I can read."

"Neither can I or anybody else. True, I use the different formations to get ideas, and I tell you, coffee ground formations can sure help your imagination. I never run out of ideas because of them. If I see a shape of a bird, it's good news, and, depending on whether the bird is pointing down or up, I tell the people whether the news is coming or going. If I see a fish, that's good fortune or success. I never run out of pictures and ideas, and people never run out of good and bad things that happen to them every day. All people. They're all the same, tourists and villagers. Even Abu–Zeid is one of them – God forgive us all."

The evening prayer came loud out of the minaret, and we were on our way back. I told Um–Sleiman I had to hurry home because my mother would throw a tantrum if I arrived late for supper. She usually prayed alone first, but I'd better be there when she was done. The prayer never lasted more than ten minutes at the maximum.

"Here," said Um–Sleiman, "take these. Eat them with your family." She pulled a stack of taboon bread and handed them to me. "Tell your mother you bought them from Abu–Zeid at the Guest House. He sells my bread."

"But I don't want to take your bread. My brothers bring home plenty of food."

"You take this right now, young man. Don't you think you are going to do the work for me for nothing. You understand?" I looked up in her dark eyes and feared her again. She was big and powerful inside. "You take some tomatoes too. I had the best crop ever this year – plenty of them – taste good too, very juicy."

She piled a small bag of tomatoes on top of my armload and ordered me to beat it.

Chapter 13

Jim called it a potluck. On Islamic weekends, we all brought an abundance of food and ate it like rodents in his hole, away from those who preferred to hunger themselves all day long during the month of Ramadan. Sometimes Aisheh would stop on her way to the hills and drop off several chunks of fresh goat cheese. Jim would bring a bag full of dry roasted peanuts in the hull. He used to purchase them from the Capital every time he took a trip up there. He said they were best when he first bought them, fresh, warm, out of the roaster, heavenly warm and full of flavor. I liked them too and told him they were the best thing that ever came out of the big city.

On weekdays, Aisheh would wait for me in our cave, or my cave as she would call it, and I would climb up there with fresh taboon bread and tomatoes from Um–Sleiman. We would slice the cheese and the tomatoes and eat them with bread, and we would talk, read in my books, and do homework. History, geography, mathematics, science, the woman hungered for all subjects. She would read and help me memorize and figure out how to solve problems and go through all the boring lessons I cared the least to learn, like the basics of philosophy and all that waste of brain effort.

Aisheh loved it and hated me whenever I chuckled at her explanation. She would read out loud, and I would lose her after the second or third statement. Then she would notice my loss and back up and try to delineate what she had read and explain it to me, until I would lose her again and chuckle and call it all fiddlesticks. After homework, on most week-days, I managed to put in an hour or so with Jim at the excavations. If not before the prayer, I helped him after supper, until it was too dark to work.

One day I fell asleep on an over–satisfied stomach. The day had been warm, and my mind remained on food until school was out. I finished my deliveries and gathered up my share in a flash. Then I hit the cave. Aisheh was there, waiting. We ate until we were full, and then I nibbled on the leftovers until all traces of food had disappeared. After that, Aisheh began to read philosophy again and put me to sleep. When I woke up she was staring at the wall. A few sun rays had marked the entrance of the cave and slashed a corner of it and hit one of the pottery pieces and exposed its natural colors. I had only seen them in artificial light, my flashlight, before, but the sun rays exposed an iridescent faculty of colors and history, all tangible before our very eyes. Aisheh's eyes were fixed on the ancient jug.

"Why don't you tell the old man to forget about his stupid caves and come and take a look at this."

"It would be easier for me to study philosophy than to convince that man to climb up here."

"Then take it down to him."

"I can't take a chance. It's too risky to move such treasures. They're too fragile and huge. I have never seen antique pottery so big and delicate. You don't just carry them around. They need to be packed properly, and I have neither the time nor the skill to do it. Besides Jim is not interested in some pottery in a cave. He's after the gods."

CHAPTER 13

I told my history teacher about Jim and his aspirations and excavations, and he said he would like to see our project and meet Jim. Mr. Rami wanted to see anything and meet anybody. He was a lonely man, tall, pale and thin, with a faint, anemic look that made him seem weak, but he had a compound, complex brain to make up for the appearance, for he could list dates, names and places and tell history like a fascinating story. He was a story teller who had come to this world with one purpose in life, and that was to tell history from the early beginnings of the human civilizations to modern times.

His audience sat in front of him and listened, and the more they listened, the better he manufactured his story. The students were most disciplined in his classroom. All the other teachers complained about attention span and order in the classroom. Mr. Rami never had to worry about that, because once Mr. Rami sat down and began to tell history, everybody listened and didn't want to miss a clue. If a student made any noise on accident or twitched his nose to shoo off a fly, the rest of the class would give him the look and embarrass him, because in Mr. Rami's class nobody wanted to miss what happened next – no distractions whatsoever. And the good teacher was aware of his talent and used it luxuriously. He always timed himself so that the bell rang at the most exciting moment in the history story, and then he would say, "To be continued," and the class would let out a morbid tone, and Mr. Rami would smile with satisfaction.

We, students, figured that the man must have been a descendant of Homer or one of those famous people who told history and passed it on orally until it finally got recorded several hundred years down the road. If those ancient historians were as good as Mr. Rami, then the history that had been handed down to us had to be precise, for the man might forget his lunch or his dinner but never a date in history.

The government had given Mr. Rami a scholarship when he went to college; therefore, he was stuck in our village. Government scholarships were usually awarded to the top students in the kingdom. They had full scholarships, tuition, food and lodging and even some pocket money to spend. Scholarship students lived like kings while in college, but once they finished their four years, they had committed themselves to the government for eight years, two years of working at the public schools for every year of scholarship, and the government had the right to place its graduates anywhere in the kingdom, which could be in a luxurious school in Amman, or in a small, cold, bare and remote school out in the middle of the desert. Mr. Rami ended up at the edge of the desert, which was not quite as bad as it would have been had he been placed further south but bad enough for a man from the big city.

The teacher had even been engaged once to a girl from Amman. He used to have her picture set in a small golden frame on his desk, and we used to stare at her like staring at an alien, a very pretty brunette, almond eyes, long wavy hair, delicate face, complete with dimples and a stunning smile. She looked different from the village girls we were used to here in Wadi Moussa – simple, crude, weathered girls, with no make-up except the black kohl they smeared around their eyes, mainly to protect them from the sun.

But Mr. Rami's girl was a city girl and would never live in a village so far away at the edge of the desert. Mr. Rami tried to convince her to come. At first she wouldn't even consider. Then she came, once, and he took her on a deluxe tour and showed her the best houses in the village to choose from, but they were still in the remote village of Wadi Moussa, which would be even too embarrassing to pronounce in the social circles of Amman. She refused to come again, and he was stuck in the mud. He went every week-end to see her and came and went and came and went, until he found out that he was burning his money on the desert highway, so he went every other week-end to see her, hoping that he would save enough money to get married. He was going to figure it all out somehow but didn't quite know how. Then he went once a month, until finally, she got tired of waiting for him and married someone else from the city.

The worst part was that Mr. Rami's girl had never told him about her plans of leaving him. He just read about her marriage in the Raii newspaper, the largest paper that covered the entire kingdom. It used to list marriages just like it did deaths, and Mr. Rami read about the death of his marriage in the paper while sipping his morning coffee at the Guest House. That day, his fiancé's picture disappeared from his desk, and when we asked him why, he told us calmly that she had married someone else, and that was the end of that.

The class was extra quiet that day. A mixed feeling of guilt and responsibility hovered over the students; some thought we should find Mr. Rami a bride from the village, but then they decided that she wouldn't be able to live with him in the city once the eight years were over, and she might even do worse than the city girl did, like elope with a shepherd or something like that. So that was a bad idea. Others thought we should revive some history characters like Helen of Troy for him. She would make a perfect bride and cause enough wars to keep history going for him, and Mr. Rami would be one happy man.

"Let's take him to Um–Sleiman," suggested one student. "She portends the future. Maybe she would give him some clues."

"He needs girls, not clues," said another boy. "There is no puzzle, just a lack of supply."

"But he needs the right girl. Maybe Um–Sleiman would tell him where to find her."

"A girl that would keep."

"One that would fall in love with him, enough to want to live with him anywhere, even in Wadi Moussa."

"He needs ideas – good ideas."

The ideas flew around the classroom for a while, and Mr. Rami sensed that the students where whispering about him, but he ignored them. He put all his frustrations in his work, and the tales of history became more interesting than ever. They became unforgettable legends. Mr. Rami became an unforgettable legend.

The students' gossip gradually dissipated, and Mr. Rami remained in our village, doomed in celibacy. Many parents felt sorry for him, and they always left some eggs, chickens, geese, pigeons, loaves of fresh bread on his doorstep. During Ramadan, the food supply multiplied, and he was thankful. He told us that. "Yesterday's food was excellent, thank you," he would say, and although it never added much meat to his bones, it was good to see him satisfied. He remained thin and single.

Jim invited Mr. Rami to spend an entire Friday with us in Petra at the excavation site. We were to meet at Jim's cave early in the morning. The crisp, cool morning air of the desert had reached our bones, and I couldn't run or even walk fast, because Mr. Rami had little experience in walking on rocky paths, and I was too polite to leave him behind. He tried to balance himself after every step and could never pick-up enough momentum to go three or four steps at a time. Each time he set his foot down, his hands flew in the air like a scarecrow, and he leaned to the left and then to the right as if he were crossing a canyon on a tightrope.

CHAPTER 13

A small day pack rested on Mr. Rami's back with our lunch in it. He had chosen not to fast that day and offered to make special sandwiches for all three of us, and Jim accepted his offer and said he would provide the drink. I remained silent. It did not matter much to me who brought what as long as the food was good. I just hoped that Mr. Rami had brought enough. His looks never promised much, but I figured if he did not provide enough to suit me, I could always find Aisheh and have some of her goat cheese or con Jim into digging some peanuts out for a snack.

When we cleared the Seeq, I tried to pick up some speed so I could thaw my blood, but Mr. Rami only walked normally. He just dropped the acrobatic motions he had demonstrated at the path to balance himself and began to rub his long thin fingers against the palms of his hands and blow on them steadily. I almost hyperventilated from looking at him. We walked up to the cave and knocked on the door.

"Come in," said Jim. "The door is open." But Mr. Rami was already in, shaking and shivering. I followed him and closed the door. "I'm Jim, and you must be Mr. Rami," Jim continued. "Lizard told me all about you."

"Who's Lizard?" asked Mr. Rami. His frown demanded clarification, and Jim quickly granted it.

"I meant Raji," said Jim. "He's a Lizard Boy. That student of yours knows how to slither better than reptiles; I tell you."

Mr. Rami was confused. All he said was "Oh", and he still shook and shivered reflexively as if his motions were battery operated. Jim invited him to sit down, and he poured a cup of tea and handed it to him. Mr. Rami hugged the special tiny glass and slurped a long sip and took a deep breath.

"Ah," he said. "You make good Arabic tea." He sat cross legged on Jim's metal trunk and his knees stuck out like those of a skeleton. "It hits the spot on a cool morning like this."

"Thank you," said Jim. He poured a glass for me and one for himself and took a sip. "I like this tea," he said. He sat on his bed and leaned against the wall. Mr. Rami slurped another long sip.

"There's nothing like hot sweetened tea."

"I never thought that boiling the sugar with the tea would make such a difference in the taste," said Jim. "It's good."

"I'm glad somebody still appreciates it this way. In Amman, we get the tea in a tea bag and the sugar on the side nowadays," said Mr. Rami. "It tastes like brewed cardboard, although, it is still better than the new British perfumed tea which is the latest fad up there. That stuff tastes like shampoo. You feel like pouring it on your head instead of taking it in."

Jim laughed. "There's one good thing about the tea in the Capital, though," he said.

"What's that?"

"It is served in a real tea cup rather than these tiny handless glasses called tea cups around here," said Jim.

"What difference does it make. The tea still tastes the same, doesn't it?"

"I tell you what the difference is. You hand one of these glasses to a foreigner, and he would not only get a culture shock, but a good heat shock too."

Mr. Rami laughed. "It is hard on the fingers when you don't know how to handle it all right," he said.

"More than just the fingers," said Jim. "Let me tell you what else you can bruise when you don't know what you're doing here." He sat up and tried to control a chuckle. "The first time I was offered hot tea in a glass like this I thought it was a cold drink of some sort. Now that was a surprise. First I grabbed the glass from the bottom instead of the top and burned my hand. Then I set it down to cool off. Everyone around me stared at me silently as if I had rejected a sacred treat. They slowly sipped their tea and made me believe it had to be cool, at least cool enough to drink. They sipped and stared at my poor lonesome glass. I felt embarrassed and picked it up again, the right way this time, and took a sip and burned my tongue. These local people must have padded tongues, I thought."

Mr. Rami and I burst into roaring laughter.

"That wasn't all," continued Jim. "As I quickly tried to save my tongue from further abuse, I spilled half the darn cup on my lap and burned my crotch. I never felt so clumsy in my entire life. Now, look at me. I can't even start the day without it."

"Neither can I," said Mr. Rami. His laughter slowly faded away. "In fact, I drink it all day long during the cold season." He frowned and continued to talk slowly. There was remoteness in his eyes and I sensed loneliness in his words. "The days are getting colder, and it seems that winter is coming early this year. They even had a hint of snow up north. This is unheard of at this time of the year."

"Who told you about the snow?" asked Jim.

"I read it in the paper."

"I hope it doesn't snow down here," said Jim. He looked very concerned.

"Don't worry; it never does."

"With my luck, we'll probably have a first. I can take a lot of rain on these paths but not snow and ice."

"For sure you won't get ice. Even up north where it snows pretty heavily at times, the temperature rarely drops more than two or three degrees below freezing, and the snow usually melts within a few days. It never turns to ice. But it does get damp, cold and windy down here, especially in the evenings. My little kerosene heater never keeps up. I have to turn on all the burners on my stove, just to keep warm," said Mr. Rami. "You don't seem to have much heat down here either." He looked around the cave.

"I have this small butane gas heater and plenty of sweaters and blankets," said Jim. "I think I'm well protected from the wind here. The hill provides a good shelter," he assured himself, "and if it gets too cold, I'll go spend a few days up at the Guest House or go on a vacation and see some other parts of the country."

"Go further south," said Mr. Rami. "Aqaba is a great place in winter. It is almost like summer in the Capital, very pleasant."

"I heard about Aqaba."

"But don't go to the resorts. I know a humble place on this side of town." He motioned toward himself. "It is a small, enclosed paradise, down toward the Saudi border. You get to eat seafood, swim, snorkle above spectacular colors of coral reef and fish. You can even get a suntan in the middle of January. The owners there are also very friendly. At the resorts, they are too snobbish and dry like the sand. At least that's the way they were with me." Mr. Rami lowered his voice, almost to a whisper. "Perhaps it was my books," he said, "and my old baggy suit does not give the impression of a rich, fat man from the Capital or a big shot from the oil countries, loaded with cash to tip those who wait on him left and right. In fact, I never tipped anybody, ever." His voice went up again. "I'll tip someday, but the receiver would have to deserve it first. He would really have to earn my tip."

"I hear you," said Jim. He tilted his head back and let the last few drops of tea trickle from his glass into his mouth and stood up. "I would like to have the address of this place you talked about."

Chapter 13

"I'll send it with Raji," said Mr. Rami. He too finished his tea and handed the glass to Jim. I had finished mine long before they did and had it set on the tray, waiting.

After the tea break, we headed for the site. Jim and Mr. Rami visited all the way, and I listened and tagged along like a servant boy. Jim said that we were going to have more company that day yet. Hans, the German archeologist, had left a message for him at the Guest House. It said that a Ms. Lux, a student of archeology, who had come from Germany to spend a year in Jordan visiting and studying with different excavators, would like to spend some time in Petra and would appreciate joining us for a day. Jim said she would meet us at the site at ten o'clock. Hans had drawn a map for her, and she should find the place easily enough.

About ten o'clock the sun warmed up, and we worked diligently, all three of us. Mr. Rami scooped the fine dirt with his skinny fingers and pulled rocks very gently, treating each one like a rarity. He hummed some of the tunes Majid had played on his reed pipe and kept everybody going with the beat. Jim relaxed over the fine dirt and worked lying on his side, scraping and scooping dirt with his tools and wiggling his foot to Mr. Rami's tune. I hauled a couple of loads to the dirt pile and then settled beside Mr. Rami who had hit a layer of broken pottery. We scraped and pulled smooth dome shaped triangles, squares and several kinds of odd pieces of man–made jumbles. I was still breathing cool, damp air from the earth with my face hovering over the dirt and the appearing pieces when I heard Mr. Rami say, "Hi."

He was the first one to see Ms. Lux. Jim lifted his head up about the same time I did, and we both recited, "Hi" to the newcomer.

"Hi," said the girl. "I am Lux, Petra Lux," she said.

"Petra in Petra?" I asked astonishingly.

Jim gave me an ugly look. "Petra is also a very common German name," he said. I nodded and pretended to go back to my work, all blushed and embarrassed. Mr. Rami and Jim stood up and wiped their hands with their pants before they shook hands with Ms. Lux, Petra Lux. I smothered a chuckling fit in my chest and turned my back, but I turned again when I heard my name being introduced. I quickly jumped up shook hands with Ms. Petra Lux and smiled politely. Her hand was soft as butter, a contrast to her name, Petra, Rock. Who in his right mind would give his daughter such a hard name, and I thought my name was bad.

Petra, or Miss Lux, as Jim started calling her, was a tall girl, about the same height as Mr. Rami. She had light brown hair and matching eyes. A day pack rested on her shoulders, and she wore dark blue jeans and a pale blue shirt, buttoned half way down her chest and then tied in a knot on her belly. Her sleeves were rolled half way up, and a notebook with a pencil tied to it rested on her forearm. The pencil had dropped down and dangled in front of her. She looked prepared for work, and Jim took advantage of her readiness and put her to work immediately. He introduced her to the project, and she too settled beside the pile of broken pottery which we had pulled out of the dirt and began to label each piece.

I felt sorry for her. We must have pulled at least fifty pieces and had many more coming up at a steady pace. By noon, I had counted seventy nine pieces of reasonable sizes. There were also tiny chips that we set aside in a different container.

At noon, Jim announced lunch time. He poured the water on our hands from a big jug, and we all washed and prepared to eat. Mr. Rami had brought enough sandwiches to feed a pack of wolves. He said he didn't know how much everybody needed, so he made sure he brought plenty, and I was grateful for that. Miss. Lux loved Mr. Rami's falafel sandwiches, and we all loved her. She ate and worked and talked easily, while we stumbled over each other in order to have a chance to talk with her. She tried to give Mr. Rami some of her sandwiches in exchange of the good stuff he had given her, but he thanked her and was embarrassed. He said he had had enough, and his face reddened like a ripe watermelon. I had never seen him blush like that before. Wait until my classmates hear all that, I thought to myself. But I never did tell them anything.

After lunch Miss Lux tried to fit some of the broken pieces of pottery together. She struggled at first, and Jim told her not to worry about it if she couldn't do it. Later, he discovered that she was an artist in her field. By the end of the day, she had put together all the broken pieces we had pulled out of the ground, and a complete, spectacular Nabatean water jug came to life.

The jug was huge, almost like what we used to call zeer in Arabic. Those clay water jugs kept the water very cool in the summer, especially when they were set in the shade. There was something about their being porous that helped keep the water cool; they breathed and dripped slowly all day long. We used to have two of them before my brothers bought our refrigerator. The jug water tasted better than ice water. I remember when my mother used to keep a small round dish under the jugs to catch the drops of water that eventually found their way out of the pores. But the Nabatean jug had special designs on it and was a bit thinner, more delicate. I could have sworn that some of the pieces we had found belonged to a different piece of pottery, but Miss Lux knew her job. She put it together and exposed an exotic rarity with an intricate design of vines and faces carved in the clay.

"There you go," she said to Jim as she gently set the jug down as if in a slow motion picture. We quit working, stood up and moved slowly toward the jug like approaching the most sacred shrine. We encircled it with our bodies and froze for a while as if enraptured in a special prayer that linked the roots of man with the branches – that brought together, the father, the son, and holy spirit, as Jim would say.

"This is a rarity," said Mr. Rami.

"It would be worth a bundle if it were intact," said Jim. There was happiness and sorrow in his voice.

"It is worth a bundle," whispered Miss Lux. She had worked hard on it.

I squirmed around Jim. I wanted to tell him about my cave and all the rarities in it, but I recalled how flat he had turned me down in the past, and I kept my peace. He would ignore me as soon as I mentioned the place. He would ignore me even more, now that a jigsaw puzzle of a rarity had been put together in front of his eyes, and it came out of his very own project.

Chapter 14

The month of Ramadan was over quickly, and a spooky play did take place in it, just like it was supposed to; the discovery of Um–Sleiman's place, the secret trips to people's doorsteps, the arrival of Miss Lux, and the involvement of Mr. Rami in the excavations were major scenes in it, and Jim, Aisheh and I thrived in the grace of such social fortune and hoped it would last for a long time.

Then came the rain. It was only October, and then came November, and the rain continued. It poured like never before. Normally, small showers of rain would mark the beginning of the winter season in my world. But that year, and by mid November, a year's worth of precipitation had soaked the ground, and the forecast was for more. The farmers up north were very happy; in fact, everybody expressed happiness and gratitude, because the country depended on good crops for its export. Saudi Arabia and many eastern European countries depended on Jordan for their fruit and vegetable supplies, especially the produce of the valley, the natural greenhouse, the cornucopia that produced all year round. But the excavations suffered, and that was no big loss to anybody around here except Jim.

"I thought this was a semi arid zone," he grumbled.

"It was," I said, "until you came. Even the weather gets tired of the routine. Remember, Petra used to have streams flowing through it two thousand years ago."

"I suppose. We'll have to quit early today. It is getting too stinking muddy to work." He threw his scraper desperately on the ground and stood up. The mud had outlined the side of his blue jeans, and he shivered and limped and almost lost his balance on the rough ground. Mr. Rami gathered up the tools in the wheelbarrow and pushed it off to the side of the road. He had been working with us every Friday and every holiday. The man had finally found something to keep him busy and entertained since he had no excuse to go to the Capital anymore. He seemed grateful for Jim and his project, I thought. A steady grin replaced the serious look on his face, and he worked with a nimble foot. He hopped and hummed and danced around the site while he worked, and looked like a silly, happy stick figure.

Jim also appreciated Mr. Rami and hoped that he would continue to help out. He certainly moved much faster than Jim, and we saw a lot of progress whenever Mr. Rami was around. But Jim also worried about Mr. Rami's dedication to the project. He seemed obsessed by it even more than Jim himself. I never told him about the failure of Mr. Rami's marriage plans. So he couldn't help but ask Mr. Rami why he never paid any visits to his family on holidays and weekends instead of coming to the project, and Mr. Rami's answer was that he had no family. His mother had died when he was little, and his father had gone off to Istanbul and married a Turkish belly dancer and raised a family there. Mr. Rami's maternal grandparents had raised him, and they both died before he finished college.

Another person, who also proved to be an asset to our project, but happened to be absent that day, was Miss Petra Lux. She came on occasion and helped us out, even though we had no luck finding anything since that first day when she put together the large Nabatean pot. She too believed that the site should be a graveyard for more treasures that might lead to a cave, more than one cave and, perhaps, eventually, to the hidden god. She was determined to help Jim find everything. In the meantime, the dirt piles turned to monuments and the excitements to frustrations.

The rain had soaked Mr. Rami well. He could no longer shake the water off what he had called water resistant clothes. They finally gave up and took the water in, clear through his pores. His black hair hung down in pointed lumps that made him look like a wet mouse.

"Why don't you just go home," said Jim. "I'll push the wheelbarrow to the cave. No reason for you to get sick yet."

"We'll take care of everything as usual," said Mr. Rami as he stared at Jim. The man was stubborn as a mule, and Jim complied. He shivered like a rag and shuffled his feet weakly when he moved. Mr. Rami walked to him and touched his forehead with the palm of his hand, saying "excuse me" as he reached over. Jim pulled away.

"You have fever," said Mr. Rami. "Do you have anything to bring it down."

"Don't worry about me," said Jim in an angry tone of voice. He looked like a child, trying to hide something from grown–ups. "Just go home – both of you," he continued. "I have all the medicine I need in my medicine box in the cave. I just need to get there."

Mr. Rami motioned for me to move quickly. We hustled down the road and headed for Jim's cave while the skies closed up and poured the ocean on our heads. Mr. Rami pushed the wheelbarrow, and I kept an eye on Jim. When we arrived at the bottom of the hill, Jim stumbled, and Mr.

Rami and I helped him up. His teeth were clattering loudly, and by the time we reached the cave we were almost carrying him.

I made hot sweetened tea and poured it into three little glasses while Mr. Rami helped Jim change into dry clothes and walked him to bed. Mr. Rami also took two pills from a jar he had found in Jim's medicine cabinet. He said that those pills were good for bringing down the fever, and he gave them to Jim who swallowed them immediately and slurped some tea after them to wash them down. We all slurped our tea and made noise, but the sound we made was smothered by thunder and lightning and pouring rain.

"It doesn't look like it is going to slow down," said Mr. Rami. "We'd better scamper out of here. The path might become hard to cross if this continues." He put his glass down and asked Jim if he needed anything before we left.

"Get out of here," said Jim. "Go home and get yourself to bed."

"I'll come back next weekend," said Mr. Rami," and I'll bring plenty of food and hot chocolate. If nothing else, we'll eat and stay warm. Meanwhile, you take care," he said to Jim. "We'll see you on Friday."

"No," shouted Jim as if he remembered something else and wanted to stop us from leaving. He lifted his head up and coughed. Mr. Rami and I stood there and waited for him to clear his throat while the storm roared outside. It muffled all noises. "I'll see you Thursday. Next Thursday is Thanksgiving day," said Jim with a rough voice. His shaking had slowed down though, and he became more articulate and calm. "Do you know what that means to an American?"

"Yes," said Mr. Rami. He knew everything, I thought. The words meant nothing to me other than their literal meaning, giving thanks for something.

Chapter 14

"Come to the Guest House next Thursday." The food is on me," said Jim. "I asked the cook up there to prepare a turkey for us. We'll eat at six o'clock. We'll feast whether we get good weather or not. I'm taking that day off."

On the way to the Seeq, Mr. Rami explained to me what Thanksgiving was all about, and I told him the old man ought to wait and celebrate it after he survived the first winter here in Petra. It had been rough on him so far, and the caves he was seeking and the gods were still no where to be seen.

"We'll celebrate again," said Mr. Rami. "After this winter, we all might need to establish such a tradition down here."

"We'd better make it a lamb instead of a turkey."

"For the Americans, it had to be a wild animal. They had to kill wild turkey in order to survive. I don't know what we would kill down here. The oryx is extinct, and I never heard of anybody eating a hyena." He scratched his wet head as he tried to think of something else. "I can't think of any other wild animal that could be hunted around here, can you?"

"Maybe we'll just turn the sheep loose and then go after them and shoot them."

"They wouldn't go too far, young man. You might trip over the dumb things trying to hunt them."

"That's okay. I don't know how to hunt anyway."

By the time Mr. Rami and I reached the path, streams had flowed down every cavity in the ground and every chink in the rock, and the Seeq looked like a low river. Mr. Rami used the ancient water canal to support himself as he walked up against the flow of water. The canal had been carved about waist high in the rocky walls, which made it comfortable to lean against when a person needed to stop and take a breath. The water had buried my rocks on the ground, and I could no longer slither. We were drenched. I could hear the water swish inside my tennis shoes in spite of all the other noises that raged all around.

Then it turned dark, pitch dark, before we cleared the Seeq, and we had no flashlight. We felt our way up and waded in deep puddles. At first, we visited and complained, but when the storm roared more fiercely, we became speechless, mostly because we could hardly hear each other anymore. I had never seen so much water my entire life. We moved silently for a long time. And suddenly I realized I was walking in silence, man silence. The wind, the rocks, the water and every object above and below me roared and proved its existence but not Mr. Rami. I stopped and let out a scream of terror, and the storm responded with an outbreak of equal terror.

The path had slowly become impassable; the stream under me gradually turned into a river, and I had to go on feeling my way like a blind man. I leaned against the canal and pulled myself forward until I finally cleared the Seeq. Then I walked up to the paved road and headed home. When I reached the yard, I opened the gate, and the door let out a loud squeaking noise. Then a voice came from behind.

"Is that you Raji?"

I turned around and felt someone's hand on my shoulder.

"Mr. Rami?" I asked.

"Yes," said the voice. "I wanted to make sure you made it home. I don't know how I lost you in that typhoon. Are you okay?"

I burst into tears. "I'm okay," I said.

"You go to bed now. Tomorrow is a school day, and if this weather continues, we might need a submarine for a classroom," he said gloomily and disappeared in the storm.

Chapter 15

It rained all night. Our roof leaked, and my mother had to put three buckets under the dripping ceiling. I wondered if the ancients intended to refill the dried–up reservoirs and riverbeds, all in one night. I thought of what would happen to us if they did. My brothers' business might have to change from horseback guided tours to row boat tours. I thought of Jim. The water would not reach him up in his cave. It was high enough, above the flood level, but what if his fever persisted? I wanted it to cease; I wanted all my tribulations to cease. It would take a miracle. I knew Jim had ample food down in Petra, and I knew the facility above him had a refrigerator in which he kept some of his supplies, but I did not know whether he would be strong enough to prepare his own food or not. I stared at the clock and listened to its ticking. Time crept worse than a turtle, and there was no sleep in my eyes. My muscles ached, every one of them, and my heart lay heavy in my chest.

I must have slept some, because when I woke up in the morning, a dream lingered in my mind, and I kept rewinding it as if it were real. I was hungry, and my father walked in and stood in the corner of the room. There was a hand extended in front of him. I couldn't see a body attached to that hand, although it seemed as if someone was there behind it, hiding, somewhere in a mixture of haze and darkness; the entire scene was black and white. Then my father pulled a large loaf of bread from his pouch and put it in the hand. I stiffened as the hand approached me and lifted the loaf of bread as if to give it to me. My father nodded, and I took the loaf and ran to the kitchen. I wanted to share Father's bread with my brothers who had been eating in the kitchen, but when I arrived there, I found only my father sitting on the kitchen floor. He ordered me to go ahead and eat the bread alone, all of it. My stomach growled, and I woke up.

It seemed impossible, but a message came from the Guest House that morning asking my brothers if they would be willing to take seven tourists down the Seeq to Petra on horseback. The path, the roaring river by now, would be navigable only on horseback, the message said, and the tourists were willing to pay triple, since the conditions were so difficult. They were desperate.

I had thought that many people were crazy, but these tourists marked the peak. Most tourists came from the different ends of the world with a list of places to see, and they believed that they had to cross off every place on their list even if it killed them. Their time was always limited, and to some, the money invested in the trip was also limited, so they were not willing to lose a penny's worth of their precious adventure; they had to go through it, rain or shine. I remembered tourists who told me that their trip was the highlight of their life, and to those who waited for my brothers up at the Guest House, this must have been the trip of their life too, since they were willing to take the risk and pay triple.

Chapter 15

My oldest brother would never pass an opportunity like that, and the others usually complied. He even asked my mother if she would convince me to join them. They could use my help, he said, but Mother said that if the weather persisted, and school was canceled, she could use my help around the house. I thanked her in my heart, and my brother knew I did. He stood by the door, looked at me and even managed to smile. He never smiled at me before. It wasn't a nasty disparaging grin. It was actually a friendly smile. "God be with you," he said. That was the common good-bye expression in our culture, and I didn't take note of it. Then he left the house, followed by my brothers.

Many tourists came in winter to avoid the heat of summer. Sometimes, snow storms surprised them in the Capital and caught them without warm clothes. They always seemed to be misinformed about the entire Middle-East area. Some people visit the desert of Saudi Arabia and think of the entire Middle-East as a desert. Others visit the snow skiing resorts in the Lebanese mountains and think of it as a European resort. The French did that. They actually called Lebanon Little France, "La Petite France." Heaven forbid. And very few knew Jordan and its own diverse weather. People could be busy throwing snow balls at each other in the north, while others bathed and cooked in the sun, down south, in Aqaba.
Petra and Wadi Moussa were in the middle, more toward the south, I should say. Their weather forecast depended very much on the direction of the front at that particular time. Therefore, they were also a good source of confusion, even to some of the local people.

The water had reached the front room of the school, and Mr. Rami pushed it out with a large broom. Then he asked me and three other older boys to help him dig a ditch in order to divert the water flow down to the valley so it wouldn't flood the school. He had rounded up some shovels and buckets from the neighbors and seemed ready to confront the storm all by himself. Everybody else stayed home.

We worked for two hours, and the rain poured on us and then faded away for a few minutes and then came back with a larger supply of water and drenched our already drenched bodies until our bodies shook as if we had the malaria, and we began to walk like turtles. But the rain wouldn't quit.

Finally, Mr. Rami threw his shovel on the ground and ordered us to stop. His face sagged and dripped, and his eyes were angry and frustrated. "Hustle," he said. "Collect all the shovels and buckets and put them inside the building." We obeyed in silence and waited for more orders. He locked up the front door and dashed into the rain. "Follow me," he yelled and waved to us to hustle. We followed all the way to Abu Mustafa's restaurant. He opened the door and walked in. Then he turned around and motioned us to get in. We all stood by the door dripping like a hundred faucets and making puddles on the floor. Abu Mustafa stared at us with wide eyes. He had been smoking his water pipe, the hubble bubble and watching the storm through the window. When he saw us, he dropped the mouth piece of his water pipe on the table and stood up.

"We need some towels," said Mr. Rami. "About five towels if you please." The old restaurant owner stood there, stiff as a wall, and tried to capture what was going on. "Would you please hustle," continued Mr. Rami. "We're about to die here."

Abu Mustafa finally moved toward the kitchen and came back with a stack of towels. Mr. Rami handed them to us and told us to dry up quickly and go sit by the wood stove, at the table in the far corner. Then he ordered a cup of warm milk and two pieces of baklava for each of us. We swarmed around the stove until the food and drink arrived at the table. Mr. Rami ordered us to sit at the table. The two diamond shaped pieces of pastry and the milk disappeared in a flash, and Mr. Rami ordered another round of milk. This time I slowed down and sipped my warm milk with ecstasy until a policeman dashed into the restaurant and asked for Abu Mustafa.

"We declared a state of emergency," said the policeman. "All hell broke lose, and a wall of water forced its way down the Seeq. There are horses trapped there and tourists. We don't know exactly where they are, and we have no way of getting to them. The army helicopters will be here as soon as possible, and we might need all the help we can get."

"What can I do to help," asked Abu Mustafa.

"I don't know yet" said the policeman. "I'm just asking everybody to be alert. If there are injured people down there, we would have to fly them either to the Kerak Hospital or clear to the Capital. In the meantime, all we can do is pray for God's wrath to ease off."

A knot bulged up in my stomach, and I felt like I could throw up. Disasters were always referred to as God's wrath in our culture. Anybody who was touched by a certain disaster was supposedly paying for a crime he had committed sometime in his life, and the strength of the disaster was always based on the size of the crime committed. I wondered about the innocent people who got hit by serious catastrophes, but then I thought maybe people were not as innocent as they appeared to be on the outside; only God knew. The Koran said that we will be judged by our intentions. The deeds of people might be good, but if their intentions were bad, God would know, and he would strike accordingly.

I tried to determine where my brothers would be at that moment, and how badly they were hit, but I had no idea where to place them. My muscles stiffened, and I couldn't get up. Mr. Rami was watching me. I saw him with the corner of my eye. He gave orders for everybody to go home. The other three boys got up and left, but my thighs felt as if they had been fettered to the chair, and I remained in my seat, gazing at my milk.

"You'd better go home to your mother," said Mr. Rami. He stood up and motioned an order for me to do the same. I pulled myself up slowly and walked toward the door. Mr. Rami followed and opened the door for me. "I'll come check on you a little later," he said. "Now take care."

Although I walked in the rain, I felt like an old broomstick, all dry and ugly, and the downpour did not bother me anymore. A feeling of alienation crept through me, and I walked apart from the wet air, under it, yet in my own, water resistant being that neither belonged to this world nor knew the whereabouts of its real home. But my feet found my mother's home, and I walked in and found it empty and quiet. Outside, the yard stood bare and wet. When I hollered for my mother, the pigeons cooed on the roof. Each pigeon had snuggled in its hole and watched the wrath of God. I saw their eyes through the holes, just eyes in tiny heads. They moved left and right and left again. Mother was no where to be found.

I dashed toward the Guest House and found everybody. Men, women, children, police officers and other government officials and army men stood above the entrance of the Seeq and watched the river that had risen and roared like a mad giant through the narrow path. The water that flowed through there was taller than the average man, and no one dared go near it for fear of getting taken in and under. The flow was fierce and threatening and daring. People stood there and waited. My mother's eyes gazed at the mouth of the Seeq. She waited.

"The flood broke through the Seeq shortly after they left," my mother said finally. "They couldn't have cleared the Seeq yet." Her gazing eyes never left the mouth of the path. They looked like the lizard's eyes, the beads that stared and wouldn't move.

"They are experienced riders," I said.

"Not in this flood, Raji – not in this mess."

A man behind us was talking to a police officer. He said that the flood had swept the village of Ma'an, the next village south of us, and left its inhabitants homeless. The government had sent out a cry of help to all the relief agencies in the country, both local and foreign.

"In that case, the help may never reach us today," said the man.

"The help we need here is different," said the policeman. "The army helicopters are supposed to be here shortly. We've been promised."

I looked around at the faces of the people who watched and waited and visited and shook their heads from time to time. Bits and pieces of their conversation pierced my ears along with the wind and the rain and the mad skies.

"Do you think they made it before the flood broke through?"

"How many were they?

"Seven tourists and three guides."

"I doubt that anybody can survive down there."

"What do they do with dead tourists? Do they send their corpses home or bury them here?"

"I suppose their embassies will worry about them."

I broke through the wall of talking people, rushed all the way to a clearing up the hill and puked my guts out. My stomach was still revolting and my head throbbing with pain when the sky roared with man-made noise this time. Two helicopters arrived and the police ordered the people to clear their landing space and move farther off. They hollered and shouted and were very busy. The visiting ceased, and the crowd of people clustered in the mud and waited.

After talking to the officials and studying the situation, the rescue teams headed back to the helicopters and took off over the path. A few minutes later, they moved further down toward the other end of the Seeq and disappeared.

"They cannot go inside the Seeq," said one of the officers to my mother. "It is too narrow and high, and the rocks bulge unevenly on either side. The rescuers will have a very difficult time if the victims are too far from either end of the path."

My mother remained silent, and her eyes now gazed at the distance where the helicopters had gone. It seemed like hours before they finally came back, and the police got busy pushing people away once again. But when I told one of the police officers that my brothers were the horsemen of this tour, he guided me and my mother toward the helicopters. One of the rescue team members looked at the policeman and shook his head. "No survivors," he shouted above the noise. "The flood had knocked the horses down, and the riders were swept with the current. We were able to pull out six bodies so far. We'd have go back for the rest. They were scattered all over."

The bodies of my two younger brothers and four of the tourists were unloaded and set at the edge of the Guest House yard. The corpse of my older brother did not arrive until much later in the day. In the meantime, we continued to stand in the mud and wait. Mr. Rami waited with us, and when the rest of the dead were brought in and unloaded, he remembered Jim.

Chapter 15

"There's one more man down in Petra; I'm sure he's still alive," said Mr. Rami to the police officers. "He's an American archeologist and lives in one of the caves by the facility. He was sick with fever yesterday. Don't you think we should get him out of there in case he needs medical attention?"

"Where can we haul him to?" said a policeman. "The helicopters are going to be loaded with dead tourists going to Amman soon, and all the ambulance cars are down south, taking care of the flood victims in Ma'an."

"Just bring him this far," said Mr. Rami. "Please. He can stay with me, and if he needs further help, I can take him by car to the hospital in Kerak. We don't have to go all the way to Amman. I'll take care of him if you just bring him this far."

The team members and the policemen considered for the while, and then decided to get Jim out of Petra. They took Mr. Rami with them to help them locate Jim's cave.

I had lost track of time. All I could do was hold my mother's hand while the relatives and the villagers took over and did all that had to be done for us. They carried the bodies of my brothers to our house, muttered prayers and wailed and cried for us. The noise that had been restricted to a storm yesterday now turned human. Nature was hushed for a while, enough to give us a chance to collect the dead and howl back and cry. Everybody cried except my mother. She remained dry until it was time to go to the funeral the next day. Then she began. The tears flooded her eyes; she began and continued to cry. I prayed that some day her tears would cease but saw no sign of dryness in her eyes again.

CHAPTER 16

I had never been to a funeral before. My thoughts roamed in ambivalent paths, trying to sort out the details. The village children and I had always followed funeral processions in the past and mimicked those who wept, prayed and wailed. We played dead, took turns carrying each other, and, just before the bereaved mob reached the cemetery, we usually swung our play-dead boy and dropped him on the ground, and he immediately came back to life and went home.

Funeral processions usually passed by, and we chased them like chasing interesting groups of tourists carrying a mystery box. The dead body always belonged to someone across the street or across town. But now, the sound of weeping, wailing and praying surrounded me and separated me from the rest of the village children. There were loud noises and streaks of silence, and then – loud noises again. I tagged along with the men and waited for the show to be over. I couldn't do what I was supposed to be doing. My uncle said I should cry and pray aloud.

"God can hear me," I said to him. "I can talk to him in my heart."

"But people need to see your grief."

"I cannot help it if I'm a lousy actor."

"Raji. Young man. Grow up, for your mother's sake."

I looked at my uncle and recited with the crowd the last few words in their prayer, "God's word is the truth. Amen."

It was over.

Both Jim and Mr. Rami came to the funeral and then followed the crowd to the house. I did not have a chance to talk to either one of them, for the house was full, and I was too busy being stunned and lost in the crowd and the conversations that rattled around me. I quietly roamed around the people and pretended they were additional pieces of furniture, objects to trip over and walk around. Every once in a while I would catch a conversation and hear words I despised, expressions of pity and sympathy.

People consumed the bitter coffee and the sweet pastry and socialized. They talked about deaths in their own families and how the survivors made it and explained to each other what we should do in order to survive and the traditional ways of handling business and inheritance. They talked as if they knew everything. I wished I could tell them to take their conversations and go where the devil would entertain better and leave us alone, but I couldn't do that for my mother's sake. I also didn't want Jim and Mr. Rami to leave or get angry with me and figured it would be hard to make exceptions in a crowd, so I continued to walk around and be idly busy.

Jim looked weak and frail, but he moved around and shared our bitter and our sweet. Mr. Rami explained the customs to him.

"The strong bitter taste of the coffee symbolizes the bitterness of the loss," I overheard him say, "and the sweet pastry that follows immediately expresses hope for happier times." I could tell him I knew some people who came only to enjoy a piece of dessert and good company, but I didn't.

Chapter 16

How often does the town have a chance to gather under one roof, I thought. And I could also tell him there were those who came with sincere hearts and those who came with a hungry sweet tooth and a tall-tale to tell, but I didn't, because Jim and Mr. Rami were among those who came to be with me and could care less about the bitter and the sweet. The two friends settled together in the corner and spoke to nobody. They looked at me every once in a while and perhaps thought I was too busy, for I put on many miles roaming the crowded floor and overhearing conversations.

"Pity, the only one left is this one over there, in the gray shirt," said a man to another. They sat next to each other, engulfed in their large traditional clothes. One had a tan cloak called gallabiah, and the other had a brown one. They smoked and exhaled thick clouds and looked content and well entertained.

"Isn't he still in school?"

"Yes, and he doesn't like to work either. His brothers tried."

"Maybe he'll get a scholarship from the government."

"Not this goofball. All he does is run around with strangers. Who knows what else they teach him."

I overheard everything and continued to roam. Some people shook my hand; others gave me hugs and kisses, and when they let go of me, I breathed in relief and continued on to the next destination, the next wall, then the next, around the corner, until I finally made it through the door and out. I climbed all the way to the roof and sat down with the pigeons. They cooed, and so did I.

The rain quit, and that provided enough comfort and hope for people to resume living again, and life in the village continued as if nothing had happened. The taboons sent puffs of smoke into the air; people butchered, cooked, baked, worked, nursed their children and ate. The children played, fought, and pushed their wire cars down the streets. The following days were marked with sunshine and warm air. And, hidden deep down, below the crust of things, were feelings of emptiness, confusion, and guilt. That was I, Raji, Rajaiiddeen Al–Mohtadi, Lizard Boy, the Goofball, the Archeologist wannabe.

I walked up to Mr. Rami's house so I could talk to Jim. Although, sometimes he seemed more confused than I, but this time, I declared his superiority, based on the fact that he was an outsider, the man from the moon, different from our colored sand. To me, he was also old, born old, for I had only known him as a man of age, and his past never existed in my time. And if age and wisdom had some connections I went to seek them both from Jim. He ought to be able tell me something I wanted to hear, I thought. The villagers failed, and my mother wouldn't talk.

Mr. Rami told me that Jim had moved to the Guest House. He had been feeling better and hoped to go back to Petra as soon as the Seeq opened up, so I left Mr. Rami's place and headed for the Guest House. Abu-Zeid led me to Jim's room in the upper level of the facility. I had never been up there in the ritzy section, and I felt like visiting a king. Jim opened the door and hugged me in. Then I walked quietly to a chair in the corner of the room and sat down. He followed me and took a seat on the bed and folded his hands on his lap. We said nothing for a long time.

"Would you like to have some tea?" he finally said.

"No."

Silence.

"There were times when I wanted them dead," I roared all of a sudden, and my crying filled the room. "But not that dead," I continued and let out very loud sobs like the braying of a donkey.

"I know," said Jim softly. "I know."

Chapter 16

"Have you ever lost someone you liked and disliked at the same time?" I scolded. For no reason, I found myself scolding Jim bitterly and asking him dead questions. He sat there and said nothing.

When I was done, Jim pulled the wallet from his pocket and opened it to the pictures of the people I had wondered about a long time ago.

"See these people?" he asked and flipped the pages. He stopped at the bubble gum face and stared at the child and smiled, unhappily. There was grief in his eyes yet a smile on his lips, an odd arrangement like sunshine and rain at the same time.

"Yes."

"This used to be my family," he said. But then he fell silent for a while, and his eyes looked as if they were searching. He took off his glasses, wiped his face with his sleeve and placed the glasses back on his nose and adjusted them again. "I loved them," he whispered. I could barely hear him. Then he swallowed and lifted his head toward the ceiling. "Life had favored us for a while," he paused again and took a deep breath, "a short while," he continued, "Because I also had a dream, something I had carried with me since I was a little boy, Raji." He paused after every sentence, and I waited patiently. "I had read many books about ancient people. They fascinated me. My father used to travel to Europe and bring me a variety of antique books and books about antiques and ancient civilizations, Romans, Byzantines, Egyptians, until, once, he brought me an old book which he had bought from a street salesman at the Quartier Latin in Paris. He told me that the Quartier Latin was covered with street salesmen who cleaned up junk yards from all around the Mediterranean and sold the trash to tourists. However, every once in a while, a tourist would luck out and buy a treasure for trifles, and this book that my father gave me became my treasure. It described strange places and unique people."

"Was it the same book, the one that described the Nabatean god we're trying to find?"

"Yes. It was written by a wealthy French explorer who roamed the Middle East area one hundred years ago. His name was Luçien Freneau, and it was mentioned by other explorers of his age. In his book, he talked about a worship place and a god he had discovered in a remote place, and he goes on to describe the place which exactly fits Petra. Anyway, Freneau said that he had plans to go back with half a dozen men to help him move this god to the Louvre museum in Paris, but apparently he died before he accomplished his project. There was no mention of this explorer again. I have searched everywhere."

"God knows, Jim. The Louvre museum has enough treasures looted from this area. The dump does not need another god."

"If I discover the god's cave and treasure of pottery, my dear boy, they will stay home, right here where they belong. But, ever since I read this book, I set my life goals, Raji. I wanted to make enough money, and go for my dream. I became obsessed by it, and I wanted to pursue it at all cost. However, when I made enough money to fulfill my dream, I also had a family, a wonderful family, Raji, that demanded all my time and money."

"You wanted them out of your way and yet didn't," I said.

Now Jim began to cry. He tried to smother his sobs, but he failed. I stared at him with fear and guilt. I had always thought of him as a strong, stubborn old man who dared do things nobody in his right mind would do. I never thought I would see him so feeble and helpless. His eyes poured. "One day," he continued, "they were all on their way home from a family gathering. I couldn't go with them, because I had to work that weekend." He rested his elbow above his knee and supported his forehead with his hand. Then he lifted his head and quickly finished the story. "They were hit by a drunk driver, and they were all smashed to death. What was I to do, Raji?"

Now the man from the moon became the man from earth, down, here, to be exact, in Wadi Moussa, the heart of colored sand, and I, Lizard Boy, was to answer his question.

"What did you do?" I asked.

"For a long time, I kept hearing someone repeating the same words in my ears. They woke me up at night, and I screamed and begged for the voice to shut up."

"What did it say?"

"Now, they're out of your way, Jim. They're all out of your way," he quoted and wiped the tears off his face with the cuff of his sleeve. "It took me this long to get over it and follow my dream. It took a long time, Raji. Don't let it take you too long. They are dead. Your brothers are dead but not out of your way; they're just where it is meant for them to be at this time. There is a time when we might think that ugly wishes do come true, but I don't believe in that now. Don't blame it on the yourself or on the wrong wishing star or on an angry god. They died simply because they happened to be in the wrong place at the wrong time. That's all, and this could happen to the saints, the angels and the devils all alike. Just pray that it doesn't happen to you. Now, you keep on going, young man – you hear?" He scolded this time, and his eyes dried up fast. He said nothing after that.

On the way home, the sun felt warm on my back, and I moved easier toward our house. All the pigeons were gone to feed, and their boxes stood empty on our roof. My mother sat on a small wicker chair on the porch and leaned against the house. She had fallen asleep in the sun and looked peaceful, weary but peaceful. Beside her, I found a bundle that housed a stack of fresh baked taboon bread. I recognized the bundle. I had helped Um–Sleiman deliver many of its kind. I pulled one of the loaves out and sneaked inside the house with it. For the first time, I felt hunger, deep down in my guts – there was hunger for anything. I had had very little to eat since Mr. Rami offered me and my friends the pastry at the restaurant when we helped him divert the rain water at the school. In the refrigerator, I found a large hunk of goat cheese and a note beside it. I picked up the note and read:

This was the last hunk of cheese I made. Your mother was asleep, and I didn't want to disturb her peace, so I sneaked in and put it away for you. I hope you enjoy it. I was sorry to hear about your brothers. It seems like disasters come in bulk these days, and all we can do is wait and see where the times would lead us. Be patient and farewell.

Aisheh

I wondered what that farewell was all about, but then, Aisheh had always had a funny choice of words. I folded her note and tucked it in my pocket. Then I picked up a knife and cut a hunk of her good cheese. The aroma filled my nostrils, my mouth watered, and I almost drooled over the food. I ate everything, the bread, the cheese, more bread, more cheese and then some more. I ate and picked up all the crumbs with my index finger and stuck them on my tongue, a few at a time until all the hints of food disappeared from my sight.

My mother woke up with a nightmare. When she saw the bundle of bread beside her, she picked it up and smelled it and gave words of praise, blessings and thanks to the giver and to God. I told her about the cheese, and she told me about the nightmare. "I need to prepare a sacrifice before the Adha holiday," she said. "It will be an early sacrifice, but that's okay. I need to do it now."

"What are you going to do on the Adha holiday?"

"We'll offer more sacrifice," she said.

That wasn't what I meant. I wanted to know how she planned to spend the first religious holiday after the death of my three brothers. I sensed that she understood what I meant but wished not to answer, so I did not pursue the issue any further.

The pilgrimage was about to start in preparation for the Adha holiday, and people had started to talk about sacrifices. The word Adha meant to give a sacrifice. People gave it as a reprimand for their sins. Individuals usually did that whenever they felt guilty for something they had done, but on the Adha feast, everybody offered a sacrifice, and all the poor were well fed. The sacrifice usually depended on how affluent the people were. Rich people butchered lamb and even more than one; others butchered chicken, and we butchered pigeons. Mother told me to get six pigeons from the roof and take them to the butcher to kill and clean, and then she wanted me to bring them back to her so she could cook them with rice and vegetables and send them off to the needy.

The woman never committed a crime as far as I could tell, but if the sacrifice would make her feel better, I thought, I would obey. The pigeons also obeyed. They just sat there as if waiting for me to pick them up.

Jim met me on my way to the butcher shop.

"Having pigeons for dinner?" he asked

"No. This is my mother's sacrifice. It is going to the poor," I explained.

"Oh yes. Mr. Rami explained to me about the feast. Where do you deliver the food for the poor?"

"I thought I would take it to the relief agents this time. They have been stopping at the Guest House every day, on their way south to Ma'an. Many people are still homeless from the flood down there, and the relief agencies have been delivering food and supplies to them every day."

"Here," said Jim. He reached in his pocket, pulled out a ten dinar bill and handed it to me. "Go buy a lamb and add it to your sacrifice."

"Jim," I said. "You don't have to..."

"Just do it," he scolded and resumed his walk down the road toward Mr. Rami's house.

The stubborn old man. He just made my job ten times as hard. I really did not want to do it, but then I decided if it would make him happy, I would do it – I would do anything and please everybody. My acquiescence made me feel like a sacrifice myself that day, and I went along with it for the lack of options. Choices had become luxury in my life. They were dreams or facts of an intangible reality, so far off, they could even be a mirage. So I sought to please everybody in hopes that I could free myself some day soon and follow that mirage.

When I took my load of live animals to the butcher, his eyes widened like a hyena's.

"Are all these animals – a sacrifice?" he asked.

"Yes." I tried to tell him that they were not all mine, but he interrupted.

"Boy. What kind of a crime are you trying to wash away?" I tried to explain, but he interrupted again, "Either that or you are trying to put in a deposit on a good one," he chuckled and spoke with merriment. I stared at him with disgust. His apron was covered with blood, the smell of the fresh kill made me queasy, and the man kept rattling on and wouldn't shut–up.

Chapter 16

"When I was your age," he went on. "My friends and I sneaked into old Mazen's yard." He lifted his eyes to the sky and said dreamily, "Ah. Good old Mazen. God bless his soul. He's been dead for twenty years now. But anyway," he continued with the same nimble spirit, "We climbed up on his roof and stole half a dozen pigeons. He had more pigeons than anybody else in the village, and we figured there was no way he could eat them all before he died, so we decided to help him out. We took the pigeons and went out to the other side of the valley, built a fire and cooked up a feast." He hung the dead lamb upside down on a huge hook that was hanging from the ceiling and began to skin the sacrifice with a fast, skillful hand. He stripped the lamb in seconds, and I wondered whether he was ever aware of what he had done. He acted like it was a simple, fun job. I would die before I killed an animal, even small as a bird, I thought. "The next morning my mother became sick with the flu," he rattled on, "and I wondered whether that happened because of my sin or not, and I promised God I would offer a sacrifice for what I did. But when my mother felt better, I procrastinated and then forgot." He spoke with his hands, and the knife he held tightly between his fingers moved with his words and made me nervous. "But you know," he continued, "I always wondered whether I should have done something about our stealing Mazen's pigeons that day. I never stole anything ever since, but it sure still bothers me."

Nothing seemed to bother him to me. He threw the cleaned carcasses inside a large box and handed them to me.

"Here you go, son. Now have a happy day."

"You too," I said.

"I will. I will."

I knew he would. He would also kill a camel as if it were a fly. I carried my load and walked fast. The smell of fresh kill coming from the box increased my nausea, so I ran to get rid of the cadavers.

The next day, my mother woke up at four o'clock in the morning and cooked all the food. By ten o'clock, the meals were ready, and the aroma of feast grub filled the house and even permeated the air clear into the far end of the yard. I wondered what we ourselves were having for dinner and heard my stomach growl several times. But I wouldn't dare ask my mother, especially when she was engrossed in preparing a sacrifice. She bundled up two huge pots (we called them hilleh), made specially for feasts, set them aside and told me to go get one of the relief agents to load them up in his car.

"This will make a good noon meal for at least ten families," she said and mumbled words of prayer and multiple blessings.

"What about us?" I asked without thinking. The words just slipped out of my mouth.

"The neighbors brought us ample food," she said. "The refrigerator is full."

I had wanted to eat Mother's food. I had been smelling it all morning. It kept reminding me that I hadn't had a good hot meal in a long time. Who cared about nightmares, sins and sacrifices. I was all three in one and even more, I thought and wished I could go to Jim's project and dig the gods out of it. Tears spilled down my cheeks as I walked up the road toward the Guest House. A row of relief agency jeeps, pick-ups and trucks were parked on the street. I walked up to one of the attendants and told him about the meals.

CHAPTER 16

By one o'clock, the meals were delivered, and Mother was at peace again. I staggered toward our house and collapsed by the gate. My head rested against the thick wood, and I felt the warm earth beneath me. The sun had warmed up the ground, and it felt good against my back. My eyelids slowly came down, and I fell fast asleep.

Half an hour later, I heard a voice calling me from a distance, but I had no power to answer. I was fettered in a dream and couldn't move my limbs. Even my lips felt as if someone had glued them together. I half opened my eyes and couldn't tell whether the voice came from a dream or a reality. Then I felt my eyelids drop down again, and I must have answered someone in my dream. A few minutes later, the voice came back. This time it was loud and close. It took away my dream and dropped me off in my yard again. The pigeons cooed all over, the chickens pecked, the horses neighed, the donkeys brayed, and the voice hovered above me.

"What are you doing here. We're waiting for you." I struggled to my feet before I realized I was responding to my uncle who stood in front of me like a palm tree.

"I just needed to rest," I said and felt my knees fold, and I started back down again. He held me up firmly and jerked my shoulder.

"Wake up, Raji. We're about ready to eat," he said. "Why don't you come in and have a bite with us."

He invited me into my own house. His entire family was there, my cousins, the old and the young, their spouses and all their children, the ones I cared about and the ones I wished I could dispose of some time ago. And the table was covered with food, lamb, pigeons, piles of rice covered with roasted pine nuts, stacks of warm sheet bread, the whole feast. I knew traditions had to have some benefits, and, for the first time in my life, I felt thankful. I ate until my guts hurt.

CHAPTER 17

The flood came and went like a tour of a ghost from Hades, and the ground quickly soaked up the water. Daily sunshine warmed up the crust of the earth, and hints of green brought hope which seemed to creep even in the most desperate circumstances. It had been declared that the town of Ma'an, south of us, was totaled by the flood. Its people were living in the neighboring schools, shacks, tents brought by the different relief agencies and with relatives in other towns and villages. Many governments, far and near, responded to this disaster and relief became abundant. With the help of the local Red Cross and Red Crescent and many of the other charity organizations that owned tough vehicles, the people of Ma'an received showers of food, warm clothes, blankets and money to rebuild the city. Rumors had it that the flood had been more of a blessing than a curse, because the town was rebuilt better than ever before, and most people were happy, thankful, and satisfied.

But the relief agents couldn't bring back the dead, and some of the homes that lost family members in the disaster rebuked their faith; others took it as a punishment from God for their sins and used it to strengthen their faith. Some people prayed for them; others visited them and prayed with them, and others pointed to them and said, "it served them well, for they were sinners." And life in the village and its neighboring towns went on in the normal way.

The Seeq was declared closed for a while, and Jim remained imprisoned at the Guest House. Mr. Rami and I visited him every now and then, and he visited with flocks of relief agents, journalists and Government officials. Abu–Zeid's chest puffed like a peacock's and his face shined with grease, for he had never seen so much attention from visitors from the Capital. Tourists usually came and went, but this time, the guests sat around and visited and drank coffee while they waited for more roads to open. They advised each other about the best ways to approach certain areas and told many more flood stories than the news had ever covered. Some of these stories leaned more toward the gossip side, but they brought all these different people together and established a spirit of camaraderie between them.

People came early every morning and had breakfast at the Guest House so they could get on with their work and head back to the Capital before dark. A journalist of the Ra'ii newspaper who came in every day at dawn and took the news back with him to Amman, the Capital, at dusk sat in one corner one morning and began to tell his non–publishable stories as he sipped Turkish coffee and ate fresh taboon bread, and a crowd gathered around him and listened and shared more stories and kept Abu-Zeid's coffee and sweetened tea brewing and his staff busy. The art of story telling came to life again, and people glued themselves to their seats the moment someone captured the audience with his wit and eloquence. Eyes of all colors were fixed at the mouth of the story teller, and necks stretched out to allow the ears to hear every word. The immaculate silence that hovered over the people would put preachers of all religions to shame.

Chapter 17

Jim, Mr. Rami and I sat at a table next to the journalist and listened.

"You wouldn't believe what happened the other day," said the journalist to his listeners.

"I believe anything these days," said an army man. "Do you know that a woman delivered her baby on a teacher's desk in one of the classrooms in Ma'an?"

"Now that's what I would call a practical lesson," said a man from the crowd. The people laughed, pushed their chairs closer together. Some rubbed their hands, wiggled in their seats and made themselves comfortable.

"Actually, three children were born at the school the day of the flood," said another man.

"Three babies delivered by one nurse," said another. The eyes widened in the crowd, and people fell silent; they listened, and the man went on. "And the babies were laid inside the opened desks," he said. "They made better cribs than the damp mattresses on the cold floor."

"One man named his daughter Forgiveness," said the first man. "Can you believe that?"

"I wonder who is supposed to forgive whom and for what."

"That girl will never forgive her father for such name."

The journalist waited patiently for his turn, and when he had a split second of silence, he took immediate advantage of it. "You know," he said. "A poor young man from somewhere around Aqaba, down south, had wanted to marry a girl who belonged to a man of status in Ma'an, but her father, the big shot, threatened the lover and kept a close eye on the girl who was very much interested in the young man. When the flood destroyed the property of the father and demolished his belongings, and when he discovered that he had more mouths to feed than he could afford, he gave his blessing to the poor young man who had hitch hiked from Aqaba to check on his girl. The marriage took place in a U.N. tent the day after the flood, and the happy couple hitch hiked back to Aqaba on a delivery truck."

"Did they celebrate with traditional village wedding song and dance?" asked a man from the crowd.

"No. They didn't have time," said the journalist. "The bride and the groom were anxious. They were afraid that the father might change his mind, because the weather kept improving and relief was coming too fast. But the crowd did sing and dance after the couple had left the premises. Even the father joined the dancers. It gave them something to do for a while."

Mr. Rami translated the jokes to Jim and his laughter came in as solos after everybody was done. People looked at him and laughed one more time.

The government officials convinced Jim to wait until the following week to cross the Seeq. The Department of Tourism had promised to take immediate action and open up the path for tourists as soon as possible. Too many tours to Petra had been canceled and the tourism business began to suffer. The government had also prepared plans to build a dam near the Seeq to prevent floods in the future, but it would all take time, and Jim had to be patient.

"Petra is supposed to open–up again by Monday," said one of the tourist agents. "You'll have a safer return to your project if you wait until someone else tried the path first."

"I hope I still have a pro...," Jim's eyes widened and his mouth froze before he could finish his word. He stared at the door and let a faint smile warm up his face. Mr. Rami had his back turned to the door, but when he saw Jim, he turned around and looked. Miss Petra Lux walked in and greeted everybody. There was an ethereal aura around her. Her simplicity and confidence pulled people toward her like as if she were a magnet. Her hair was braided and then twisted like a doughnut at the back of her head. She had on a pair of dark blue jeans, and a khaki jacket with a large hood. Her notebook rested on her forearm, and a pencil tied to the notebook with a string dangled loosely at the side.

"What in the world are you doing here?" asked Jim.

"I came to check on you," she said. "We've heard nothing but nightmares about this place in Amman. Hans gave me his project jeep. He said he won't be needing it for a few days."

"That's nice of him."

"He's also worried about you, and so are the Schnellers and the Breners. They all want to know how you are doing, where you were during the flood, and how your project survived the disaster."

"Well. Here I am," said Jim. "And only God knows what my project looks like."

"You haven't been down there since the flood?" asked Miss Lux.

"No," said Jim, a bit surprised. "The road is still closed."

"Why?" asked Miss Lux.

"What do you mean why?" said Jim with a scolding tone and a frowning smile.

"The ground should be dry enough by now. It doesn't take very long for this sandy soil to soak up the water. I think we can go anytime."

Mr. Rami lifted his eyebrows as high as they could go, and his lower lip dropped low. "Do you know what it is like down there, Ma'am" he said.

"Do you?" she asked.

"I crossed the Seeq the night before the flood," said Mr. Rami. "And let me tell you. For a while, I thought I was going to join the gods we were trying to excavate the last few months."

"But that was a long time ago, gentlemen." said Miss Lux. "It's time to go back to work; don't you think?"

"That was less than a week ago," said Mr. Rami.

"That was almost a week ago," argued Miss Lux, "and it hadn't rained since. The path should be passable by now. Don't you think?"

We all stared at her persisting eyes and waited for more instructions.

"Sit down and have some coffee first," said Jim. "I think she's right," he said to Mr. Rami. "We don't have to wait for anybody. We can give it a shot today, all four of us. What do you say?"

Mr. Rami shook his head at the defeat. "I suppose," he said. "I had hoped to spend my weekend, all of Thursday and all of Friday," he enunciated, "idling. The flood clean up at the school, and trying to put everything and everybody back on the right track just about killed me. What the heck," he finally concluded.

"That's the spirit," said Miss Lux. She smiled gaily at Mr. Rami. "You can idle during the Adha holiday. It's coming soon."

I stood up and told Jim that if I were to go with them, I would need to go ask my mother first. He said I didn't have to go, but I told him I wanted to. I wanted to go down there in the worst way. I begged him not to leave without me.

While I was gone, Jim and Mr. Rami filled Miss Lux in on what had happened to my brothers. When I returned, she stood up and shook my hand and pressed it tightly. Tears were rolling down her cheeks, and she sobbed softly. Her eyes were red, and I could tell she had been crying for a while.

"I heard the bad news on television, but I never knew that the victims were your brothers," she said.

Chapter 17

I never thought anybody could be so versatile. One minute she was tough and ready to challenge the men, and another minute she was soft, sweet and compassionate. I had never seen a person like Miss Lux before. Of course, there was Aisheh, but Aisheh had more crude and weathered looks and bubbling tempers. I guess I loved Aisheh because she was wild as the black iris on the hillside, and I loved Miss Lux because she came from some exotic flower garden.

"Are you ready to go?" asked Jim.

"Yes, and I brought four horses," I said. "I think it would be a good idea to go on horseback this time."

"You didn't have to do that Raji," said Jim.

"I know, but we have them, what's left of them. We might as well use them. Besides, they need to get out every now and then, until we decide what we do with them." The party complied, and we mounted the horses and trotted slowly toward the mouth of the Seeq.

As we rode down toward the path, a crowd of people followed us with their eyes. Their murmurs also followed us until we disappeared into the Seeq.

"Are they crazy or what?"

"Has anybody been there after the flood yet?"

"What people would do to get famous. Tomorrow, the news would announce the first ones to cross the Seeq after the flood."

The road was soft but not impassable; thanks to the abundance of fine rocks. The flood had rearranged the stones here and there and added several bumps, some of which we removed by hand in order to make it through. The cliffs still towered above us and bulged, but none of them had fallen off or seemed threatening. Each bulge continued to be part of the monolith that was split to form each side of the Seeq. The horses complained every now and then but kept on going slowly down the path. A strong smell of dampness filled our nostrils and an eerie feeling crept through me. The Seeq I had treaded daily with certainty and confidence now turned into an adventure path and gave me the feeling of an alien who had been robbed by an even more alien intruder. I felt the loss for the first time. It had been bigger than I thought. I had been numbed until that moment, the moment I saw the carcass of our first dead horse or what was left of it. It lay all black and ugly at the end of the Seeq and was caught between two large rocks on the right side of the clearance. There had been wild animals, perhaps hyenas and foxes, munching, and there were flies and bugs feasting on the sacrifice. I knew I was walking inside the scar that had been carved by a natural disaster, an upheaval that could neither be overpowered nor avoided by man. I looked at Jim and felt all the eyes staring at me. A fetid smell arose from the dead animal. I nudged my horse, and it took off galloping down the main road toward the dry riverbed.

What we used to call the dry riverbed was no longer dry. The water had puddled in it and waited to get evaporated by the warm sun or interred by the tepid earth. Other than the little details that could be found by tracing the tracks of the flood, Petra stood still and solid like it had been for two thousand years. An overview of the place gave peace, the kind that had been handed down from century to century after surviving many a cataclysm.

Jim was nervous as we approached the project. He squirmed on his horse and stalled behind and let the others go ahead first. The horse sensed his uneasiness and grunted a few times. Mr. Rami and Miss Lux nudged their horses and hurried to the edge of the enterprise. Then they dismounted their horses, tied them to a rock and ran toward the excavation site. Jim kept his eyes on the ground, and his horse almost stood still. I stayed with him.

Chapter 17

"Come look at this, Jim," Shouted Mr. Rami. "It looks like the gods did all this to help us out."

Jim and I moved toward the site. The mounds of dirt we had piled up were washed down the valley, but the water had also washed out a layer of the ground. A capital of a pillar peeked through the mud. Its intricate designs had been protected by the earth. The carved edges were sharp and crisp although one side of it was cracked. The fall had done it; the fall, the trace of a cataclysm from centuries ago. It had waited all this time for us, in the year of the flood, to track it down.

Jim's grin came back, and I could see hope in his eyes. He kneeled down and touched the carved capital, going gently around the edges. It was another baby for Jim. He looked like a proud father.

We messed around the project for a few minutes and then headed toward Jim's cave for a cup of tea. Jim checked his supplies at the cave and prepared a list of things he needed to have.

"I'll go to the Capital tomorrow and spend the rest of the week there," he said. "Monday I'll get back to work."

"If you wish to go today, I'll give you a ride," said Miss Lux. "I'll also bring you back, because I intend to come back and help you on Monday, Jim."

"What about your work up north?" asked Jim.

"They are on hold for now. I can do whatever I want for a while, and I was thinking of renting a room at the Guest House for a few days to help you resume your work again."

"I'll come too, whenever I can," said Mr. Rami. "Even after school on school days."

"I'll be here, Jim," I said.

Jim's face relaxed and he looked healthy again. The tea he made tasted good and sweet. We all took seconds and thirds, while we waited for him to pack his clothes and get ready for the trip to Amman. When we left the cave, the sun was shining on the hill where the Nabatean tombs stood vacant. The sun rays exposed brilliant layers of colored sand. They towered up and up the hill, above the tombs and the searching eyes.

"Look," whispered Miss Lux.

"Colors," said Jim.

"Purple!" said Mr. Rami.

I looked and remembered my cave and its colors. Who would listen to a poor peasant boy, I thought as I mounted my horse and followed the party.

Sunshine and silence.

We arrived at the Guest House early in the evening. Abu-Zeid looked at us and sighed. "There you are," he said. "I thought you'd never come."

"Why?" asked Jim.

"Your turkey arrived from Amman this morning, and I cooked it just like you had asked. I began to wonder whether to serve it to the customers or wait for you to show up."

"It is Thanksgiving day today," said Jim, fully surprised at the realization. "I forgot all about it. I was going to borrow your oven and bake a pie," he mumbled innocently to Mr. Rami. His face sobered. Mr. Rami and Miss Lux looked at him, winked at each other and smiled. "But that was before the flood," Jim continued. He sounded pathetic.

"We'll have baklava instead," said Mr. Rami. "You can call it pistachio pie if you wish."

Abu-Zeid cleared his throat and led us to one of the side caves. "I arranged a private room for you," he said. "This way please."

A Mid-Eastern colorful chandelier hung from the ceiling of the small cave. It threw a variety of reflections on the uneven walls. Under the chandelier, there was a table covered with food. A turkey, used as a centerpiece, all shiny and brown, shimmered in the light. There were mashed potatoes, gravy, peas, carrot sticks, salads, and two apple pies, one on each side of the turkey. And there was a small tray of baklava, crowded in the middle. My mouth watered at the site. I had never eaten a turkey before. Jim had talked about it for so long and described it many times to the point that I could taste it without ever putting it in my mouth. He did the same with the pies. I recognized what they were without ever seeing one before.

"Where did all this come from?" asked Jim. "I only ordered the turkey."

Abu–Zeid looked at the company and smiled cynically. "Have a seat everybody and happy Thanksgiving," he said and darted out.

I sat facing Miss Lux. Mr. Rami and Jim faced each other, and Jim asked us to hold hands for the table grace. Thinking of him as a Christian, and knowing that Christianity is one of our mono–deitic religions that shared the same roots with Judaism, I had expected him to say something Godly, not too far from what we, Moslems would usually say, something like, "In the name of the God, the Merciful and Compassionate," but he didn't. What he said was bizarre. It started out all right but ended somewhere in the desert, all rough and dry. I had my doubts about the Lord's acceptance of such words. His Almighty seemed to have trouble accepting much milder and more civil and complaisant prayers. Deep in my heart I prayed for mercy and compassion for Jim, because his prayer went on, something like this, "Thank you Lord for your generosity and love, the pillar capital, the carvings and the colors. Your ways are sure different, Lord; your canyons are too deep and your hills too high, and every time we make it, be it up or down, it seems like we leave somebody behind. What do they think of all this, I wonder? That's the reason why I hate logic, Lord. Now, you take it easy on us. Amen."

Jim invited everybody to dig in. I waited for someone to comment on his prayer but nothing was uttered, and I concluded that I was the only one bothered by it. The rest of the company seemed to accept it for all its worth. Jim stood up and began to carve the Turkey and stack a few pieces of everyone's plate.

"In the name of God, the merciful and compassionate." I found myself mumbling quietly over and over while Jim served.

I ate until my guts hurt.

Chapter 18

The balmy weather that followed could not freshen the stifling air left by loss and decaying hope. People hung on and waited for the air to move. Mr. Rami and I settled into a routine that confined us to the school and Jim's excavations. This pattern helped me avoid the villagers and the school boys who insisted on knowing what I planned to do next. "I don't know yet," seemed to work well enough whenever a confrontation became inevitable. The words stopped the investigations and ended the unwanted conversation. After that I was free to go. Some tried to give me advice, and I still said, "I don't know yet," until they gave up and left me alone.

Mr. Rami continued to find entertainment in the archeological enterprise. It saved him a trip to the city and provided something that isolated him from the school yet kept him in close contact with history. Although he had no hope left in finding caves in that particular spot, he found enough ancient objects that fascinated him and enriched his stories in the classroom.

"I'm afraid, the old man is going to leave here disappointed," he said to me once as we left the excavations.

"Jim is finding many pieces of pottery, though, and according to his book, the place was supposed to be rich in pottery."

"True, but remember that pottery used to be the main item in those days. Every place you dig can be rich in pottery. I don't see any indication or hope for a set of caves up there. That bulge in the hill Jim had put his bets on is too flat now to make a cave. There are no caves on the site."

"Don't tell Jim that."

"He knows, Raji. He knows. But as long as he keeps finding things, he cannot quit. He has to go all the way through now. Besides, he has no time to move on to another site. His year here is going to be over soon, unless he renews, of course."

"Do you think he will?"

"It depends on how much energy he has left. This is not an easy life for someone his age. When I get that old, the last thing I wish to do is dig in the dirt. I'd rather see people, travel, visit historical places around the world. What is still buried in the ground would not interest me when I myself am not that far from being buried in it. What would you do Raji?"

"I don't know yet, Mr. Rami," I said unconsciously. But when I heard my own words, I recovered quickly and amended the answer. "I don't even know what I'm going to do in the near future, let alone after retirement."

"You'll make a good archeologist, young man. I can get you started and give you ample recommendation to get you anywhere."

"But my mother." I paused. There were no more words ready to explain what I wanted to say about my mother.

"What about your mother?"

"She's left alone."

"She has her house and life down here. You need to get yours started, and you'll both be fine."

Chapter 18

I remembered Um–Sleiman and what had happened to her because she lived alone. First, she had been cursed because she bore no children, and then doubly cursed because her husband had died and left her alone. Now my mother would be treated the same. I could hear the villagers say, "She couldn't keep anybody. Her husband and three of her children died, and, the last one left her to seek better luck somewhere else." She would definitely be treated as another cursed woman. The villagers are hard on lonely people. Their gossip hurts; it stabs like knives.

"Do you know Um–Sleiman?" I finally asked Mr. Rami.

"The fortuneteller?"

"Yes. Do you know how the villagers treat her?"

"I do, but, do you know why?"

"Because she's lonely."

"No, Raji. Because she wants them to leave her alone."

"What?"

"Yes. I have watched that woman enough times and came to know her very well." Everybody had been watching everybody else in the village, I thought. First Um–Sleiman told me she'd been watching me as well as everybody else, and now Mr. Rami had been watching her, and Abu–Zeid watches the entire gamut of watchers. I concluded that our town would never be short on guards. "Um–Sleiman is doing well all by herself," continued Mr. Rami. "I have seen her leave wonderful meals, hot casseroles and fresh baked taboon bread at my doorstep. She likes what she does and prefers to keep people at a distance. There's nothing wrong with that, but your mother is miles from being that way. She has friends in the village and had a very prosperous social life. She'll never be treated the same way."

That was a flicker of hope for me, and the following week I found lamps, ancient lamps that made that light brighter in my life. While I was scraping against the hill, I came upon a final section of a man made stone wall. Fine dirt had filled in the cracks, and I worked on loosening it all and scraping it out. But the dirt above the wall kept falling on me, and I decided to get rid of it first until it quit sliding down, and in the process, I confronted three Nabatean clay lamps, one of which was of a medium rarity. It had a place for three candle wicks. Jim said that if the Department of Tourism would let us keep the two common lamps, he would give me one of them.

"You earned this one, Lizard. You earned that baby," he said.

"What would I do with it?" I said, remembering the abundance I still have to contend with in my cave.

"When you become an archeologist, you'll be very proud of it, Raji. You'll remember this day and be very proud."

I would be if what Mr. Rami said would come true, I thought. If I ever become an archeologist, I would work on my own collection of antiques, and this would be an addition to the pottery in my cave. I already have a collection, I thought. If I could ever find a way to get it down. An archeologist would know a way. I would know a way, in due time.

Jim and I went to eat at the restaurant in town that evening, because the next morning, he wanted to have a head start toward the Capital. No sooner than we stepped in, we discovered that the pilgrims had had the same destination – Abu–Mustafa's restaurant. It was popular among the Turks, and they remembered him from year to year. Jim was concerned about the commotion when he saw the Turks, the poor Turks flock into the restaurant. It was quite a sight in a small quiet village. These Turks were the ones who could not afford airplane tickets from Turkey to Mecca. They drove all the way from their country up north, across the Jordanian desert, and then they would continue on down to Saudi Arabia.

Chapter 18

Three cars packed with people and their belongings pulled in front of the restaurant as we walked in. The rear view mirror of each car had hundreds of beads of all sizes and bright colored, decorative objects dangling from the mirror, all the way down to the dashboard. Also, each car had a top rack on its roof. It was heaped with luggage. It towered far above the car and made it look as if it were a double deck mini bus. The load was tied down and secured with an abundance of rope. It crisscrossed every which direction to secure the load.

"Pilgrims," I said to Jim. "Low income pilgrims." He stared at the sight of people and bundles and more bundles and people and colored beads and scarves. The strong smell of cheap perfume immediately permeated the air in the restaurant and restricted it to a near suffocating level. "They came all the way from Turkey," I continued, "heading for Mecca. The rich ones fly, and the poor ones rent a car. They car–pool and do that every year."

Jim was amused, and he looked pleased with himself. He had had an eventful day with my discovery of the unique Nabatean lamps, and now his day was topped with evening entertainment. I could tell he had never seen pilgrims before, for his eyes were fixed on them. It was embarrassing. When the waiter came, I had to order our meal all by myself, because I couldn't get the old man's attention enough to know exactly what he had wanted. I knew he had come here for the daily hot meal but didn't know exactly what he wanted for a drink, and I didn't think he cared much. I ordered what I wanted for both of us.

Then the place fell silent all of a sudden, as if the people were knocked on their heads with a stunning bar, and the room that roared with noise a minute ago became quiet like an empty tomb.

"What happened?" asked Jim. His eyes grew wide with shock and concern again.

"Didn't you hear the prayer call?" He listened to the sound coming from the minaret of the mosque. "It's prayer time, Jim. Remember, these are pilgrims. That's all they do these days – pray."

Each pilgrim had a prayer rug rolled up under his arm. One of them approached me with a question in his eyes, and I knew exactly what he was seeking. I pointed south to him, and he gave me a thank you salute with his hand and went on to inform the rest of the party. They unrolled the long narrow rugs and set them side by side against the wall that faced south, took their shoes off and fell on their knees. They mumbled their prayers, and the stifling air was filled with a mixture of humming noise and smell of cheap perfume, food and feet.

"What did you tell them?" asked Jim.

"I directed them toward Mecca. They have to face Mecca when they pray – straight south of here."

"And they practice that everywhere they go?"

"Five times a day."

"How come you don't do that?"

"Because."

"Just because."

"Yes. Besides, I think my mother prays enough for both of us." Jim shook his head. "What are you shaking your head for? I scolded. "The only time I saw you pray was at the Thanksgiving dinner, and that wasn't much of a bargain prayer either. It was embarrassing. I felt obliged to pray to God for you so he would have mercy on you. You told me that you go to the International Christian Church in Amman to see your friends there on Sunday, but you never mentioned prayer, old man. Your faith is just as lousy as mine. Do you even believe in God?"

"Do you?"

"I asked you first."

Chapter 18

He rubbed his forehead with the tips of his fingers as if he had to think about it, but his cynical smile ruined his sagacious appearance. "I believe in God all right," he finally said, "but not the same way most people do, I guess."

"What do you mean?"

"I mean, they all have the right idea but the wrong attitude, even those who seem to be wonderful on the outside. They point wrongly to people of different beliefs and make enemies out of them, and the right idea gets lost and war goes on. I hate fanatics is what I mean to say, and I haven't met too many open minded pious people in my life."

"What is it like at the International Church in the Capital."

"Now that place is different from any church I have ever seen." He giggled at the thought. "The people there are mostly foreigners in the country – embassy people and foreign workers, British, American, French, Indians, Chinese, Japanese, you name it, people of all denominations who cannot go to local churches, because the services there would be in Arabic, and they wouldn't understand it. At the International church, the service is in English, which is a more universal language; therefore, it attracts all those who understand English. The unique thing is that they all have to muffle their differences and learn to accept each other for a change, and it works – at least during the service. They all keep their differences at home and come and worship together. Now, that keeps the right idea in focus, and I don't mind that at all."

"Maybe that's what we need – a world full of foreigners."

Jim laughed. "If we stop and think about it, Raji, that's what we are in this world – a bunch of foreigners, just a bunch of foreigners," he repeated dreamily.

Jim and I were certainly a couple of foreigners or at least a weird combination at the restaurant. I could feel many Turkish eyes staring at us as the mouths jabbered in Turkish, words I could not comprehend. Soon, the waiters came with an abundance of food. There was rice, pocket bread, lamb cooked in vegetable sauce, olives, fresh green onions, and yogurt. I had ordered kebob for me and Jim, and it came with a wealth of condiments and pocket bread. Jim looked at his food and frowned. "Funny," he said. "I don't remember ordering this."

"I did, Jim. You were busy staring."

"You, Lizard. I ignore you when you speak Arabic, but from now on, I'd better watch it, especially when you order my food. I never tasted the kebob in here before." He pulled a bite of meat from the skewers and put it in his mouth and chewed vehemently. "Good food. You lucked out again," he said and pulled another one.

When all the food was consumed, Jim headed for the Guest House and I home. The streets were empty and silent except for Um–Sleiman's cart. It came roaring around the corner as I turned toward the house. She wobbled behind the handle bars and mumbled a mixture of song and pain. When she saw me, she stopped and motioned for me to go to her.

"What do you need?" I asked.

She reached deep down in her dress and pulled a small bundle from her pouch. She opened it and exposed a small charm made of clay. It had a face surrounded by very intricate designs and was well made. "Take this to Jim," she said. "It is a lucky charm which the Nabateans used to wear. An excavator told me that once. He was looking for the real thing and showed me a picture of it and said that the real one would cost a fortune. That was many years ago, but I couldn't forget that face in the picture. I went home and worked hard on it, and then I set it aside and didn't have a chance to get back to it until now. I want you to give it to Jim and wish him good luck. Tell him you bought it from the souvenir corner at the Guest House."

"Are you sure this is not real?"

"Yes I'm sure, silly. I made it. Who do you think makes all those antique imitation souvenirs at Abu–Zeid's corner? But this one is a first and probably a last of its kind. Making faces that small in the clay is no easy work, but I always wanted to imitate that picture. The eyes are powerful in it. They stare. See how they stare?"

"You made these things!"

"Shhh. I make them and Abu–Zeid sells them for me."

"And I thought these souvenirs came from some fancy company in Amman."

"No, silly. When I started making them, Abu–Zeid even tried to sell them to tourists as real antiques. He thought he could make a fortune, but he couldn't get away with it, and I was mad at him. I told him I would tell on him if I ever caught him selling my souvenirs for real antiques. I want no illicit deals to bust my blessings. God gave me a good hand and a good eye. I can imitate anything I see, and I intend to keep it that way, and if my work gets into dirty deals, my hands will be cut off and my eyes plucked out. Yes Sir. God doesn't like dirty deals. Neither does the Tourism Department. I told Abu–Zeid that, and he agreed."

I was inspecting the charm and listening to Um–Sleiman at the same time. "Did the excavator find the real thing then?" I asked without taking my eyes off the masterpiece.

"No. The poor thing got bitten by a snake and died before anybody had a chance to reach him."

I had seen that face on the charm before, but I couldn't remember where until I looked into Jim's eyes when I went to deliver it to him at the Guest House. Jim's wife. Her picture. The charm on her breast. I remembered. It had the same picture. When Jim saw the charm, his eyes grew wide.

"Where did you get this from?" he scolded.

"It's a long story. Let's just say from someone who likes to imitate antiques. He (I felt that I had to change the sex in order to hide Um–Sleiman better) told me this is supposed to be a Nabatean lucky charm."

"A lucky charm indeed."

"Is this the god you're seeking?"

"His very own self. I wonder where your friend learned about it."

"He said that an excavator was looking for it many years ago and that the excavator showed the picture of the god to this antique imitator, and he molded it. This is his first piece of this charm. He says it isn't easy to imitate such designs."

"Could you do me one more favor, Raji?" Jim's eyes drooped, and his face saddened.

That's all I do these days, I thought. "What do you need?"

"Just ask your friend next time you see him whether that excavator had found what he had been seeking or not."

"No, Jim. The poor thing died of a snake bite."

"A snake bite?"

"Yes, Jim, a ssssnake bite. He died before anybody could get to him."

"I see."

"Does this mean we still have hope?"

"I hope so, Lizard. I hope so." He looked at me with a sad face. Then he went back to his lucky charm and felt it over and over again. He never saw me leave.

Chapter 19

First came the Adha holiday, and the village streets filled up with children gobbling down cheap candy. The little girls drooled over their ruffled, bright colored dresses, and the boys decorated their wire cars with the hard candy, just like the pilgrims did with colored beads. They dangled on all sides of the flimsy cars until they were pulled out, one at a time and consumed by their owners. And the rest of the villagers awaited their whole–lamb meals with hopes and expectations.

In our house, the day came and went like any other ordinary day. I tried not to make a big deal of it. Mother had cooked a flock of pigeons in spinach and served them with rice. My brothers used to butcher a lamb, a holiday treat that relieved us from pigeons for a change, but Mother said she didn't feel like lamb this year, so we ate pigeons again, just like the day before and the one before that. My uncle had invited us to spend the day with him and his family, but my mother declined. She insisted on staying home to pray and cook another sacrifice and a meal, all by herself.

She sacrificed three pigeons that went to a beggar in town. He was a middle aged man who had lost both legs for reasons unknown to me. One rumor said he had been injured during the war with the Turks; another said he had been hit by a train during the Turkish time. Whatever the reason was, the Turks seemed to have something to do with it. He used to crawl up and down the village streets on all four and end up at the Guest House, where the tourists had provided most of his income. I dropped the three cooked pigeons off at his shack and came home and ate with my mother – whatever she had kept.

It wasn't until then that I realized that my mother hadn't talked to me. She had always been a woman of a few words, but they had become fewer yet since the death of my brothers.

"Are you going to keep the rest of the horses?" I asked, trying to fabricate a conversation.

"I don't know yet."

Those were my words, I thought. She couldn't use them on me. That was how I answered people's questions, but I didn't tell her that, even though they sounded sharp and piercing. "My uncle and his children seem to be taking good care of them so far," I said. "But are you going to let them keep doing that?" I wanted her to talk, just like the villagers wanted me to talk, but she shrugged her shoulders and continued to eat quietly. "Do you want me to quit school?"

"No," she said firmly. My words woke her up and forced her to be alert and say something, minute but worthy. "That's your dream, young man, and you are going to follow it through."

"Why?"

"What do you mean why?"

"Why don't you want me to do something that's worth doing around here, something practical, like most people advise."

CHAPTER 19

"Look, Raji. All the other men in this house died early while trying to do something worth doing around here, something practical and useful for the moment. You're different, and I like that and want you to remain that way." Then she mumbled softly as if to scold fate. "Perhaps you'll live a little longer." Her eyes filled with tears, and she quit eating.

"But what is to become of you and the business?"

"I'll take care of that. Now don't you fret about it."

"Aren't you going to tell me at least what you are thinking of doing?"

"I told you. I don't know yet, and when I do, you'll know. Right now, we have enough money to get by, and I'm in no hurry. I don't need to make hasty decisions."

After dinner, I climbed on the roof and sat down beside the pigeon boxes and read for the rest of the evening. There was nothing for me to do anywhere. Jim and Mr. Rami had disappeared for a few days. They had gone to the resorts of Aqaba to spend some time snorkeling, swimming and cooking in the sun by the Red Sea, and the rest of the people were indulged in their own affairs and feasts and family blessings and feuds, so I sat down with my books and inhaled words and exhaled boredom. I read until my eyes hurt; then I fell asleep; then I woke up and read again until my eyes were tired, and I went back to sleep again.

When Jim and Mr. Rami came back, Jim looked all tanned and burnt in spots. His nose was all peeled off and his half bald head all red and shiny with grease.

"I never had a sunburn in winter before, not in America." he said gaily.

"You do look odd, even in Jordan, Jim," I said. "The weather is for a late snow storm up north again, and it has been on the cool side even here. We didn't get any of your Aqaba sun."

Mr. Rami looked darker and somewhat healthier. He had some color in his face, but I couldn't tell whether it was real or just a reflection in the twilight, and, if my imagination didn't do away with my senses, the man had even put on some weight, real flesh that covered his poking bones. Even the students noticed the change in him and were sure he had found a girl somewhere in Aqaba, but I assured them that the entire godsend was the old geezer, and that was by no means a serendipity.

Shortly after the Adha holiday came Christmas, during which Jim disappeared again for a few days. He went to Amman and its suburbs and spent some time touring the Byzantine ruins with his German friends. When he came back, he was ready to excavate again. He had finally missed his hole, and I gave thanks for that, for I had missed his hole too. I had missed everything, even Aisheh's goats. I had seen neither the shepherdess nor her animals for a while. I had seen only words on pages, sad and happy words that told about other miserable people in far away places.

When Jim came back from town, I saw him jump off the taxi, pay the driver, and hop gaily toward the Seeq. He even skipped in nimble feet, although the back pack was resting on his shoulders. It bulged but didn't seem too heavy. Still, it surprised me to see him acting so agile and light. I had spotted him from our roof where I had been reading and dashed down as fast as I could and caught up with him before he entered the Seeq.

"Did you bring some peanuts?" I hollered.

He turned around and saw me walking toward him. "Fresh, dry roasted, in the hulls," he said. "Here," he leaned over toward me with his back pack, "smell them? I could smell them all the way from Amman." I sniffed the air around his back pack and smelled the peanuts all right. "What did you do while I was gone?" he asked.

"Nothing."

"Nothing?"

"I read a translated book."

"What is it called?"

"Les Misérables, by Victor Hugo."

"Damn French miseries. Why don't you find something more cheerful to read about, young man?"

"There is none. Besides, this wasn't bad. It was long, and I needed a long story to keep me busy while you were gone."

"I brought you something else from Amman."

"What is it?"

"Wait until we get to the cave. It's in a box, and you'll have to open it and find out. Maybe you'll forget about the stupid Misérables." He tried to mimic the French pronunciation sarcastically. His lips formed a sissy kissing position, and he half closed his eyes and held that face for a while.

In his cave, he dropped his load and pulled the peanuts out and then a gift box, all wrapped up nicely. He handed it to me and said, "Here is an Adha, Christmas, whatever you may call it gift. Happy holidays."

I opened the box and found a camera, a real honest to God camera, loaded with flash, film and everything.

"This is for me?"

"I couldn't sacrifice it for the gods."

"You didn't have to do this, Jim." I pulled the camera out of the box and turned it over and over.

"Why not," he said, sounding as if he got rid of a pain. "I got tired of you coveting every camera you see. I thought maybe this will cure you once and for all. Now, you may covet something else for a change."

"I don't covet, Jim. I just fancy things is all. Everybody fancies things, some more practical than others, but everybody fancies things."

"What do you mean some more practical than others?" He was scolding as if he knew what I was talking about him.

"I mean, at least, I wished for a camera not a god in a two room apartment–cave."

"Now off with you, young man," he squeaked in a sharp tone of voice. "You got your wish. Just see to it that you come back tomorrow to help me with mine. We'll see whose wish is more practical. Off with you, infidel lizard."

He shooed me off, and began to unload the rest of his back pack. I picked up my box and headed for the door, but before I left, he turned around and yelled, "Hey, wait. Don't forget this." He piled a large bag of peanuts on my already loaded arms.

"Don't you want to keep some for yourself?"

"Nah. I had my fill in town. Your mother might enjoy some too. Just take it." He turned me gently toward the door and headed for his back–pack again.

I took two steps and turned around.

"Jim," I said.

He turned around again and half closed his eyes to express loss of patience, "Now what."

"Thanks."

"For what?"

To that, I gave no answer but secured my prizes in my arms and headed home smelling peanuts and feeling a camera box, full with the real thing it said it was. When the weather turns decent, I thought, and Aisheh is out with her animals, I would take pictures. The first one would be of the shepherdess by the cave and then the cave and then the pottery and then, of course, Jim.

Chapter 20

Time stalled again; winter faltered and howled like a crippled dog. The seasons had always been equal to me until this year, the year that went down in history as the year of the flood. I had heard people complain about long winters and short summers and could never understand why. Each season in my life had always had its natural length, three months. They mingled and blended their ends together every once in a while, but they were more or less equal, and I was happy with that arrangement and satisfied. This winter, however, went on like the day after doomsday. The early start of wet cold weather had overwhelmed autumn and chased spring clear to the verge of May. There was a very unusual April snow storm up north and nasty cold winds that carved the faces like sharp claws down here in the south. The old saying accused people's lack of faith of being responsible for severe weather changes; the weather man called it a change in the cycle, and the migrating birds did not seem to know what to call it. They were confused and flew in circles northeast of the country, near the oasis of Azraq, where they usually rested on their way to and from Eastern Europe.

Jim puttered around. He totally uncovered the capital of the pillar that had been exposed by the flood and pulled a few other broken trinkets that poked through the weary earth. Although Miss Lux, Mr. Rami and I continued to help Jim, we no longer saw signs of auspicious progress. The hidden gods seemed stuck in the mud just like the people who sought them. For the first time in my life I experienced dead ends and realized that there were actual limits, borders, and ends to everything, even dreams. Prior to this confusion, my dreams had penetrated all barriers and caused them to diminish. Now, even the fantasies had been trapped, overpowered by boundaries of fate, weather, and uncontrolled agents. The only docile power I possessed remained in my books, the sole malleable medium that relieved me from the rut I had fallen into, and I held onto them, tightly.

Mr. Rami was pleased with my academic progress. He told me to keep it up, and I did, not because he said so, but because the books continued to help revitalize my imagination. I had spent many long hours on the roof of our house reading to the pigeons, watching the villagers go about doing their work, and reflecting on their life and my death. I filled up my diary, and it spilled over onto my school papers. The teacher said I had a natural talent in writing. To me, the talent was rather a need, and without it, even my dreams would have been buried, not in the ground but in the emptiness of the space where no one can excavate them but the spirits.

My mood and my feelings toward the surroundings changed every day and my writing reflected this fickle attitude. One day I praised the tranquility and majesty of Petra; other days, I cursed its mute rocks and their impaired images that expressed nothing but the brutality of disaster. All was ruins. If strangers were to read my diary, they would call it a compilation of diverse meditations written by a number of authors that expressed different attitudes toward the same thing. My pen played the devil's advocate and camouflaged my true ego in the words. Meanwhile, I kept trying to maintain faith in my existence.

The signs of life I observed from the roof were skimpy; the first tourists to appear since the flood arrived in late March, and after that nobody came until May, when a sudden wave of hot weather hovered over the south like an evil spirit. Before that, even the sound of sheep and goats could scarcely be heard in the valleys, and the shepherds found other jobs on the outskirts of Wadi Moussa. I saw no trace of Aisheh during winter and would never dare come close to her farm on the far side of the village. Her father's wrath would be undesirable, according to her. I just waited patiently for her to make her spring appearance one of these days as usual. Winter had been heavy with penitence. Other winters had only confined people to their dens and taught them how to be patient, but this one added grief and despair, and I felt the need for more than a book. My soul yearned for a human friend to talk to in a loud voice, very loud voice.

Although springtime was felt sporadically at the beginning, its signs had crept through the ground and gradually covered the surface of the earth with rich green grass and wild flowers. By the end of April, the ground showed colors again, colors that would fade away and dry up in this semi arid part of the country by mid August. Researchers had found four hundred different kinds of wild flowers in the green parts of Jordan. I tried to count them once and discovered that I had counted the ones I liked several times over and gave up. I believed in the more conspicuous flowers, the large red poppies, white daisies, and blue iris. The latter ones came in all shades of blue. They ranged from very light, almost white, to the deepest blue, almost pitch black. Tourists called them black iris and thought of them as strange and exotic. The petals of the black iris started with a deep, dark blue color at the center, and they gradually darkened more and more until they looked black toward the lacy ends.

Many tourists had scoured the ground and pulled out bulbs of black iris to take home with them. The land was a haven for robbers, for, not only did they rob the historical artifacts but also the flower bulbs, and, if they could, they would have lifted off the carved monoliths and moved them to their own land and claimed them and confused history to no end.

Then the millipedes crept out of the ground. Millipedes looked like centipedes, except they were much bigger and safer. They had no poison in them but were enough of a nuisance to make up the difference; black moving twigs crept on the rocks and wandered all around for people to trip over, squash and trim, a piece here and another one there. Many tourists screamed at the sight of millipedes. "Centipedes" or "baby snakes", they would say as they screamed and made me chuckle. I used to tell them that I would scream too if the slim buggers were snakes and assured them that they were nothing but a safe nuisance.

Aisheh still hadn't shown up, and that wasn't just a safe nuisance, for April had begun to crawl out of the calendar already, and there was no trace of her anywhere. I had surveyed the hills, the valleys, the cave, and every place I could think of that might have been of use to her at one time or another, but she was nowhere to be found. Something was the matter, and I had to find out what it was.

It took me a while to gather enough courage to go ask about her. For a young man to be asking about a young maiden in a small village the size of Wadi Moussa was quite a suspicious gesture, but I decided to do it anyway. Her brother had owned a small business out by the main highway. He made coats and rugs from sheep and goat skin and mattresses from sheep wool and sold them to tourists and local people. I walked up to his store and stood at the door for a while. The unpleasant smell of fresh wool filled my nostrils, and I felt nauseated.

"What can I do for you?" he asked. He was a husky man, the size I wouldn't care to jest with unless it was of extreme necessity. His eyes were large and dark as the night, and he had a bushy, thick mustache under his nose. A tiny piece of lint from his shop was stuck on his eyebrow, and it moved with the shaggy, unkempt hair up and down as he talked. When I said nothing, he repeated the question, and I think he sensed my fear and confusion. He smiled gently, and with that, he erased the savage feelings I had initially experienced about him, and his looks softened a little. "What can I do for you, lad?"

The words wouldn't come out of my mouth. I tried and tried, and all I could do was stare at him. "Are you okay?" he asked.

"Yes." Finally, I was able to say something and prove to myself that my speech had not been affected by my mental paralysis.

"Is there something you need?"

"Is Aisheh okay?"

He hesitated a little. His eyes studied me from head to toe and made my marrow twitch inside my bones. "Yes," he finally said. "Why?"

"Her goats," I said. "I don't see her goats in the hills anymore. I was planning on buying one of them. I had my eye on the large one, the one that kicks too much and ventures off all the time. Aisheh said she would talk to her father about it."

"I'm sure you do see the goats out there, lad," said the man. "It is Aisheh you don't see anymore, and I doubt that you ever will," he whined in a high voice, and his eyes stared in a reverie. "She's been married for quite some time now."

"Married". The word was repeated as a statement, all natural, nothing to it, a fact of life.

"Yes. An oil rich man from the Gulf came last fall and asked Father if he would allow him to marry his daughter." He chuckled, shrugged his shoulders, shook his head, and resumed his work with the large needle. "Money talks these days, you know," he continued, poking the needle in and out. "Father gave his blessings, and Aisheh flew away with her husband. He sure was loaded – very greasy, bailed father out of debt and replenished the stock too."

"Married." So that was the farewell in Aisheh's note, I thought. She had meant it.

"Yep. It all happened in a week's time believe it or not. Before they knew it, the goats were stripped of their shepherdess and were assigned a shepherd to obey and drive wild. They are still out there, healthy as ever, and their young master is trying. He's not doing as good a job as Aisheh though. One of the stubborn animals, and I think it's the one you're talking about keeps giving him trouble, and Aisheh wouldn't give him a hint on how to deal with that goat before she left. She wouldn't talk to anybody. I'm sure the shepherd would be more than glad to get rid of the crazy thing. He would give it to you for free; my father would rip you off." He laughed aloud at his own joke, but when he noticed my grave face, he sobered and squirmed and cleared his throat.

I nodded and turned around to leave, forgetting the excuse I had made for asking about the girl. But the man didn't forget. He hollered after me, "Do you still want to buy that goat?"

"I'll see. I need to check with my mother first."

His eyes checked me again with interest and suspicion. Then he smiled, nodded and finally said, "If I were you, I wouldn't; neither would I ever ask about Aisheh again. Go in peace."

Chapter 20

I did.

Jim was shoveling large clumps of dirt from the ground when I reached the sight. He didn't see me come until I walked up to him, yanked the shovel off his hand and sent it soaring like an arrow toward the hill. He stood back and stiffened up. "What the hell did you do that for?" he asked. "Have you gone mad?"

"Aisheh is married," I shouted in his face.

"What?"

"You heard me."

"To whom?"

"To a rich son of an ass from the oil countries."

"You must be really hurt, young man. I never heard you talk like that before." He watched me walk around him in circles and kick dirt into the air. "Have you ever told her that you loved her?"

"No."

"Then what did you expect her to do, watch you turn into an old geezer?"

"We don't talk about these things around here, Jim, " I said. "We ... just know."

"Sure you do."

"Sure we do. We talked, studied, played, and chased goats together. She knew how I felt about her, and I knew how she felt about me."

"In that case, so did the goats and the millipedes."

"Jim. You don't understand. She probably never even had a chance to see her husband before the wedding day. It was a monetary deal. She complied just to save her father from debt."

That shut him up. He then let me kick dirt around him for a long time and went back to his work and dug, first in silence. Then he started to hum and fill the wheelbarrow and move around me as if I were a boulder, lifeless, yet moving in odd directions by mysterious forces. When he heard the noon prayer from the minaret, he stopped for lunch. I continued to walk in circles.

"Lizard," he finally said, and when I did not respond, he called me again and again. Then he stood up, walked behind me, grabbed my shoulders and knocked me down to the ground. I landed with a thud on my rear end. It was fortunate that I hit soft dirt.

"What did you do that for?"

"Now that I got your attention," he said and slowly lowered his body and sat down beside me. "You are a very young man."

"I sure don't feel like it."

"There is still high school to finish and then college, and somewhere along the line, another Aisheh will come to you. You are a fine young man. Let this Aisheh go and wait for the right one to come at the right time. Just make sure you tell her how you feel about her this time, right from the beginning. Women like that. There is nothing you can do right now. What happened happened. It is past. All you can do now is get off your flattened bottom and lend me a hand. I am ready to dig out another layer on this side." He pointed to the northern section of the project. "It seems like it had been elevated from the original ground on purpose. I see the edge of a stone platform. We might have hit an altar of some sort. My wish might yet come true, and we'll have a talk again, you and I, and I'll show you how practical my wish would be to someone who discovers the past as a rarity, rather than dwell on its disasters and bury himself with them."

In one corner of the northern section, Jim had brushed off a small part of a smooth stone layer. The stone was thick and heavy. We couldn't see its bottom, for it seemed to be buried deep down into the ground. Although I had no interest in working that day, the discovery of this corner, the platform caught my fancy. It was heavy and ancient and had been hidden in the ground for thousands of years. The uncovered corner looked as if it were waiting for us to get the job done and unveil its history. It stared at us in rock silence, literally. Jim looked at me and waited.

"What do you think?" he asked.

In a reflex action, I grabbed the shovel and gently, began to scrape off the thick layer of dirt above the stone. Jim joined me, and we worked in silence. We dug and shoveled, and I hauled away. When he stopped for a drink, I went on; when he stopped to catch his breath, I went on, and when he stopped to rest his back for a few moments, I went on. By sunset, half of the north section was cleared, and I noticed that Jim had given up on me. He stood at the edge of the road and watched me slave over the dirt, oblivious of the world that surrounded me, indifferent to the time that had rushed by. Each moment could have been an hour, a year, or even a century. Even space had reduced itself to the hole I stood in, the hole I dug out, and the dirt I pushed away. The outside world of people, goats, sheep, and music faded away into complete darkness, the kind that had no sun, no moon, not even a fragment of a falling star.

"We'd better call it a day," Jim hollered. "It's going to be too dark to see pretty soon."

"I can see in the dark."

"I know you can, Lizard, but I can't. Go home, young man. I want to quit for the day. Go home, young man. Quit."

I pushed the shovel into the ground and took off.

Chapter 21

Two thousand years ago, in the city of kings, merchants, and passing caravans from the far east and all the way to the far west, people gathered around. There were preachers, orators, teachers, lovers, magicians and other entertainers. There were princes and princesses, noblemen and women, and beggars, vagrants and loafers of all ages; they listened, traded silks, perfume, spices, gems and laurel; they ate, sang, danced, and quaffed their date liqueurs and grape juice; they loved and hated, hugged and fought, laughed and cried, and then they were gone.

Now, many centuries later, in the same city of carved monoliths of colored sandstone, still reaching for the vacant skies, amidst a sea of ruins and half barren hills, where simple shepherds led their herds and sang to them between the valleys songs of sunrise and sunset, songs of love and thanksgiving, while the hills carried the sound of music to the tombs of ancient kings, merchants, friends and foes, in the midst of this same city, there stood four people, searching for a reason, or a pretext that might justify the extinction of the ancient civilization and its mighty gods. The figure of a young, slender orator appeared on a small platform, between the ruins, and another actor lay before him as if dead. The dead, however, was older in age and rounder in figure. Mr. Rami raised his hands above Jim, looked at the audience and recited from Shakespeare:

'This was the noblest Roman of them all;
All the conspirators save only he
Did that they did in envy of great Caesar;
He only, in a general honest thought
And common good to all, made one of them.
His life was gentle, and the elements
So mix'd in him that Nature might stand up
And say to all the world, "This was a man!"'

The crowd, Miss Petra Lux and I, applauded and cheered as the teacher and the old man took a bow and stepped down from the newly discovered platform.

"Tonight, Shakespeare, tomorrow, more Shakespeare," said Mr. Rami.

"How much of Shakespeare have you memorized," asked Jim. I thought you were a historian."

"Shakespeare gave history a character. I read only his historical plays. I can do without his summer night dreams. They give me nightmares. But his historical plays are grand."

"They are nightmares too," said Jim.

"I don't mind historical nightmares. I think there should be a play for every historical figure and main event. I wish I had the talent to write them. There would be a revolution in the art of history teaching."

"One Shakespeare is enough to burden the poor students around the world," said Jim. "Don't make yourself so unpopular."

"But this would teach history. Teachers would combine history and literature lessons together and make better use of their time. Can you imagine that?"

"No," said Jim firmly.

CHAPTER 21

It suited Mr. Rami to be an orator and an actor. The man had to be more than just a humble teacher, for he possessed internal power. Although his thin body never reflected an authority to be feared and respected, but his powerful eyes and gestures filled in the gap. There was something about his eyes and agility that captured the audience, be it the students, the spectators or just the friends around him. He hypnotized his listeners and took them on a journey to his own dream land, where his memory had carved a space in history and escorted the guests on a tour of a special time and place. When Mr. Rami talked, everybody looked at his eyes and listened with interest and fascination and with disregard to the skinny body below.

Jim had held a party on the site to celebrate the new discovery. After we finished sweeping, brushing, and manicuring the stone, Jim brought an assortment of sandwiches, potato chips, and soft drinks, and we picnicked at the site. After a conference with all members of the excavation project, it was decided that the discovered corner of the site was not an altar but a side platform for less formal orations or speeches; however, in spite of all the excitement that emanated from the discovery, there was no doubt left in mind that it had hid the mysterious god we were looking for even further into the ground. But Jim didn't seem too concerned. He was excited, just like the rest of us. After all, we discovered something that had waited to be discovered for about two thousand years, and that's no trifle matter in a man's life. We also ate all the food, down to the last crumb.

"That was a good party," said Mr. Rami. He took a long drink from his canteen and poured the rest on his head and washed his face. "Thank you, thank you, Jim," he chanted.

"My pleasure," said Jim humbly.

Mr. Rami lay down on the ground and closed his eyes. "Now we should have some music," he said.

"Darn it," said Jim. "I forgot to turn on the tape player. I carried it all the way here for nothing."

"What else have you carried all the way here?"

"I had a full wheelbarrow and a backpack."

"Good thing you didn't have a vehicle. Let's hear some music anyway. We still have time to listen and loaf."

Jim turned on the tape player as loud as it could go. But instead of putting everyone to sleep, the merry and cheerful music echoed through the valley. Mr. Rami raised his eyebrows in surprise. "I thought you had soft music for us," he said.

"Soft music is not for parties and celebrations," declared Jim. "You want soft music, go to a funeral. This is a celebration."

"All right," said Mr. Rami. "Be that way. I guess we won't listen and loaf. You want to party; let's make it a real one." He stood up and walked toward Miss Lux. "May I have this dance, please?" he asked courteously as he bowed before her, extending his right hand with extreme civility. Her eyes widened with surprise. She took his hand, stood up, and they walked to the platform and danced like city folks. I wanted to dance too but didn't know how, so I swayed my body back and forth with the beat and saw Jim doing the same, except he was coveting; I could tell.

The warm breeze, the bright sun, and the full stomach made everybody drowsy after a while. One dance was all anybody could handle. We spread out, lay on the rough ground, and stared at the empty sky. Even the merry music couldn't keep us awake; some of us drifted into daydreams; Jim snored heavily like an unhappy goat.

"Mr. Rami," I whispered. He was lying close to me, and I didn't wish the rest to hear.

"What, Raji."

"Is this the end?"

Chapter 21

"What do you mean?"

"I mean. Have we hit a dead end in the excavations?"

"I don't know, Raji. Jim still wants to clear the area around the platform. He might hit some more things yet, but I don't know what else he has in mind."

"I do not want Jim to go, Mr. Rami. I don't want this to end."

"I know that, Raji. I know that." He said his last statement so softly and then closed his eyes as if he were drifting off to sleep too. I gathered he didn't wish this enterprise to end either. It would be another breach to a happy phase in his life.

On my way home that evening, I saw my uncle and two of my cousins walking our horses to their stables. They greeted me with smiles and watched me go home. I felt their eyes follow me all the way to the yard gate. There was something on their mind. Although they always talked sparingly with me, their timid reception of me could not be so restrained unless they had something on their mind; it concerned me.

When I reached the house, my mother met me at the door. I knew she had something serious on her mind too. She always met us at the door whenever she had something sour to tell. I couldn't fancy the worst, however, because I thought it had already taken place. The father died. The brothers died. What else could there be. She was still standing, alive, before me, and that was a good sign as far as life and death went. Nothing could be that wicked. But her expression told me otherwise.

"What is it?" I asked.

She walked to the kitchen and let me follow her. Then she put the tea kettle on the stove and said without turning around to look at me, "Would you like some tea?"

She didn't have to ask. I always wanted tea, and she knew it. "What is it?" I demanded.

"It's your uncle."

"He can't be dead I just saw him walking the horses home."

"He wants to buy the business," she said. "He and his family have been helping us take good care of the horses, and I know they will do well if they took over the business. But I told him, first, I need to let you know of his interest and see if maybe you have any other ideas."

"I have none, Mother," I said. "You may do with the business whatever you see fit."

"What about you."

"I thought you wanted me to go to college."

"I do, but what if you do not get a scholarship. What are you going to do? I believe it is time you began to figure things out, Raji."

"No, Mother. It's not time yet. I'll figure something out. Don't worry," I said. "When the time comes, I'll worry about it." I collapsed on a small stool and pushed the back of my head against the wall. I had no idea what to do, but running the business was the last thing in the world I wanted to do, and my mother knew that. She knew that I'd rather starve to death than run the horses back and forth through the Seeq. "Go ahead and sell the business," I said.

"Your uncle would like to buy the house also," she said.

"What?"

"His son is getting married next month and wants to share and expand the business with his father. They want this house too, Raji."

"And where are we supposed to live, in the dump?"

"Listen, Raji," she said calmly as if she had it all figured out. "The business and the house belong together. You have no intention to stay here in Wadi Moussa anyway, and I have no need for such a big house. Why don't we sell this place and buy a small one up in the new area. There are several houses for sale out there, all newer and much more comfortable than this."

"Mother, I am planning on returning to work here in Wadi Moussa," I said. "I am going to be an archeologist, and I belong right here in the heart of all historical sites."

"When you get back, you can build your own place, Raji. You can build a home that is not surrounded by horse stalls and chicken coops" she said. I knew she was right, but the idea of selling my childhood house made me feel like a fowl, with its feathers being plucked off while still alive. I stood up, picked up my book and headed straight for the roof. The pigeons were settling down for the night. They cooed as if to object to my late visit. I sat down at the edge and looked at the hills as they began to fade into darkness.

A lump settled in my throat, and I couldn't talk much. For many days, I had to swallow and hold back my tears before I said anything to anyone. On Fridays, I brought my lunch with me to the excavation site and ate with Jim. Lately, he had become fond of plain common falafel sandwiches, stuffed with deep fried bean patties and salad greens. He bought them faithfully from Abu–Mustafa's restaurant. The man had become well culturalized, I thought.

One Friday, I too bought myself a falafel sandwich, just before I went to join him and ordered some extra hot sauce, called shatta, on the side. Jim watched me pour the hot sauce all over my food. I offered him the last drop, and he opened his sandwich and let me dump it in.

When he took a bite, his eyes bulged, and his face reddened with an enormous flow of blood. "Now, that's what I would call real penitence," he said. "This stuff is fire, young man. What did I do to you?"

"I'm doing it to myself too."

"It is hotter than hell."

"I don't mind the fire," I said pensively. "I am used to it."

"My mouth burns so bad; I can't even taste the falafel in my sandwich."

"They're there," I said. "You just need to train your taste buds to sort out your food better."

"My taste buds are dead. Your hot pesticide just killed them all." He grabbed the water canteen and drank what was left in it and shook the last drop into his mouth. "Easy on yourself, young man," he advised. "Life is not that bad."

"If life is not that bad, then this stuff is not that bad either. It gives your food some flavor."

"Well it gave me heart burn, and I can't feel my lips anymore. Good grief, young man, I don't remember your food ever being so hot."

"It beats drinking, Jim. It numbs your flesh but keeps your brain working."

"Numbs my flesh. It darn well mummified it. Don't be too hard on yourself, Raji. Life's not that bad."

"Bad enough."

Jim studied my face. I could see him with the corner of my eye while I stared at the horizon. "What is it now," he whispered. "You've been acting this way for a while. I have never seen you so quiet, so full of apathy and hot sauce before."

"My mother sold the house and the business."

"She did?"

"We are in the process of moving to a smaller house at the other end of town."

Now, Jim was quiet, and neither one of us said much for many days. We cleared out the area around the platform and made it look clean and presentable for visitors, and then we got stuck in the mud again. Jim decided to dig out several deep, narrow, and straight tunnels in all directions around the site to see if there was a hint of hope for finding anything of interest. We labored in silence, and when Miss Lux and Mr. Rami joined us, they too slaved quietly as if everyone had been deprived of the human language.

There were eight eyes and four heads communicating and eight hands digging, scraping, shoveling, and hauling dirt and fine rocks over and over again. Words were futile when they served no purpose; however, physical work seemed to keep a balance between the mind and the body, a cooperation that kept everybody in motion so they wouldn't drift off into the undesirable paths, which the holy books had condemned. At school, we were constantly reminded of the "straight path" and warned against "the crooked path" of life and how difficult it was to remain on the straight road without falling into some kind of a booby trap set by the devil.

I found myself standing in the middle of an intersection, somewhere between all paths. Mr. Rami, however, faithfully searched the ground for a substitute adventure since his marriage plans had fallen apart, and even though the excavations provided a short path for him, it was a straight and convenient path, and he found hope and good company in it.

Miss Lux, because archeology had been her specialty, thrived on every little discovery, and she was always kind and gentle and possessed all the Godly adjectives. I envied her for the freedom and fortune that helped her mold her own path. And Jim, poor Jim, his path turned out to be a cul–de–sac. His intentions and conduct were straight, but his windfall ran out of wind. He had followed his itinerary in full gear and now fumbled on the way back.

None of the archeological team members had an answer or even a clue about the next step in their life. But they all worked diligently. I slaved so I wouldn't think of the future. To me, the very existence of both human and object seemed too fragile and delicate and therefore, too ephemeral, and the paths, both crooked and straight, were tangled up in a knotty ball, too tight to untangle and go through. The Nabatean Kingdom was of a great value and an asset to the world trade thousands of years ago. It too must have fallen into a messed up thoroughfare that led to its destruction. Now, it is but a lesson in history, and we can't even learn from it because we still have the same human strength, which can help us maintain a glorious existence for a while and the human weakness, which will eventually fold us into the crust of the earth, and we would join those who preceded us and become the same lesson in history ourselves for those to come and tread our graves and dig out our belongings in search of a clearer path.

"If the paths were all clear, and we all knew the answer to everything, life would be so damn boring, I wouldn't want to live it," said Jim when we finally talked. We had spent that Friday and the previous one alone. Neither Mr. Rami nor Miss Lux had shown up, so Jim and I puttered around by ourselves. Then we sat down and loafed for the rest of the day. "Mysteries and hardships make great men," continued Jim. "Those who have it easy, do not make it into history lessons. They disappear into the elements, fertilize the soil with their rotting bodies, add gases to the air, and fatten the inferior life below the ground. They are all important, mind you, but they do not provide direct mind teasers for future generations, and, therefore, they add to the boredom of life."

"I'm tired, Jim."

"Here," he searched his pockets and pulled out a bag of licorice candy and handed me one. "This should perk you up a little."

Chapter 21

"You have an immediate remedy for everything, don't you." I took the piece of candy and threw it in my mouth. It was fresh and soft and chewy.

"Now, admit it Lizard, that did change your mood, didn't it."

"I don't know. I need another one to decide."

He pulled the whole bag and threw it at me. "Here, take this home and work on it until you make up your mind."

"I'll take a few more," I said. I was embarrassed.

"Take the whole thing. I don't need it."

"Your company enjoys your treat. Are you sure you don't want to keep some."

"You're my only company, Lizard. I'm stuck with you."

"I wonder what happened to Mr. Rami. Did he start going to Amman again on Fridays?"

"Beats me, and Miss Lux must have found a gold mine up north. I haven't heard from her for a while."

It was still early. Instead of going home, I climbed up to my cave, pushed the door open and let the bright sun rays shine clear to the far wall. Aisheh and I had never done that before. We always opened it about half way for convenience and to keep the contents protected from exposure to light and wildlife. Also, if the clumsy, heavy door was pushed open too far, closing it and securing the boulders behind it would be a difficult chore. This time I didn't mind the chore.

On the wall, the sun patch revealed to my eye, for the first time, a patch of tiles that were fit into the wall like a picture frame, about one square meter in size. The tiles looked as if they had covered a hole behind them. I had always glanced at that wall without taking the time to study it carefully, mostly because the tiles had been covered with a thin film of dirt that had been shaken down to the ground. I assumed the dirt shook off gradually, each time I removed the door and shoved it back and rolled the boulder behind it. I brushed the rest of the dirt off the wall with my fingers and noticed the bright colors of the exposed tiles. The variegated colors blended precisely with the wall that surrounded them as if the tiles had been cut out of the same spot and then pasted back on. The lines around these tiles were camouflaged until the sun hit them directly and gave them away. I ran my fingers around each piece, over and over again until I could hear my heart pound inside my chest. I had heard of secret treasures before but had no idea what that one could be like.

"Jim," I mumbled to myself. "You've got to come up here, Jim, even if I have to carry you on my back.

Chapter 22

An incident in the Roman castle on top of a hill, in a town called Kerak north of Petra had discouraged Jim from taking any further risks. I had tried desperately to convince him to climb up to my cave. I begged; I pleaded; I threatened and shouted, but the stubborn old monster wouldn't budge. The catastrophe in the Kerak castle had involved a British archeologist who came to dig around the Kerak area and found himself standing on top of the castle that overlooked the hills and the valleys, all the way down to the desert.

The town of Kerak was located on a hill that surrounded the ancient castle, which was first built by the Romans. When the Roman and the Byzantine eras were terminated, the Islamic, and then the Crusader eras took over. After each era, the castle had been destroyed and then rebuilt to suit the needs of the latest inhabitants. The strategic spot of the castle had allowed the viewer at the very top to spot the enemy for miles and miles around. Now, the visitors savor the spectacular scene of green hills drifting off into the desert all the way to the Red Sea. The spot had attracted many artists, archeologists, historians, and other professionals and non–professionals. They came to paint, draw, dig, and watch history from the present moment, from a castle that stood there in majestic magnitude. Its walls were built of heavy boulders that promised security and shelter in the days of successive invasions.

The huge and heavy boulders that covered the roof of the castle had always seemed so securely built, and the fact that the castle had been strong enough to withstand the elements for many centuries left no doubt in anybody's mind of its stability and magnitude. However, what seemed to be everlasting and gigantic in the mortal eye, was but ephemeral and fragile in the hands of time, so, when the British archeologist set his foot on one of the large boulders at the north edge of the castle, it gave way, and man and rock came tumbling down the castle, all the way to the wide dirt road that surrounded it.

A few hours later, a helicopter flew the archeologist from the small, local hospital in Kerak to the Medical City in Amman. The castle guard who had found the victim still alive rushed two blocks down the road to the local hospital and screamed for help. The poor guard had never encountered such a disaster in his life before. People at first thought he had gone mad. His eyes bulged and his face swelled, and both his hands pointed toward the castle. "A man fell all the way down," "He fell with the rocks," the roof," "all the way down," "the roof of the castle," the man, the archeologist fell," "all the way down," was all he could say.

The paramedics were able transport the victim from the bed of rubble he had fallen into to the local hospital. He was still alive and even mumbled some unintelligible words. They sounded like small clusters of consonants without enough vowels to support them. "He pronounced lots of m's and l's and f's," said a young nurse, "but no one could hear real words. They could have been his last wish," she sobbed. She too must have never seen such a monumental disaster. But the man had suffered from major head injuries, and twenty four hours later, he was pronounced dead. History had claimed another victim.

Such news spread like wild fire between small towns. When Jim heard the story in different, but similar versions from each and every person he had encountered, he declared incompetence. He would no longer take an unsure step, nor would he listen to me when I tried to explain to him how easy it would be to climb up to my cave.

"What do I have to do to convince you, Jim," I shouted. "You've got to see this place."

"I'd like to see many places, Lizard, but, at my age, I'd rather stick to the ground, as low as possible."

"You still have to fly back to America and cross the stupid ocean, Jim. That includes much higher elevation and more risk than crawling over a hill."

"It's too steep."

"I'll dig out steps for you."

"Home–made steps, like ancient steps, cannot be trusted."

"I'll dig the steps in the hill for you; I won't balance anything on rocks. I promise; I swear."

"Home– made steps..."

"You and your home–made steps."

I couldn't get anywhere with the man. He was stubborn as a mule, and that made an even more stubborn mule out of me, for I was determined to get him up there at any cost. I tried to describe the place to him, but he wouldn't buy my words.

The next day, Mr. Rami dismissed us early from school for no apparent reason. This action did not take place too often in our school system. In fact, the teachers had never done that before, not in my lifetime, but we assumed that Mr. Rami must have been extremely sick and were glad to be relieved from the burden of his homework for one day. On the other hand, in spite of Mr. Rami's skimpy appearance, his good health, endurance and commitment never allowed him to get sick very easily. The puzzle of this early dismissal action grew bigger with further discussion between the students. They finally decided it was about time for a weakness to prevail at least once in the man's life. After all, he was human – teacher but human – and was due for something precarious that would bring him down from the celestial pedestal to the human level. "Perhaps the teacher is sick" became the topic of conversation at school upon the announcement of the dismissal.

The students jabbered as they left the school, and Mr. Rami overheard and smiled wryly.

"He's not sick," I whispered to one of boys.

"How do you know? Look at his face."

"His face always looks like that."

"Now, don't you spoil it for us. He looks sick and maybe he will stay that way for a few days."

"He doesn't look sick to me," whispered another boy.

"He never looks sick."

"Why do you suppose we're dismissed so early?"

"I don't know. Maybe he's dying."

"What if he is dying."

"Maybe we should do something."

"Wait until we know for sure. You can't bury the man alive."

"He might die while we're waiting."

"What do you suppose we should do?"

"Find out for sure what the problem is."

"How do you know it's a problem?"

"I don't know. Let's think of something."

"Let's not."

"Why?"

Chapter 22

"Go home and enjoy the holiday. He'll be fine before you know it."

As I was leaving, I turned around just in time to see Mr. Rami shake his head at the departing students. His smile had grown wider and his face gleamed with a touch of color. He looked healthier than ever.

It was too early to be home, and, instead of going to Jim's project, I headed for my cave again. I carried with me a lantern, a flashlight and a few tools which I had gathered from our house. A persistent idea to lead my own excavations in my own cave overtook me, and I complied. The early afternoon sun was burning hot, and the lacking breeze made the breathing heavy and short. With my large bundle on my back, I climbed up the hill and headed toward the cave. The sound of goats echoed in the valley and followed me to the top, but I could see no shepherd or shepherdess around. "Aisheh," I muttered. Then I heard the music of a reed pipe coming from below and was able to spot the shepherd that played it. "Aisheh is gone," I said to myself out loud.

I lit the lantern and set it on the floor in the center of the cave and carried the flashlight with me. Although I was hot from the sun that baked the life out of the living things outside, a chill crept up my body. The cave had provided enough humidity and eerie cold breezes that sent tingles up my spine. Going to the cave, just to hide by the door, visit with Aisheh, and relax was one thing, and going with an explorer's mind was another. My hands shivered as I started to carve around the top row of tiles to loosen them up.

Although the colored sandstone of Petra was easy to carve, someone must have used a bonding of some sort to build the tiles in the cavity of the wall. I worked clear into the evening and was still unable to remove any of the tiles.

I was afraid to whack them out of there, for fear of destroying a sacred secret from the ancient man that might be hiding behind them. Jim had taught me how to be gentle in the land of history, and I tried my best.

Two of the tiles moved freely in place but wouldn't come out. I wanted to pull them rather than push them into the unknown, for behind them there was an echo that indicated emptiness, a hollow space of a sort. The drumming – echoing sound kept getting louder as I pulled and jiggled the tiles, and I began to think of them as a facade of a sizable room. My fear was that if the tiles fell into the unknown side, they might destroy something of a value that could be resting somewhere behind them, and I remembered Jim's words, which he repeated frequently as we excavated. "There is no room for an accident in an archeologist's work," he would say. "It would be most embarrassing to break a piece that had survived the centuries." When the two, ten centimeter thick tiles finally broke out of their places and came loose in my hand, I heard a faint whistle that sent more tingles up my spine and raised goose bumps on my skin. Sometimes, archeology makes a person feel as if he were trespassing on mysterious dimensions, where time and space connect again in such wholeness held by an omniscient power.

When I laid down the two tiles on the floor, my light fell on a small piece of carved rock that was stuck in a chink under the wall. I picked it up and stuck it in my pocket, for I had no time left to do further research. Darkness had crept into the cave and left nothing but the faint light of the lantern to throw eerie shadows all around me. The moon had diminished into one of its minute phases and left the stars to glow all alone. I left the tools and the flashlight on the floor of the cave, turned off the lantern and walked out. I pushed the door shut and shoved the large boulders behind it to secure it and ran down the hill, along the dry riverbed and began to turn toward the Seeq, when a faint light caught my eye in one of the tombs at the bottom of the hill. I stared at the light and saw it flicker alone in the darkness. The rest of the ancient city had slumbered in morbid silence. The goats and their musician had gone back to their home in the outskirts of Wadi Moussa. There was a light in the facility up above Jim's cave on the opposite hill. I figured that Jim must still be there washing or cooking. But the light in the tomb was foreign, and I had to find out the source of it. Nobody had lived anywhere near the tombs for a long time; I was sure of that. Who could have moved there all of a sudden? Another Jim?

Being a lizard, as Jim would put it, helped me slither without making too much noise. I slowly moved up the rocks that were scattered between the road and the edge of the hill. It was easy to do that since I left my load at the cave. The light continued to flicker in the tomb, and the smell of barbecued lamb reached my nostrils. I almost drooled on my shirt, for I was hungry and tired. Suppose the newcomer would be as generous as Jim and invite me for a bite? I let this dream linger in my mind as I approached the mouth of the tomb from the left side and saw the dying fire of the barbecued meat. I leaned my body against the outside wall by the entrance and tucked my stomach in as flat as it would go. It growled, and I slapped it gently and eased my head forward, just enough to see inside the cave, and there, before my very own eyes, was Mr. Rami and Miss Lux, all wrapped up in each other's arms, kissing and whispering unintelligible words in each other's ears.

"That pervert," I mumbled. "So that was why he dismissed us early from school. That poor, dying, sick teacher. We even felt sorry for him – not much, but we did some. Wait until everybody knows about this, I told myself. I watched for a while and then leaned my head back against the wall. It was a beautiful sight. I giggled at my discovery.

I wanted to shout and let the world see what I had seen. It was quite a sight, weird, strange, of conflicting contents, but beautiful. No, I wouldn't tell tell anybody. Would I do such a thing? Sure I would. At least I should tell Jim. He should know; shouldn't he? It was his privilege. After all, they met on his premises, at his very own excavation site. No, I wouldn't tell Jim.

Then all of a sudden, embarrassment and shame overtook me and smothered my cynical thoughts, and I decided to leave them alone. After all, I thought, what they did was no business of mine – or was it; I didn't know. There was confusion in my head. My brain sent contradicting signals to my conscience, until I finally decided to leave. I was jeopardizing my rapport with Mr. Rami. Our relationship had exceeded a teacher–student relationship recently – thanks to Jim, and the excavations. I slithered away and walked home like someone who had just met up with a friendly ghost. My mother asked me where I had been.

"I saw a strange smile on your face, Raji, and you were talking to yourself as you walked into the house," she said.

"I was just thinking out loud, Mother" I said. "Sometimes it is hard not think out loud."

She mumbled words of prayer to chase away the evil in case my wits were fading away, but I assured her that I was fine.

Secrets were tough indeed. In my diary, the next day was marked as the longest day in my life, for I walked like a proud peacock and talked like someone who had just had a stroke and lost part of his speech; I mumbled and stumbled over my own words and feet. I walked with knowledge in my head and palpitation in my heart; I walked like the only student in the entire school who knew something nobody else knew; I walked like a secret bearer, ready to burst. I wouldn't tell. I couldn't tell. It would be immoral; it would be a blasphemy; it would be wonderful, but I wouldn't tell.

I also tried to avoid looking into Mr. Rami's eyes, but that was difficult also, and I could swear he looked at me and called on me more than he ever did in his entire life before.

"What's wrong with you, Raji," he said at the end of the day. "You didn't seem to be all here today."

"I... I am here, Mr. Rami," I said. "I'm everywhere," I muttered and dashed home.

Jim had come to eat supper at the restaurant in town that night. I saw him walk up the hill and stopped to talk to him. I wouldn't say a word about you know what. I promised myself and pressed my fingernails in the heels of my hands. I wouldn't say much. But then I visited with him long enough for him to discover that I had something hiding in my guts.

"Why are you so antsy?" he asked.

"I don't know. I'm just happy," I said, "for no reason at all."

"I'll give you a reason," he said with a positive firmness in his voice.

"What do you mean?"

"Well. You might as well know now," said Jim. His eyes glittered; his forehead shimmered, and his smile made me sick. "I'm sure you'll be involved in the ceremony, one way or another."

"What ceremony?"

"Mr. Rami and Miss Lux are planning to get married soon," he said. "They want to make it a town celebration and involve all the students and their families. The ceremony will take place at the school, Raji."

I watched Jim rattle off my secret as if it were announced on the news. He took away all the mystery and the fun of the entire discovery, and I was mad. "I know," I said.

"How did you know? Did he tell you already?"

"No. I mean. It was obvious that they were in love," I said. For the first time I had put my foot in my mouth but managed to pull it out at the proper speed.

"Do you really think so?" said Jim. "I would have never guessed they were in love. It was a surprise to me."

It was a surprise to me too, I thought, but then I said, "Remember how they danced on the platform the day we celebrated its discovery? They were so close together, closer than the Holy Prophet to Mecca."

Jim laughed at my ignorance, his eyes filled with pity and sarcasm. "Yes, Raji," he said, "but city folks always dance like that."

"Holy, holy, holy. City folks sure know how to live. If we peasants danced like that we'd either be married or dead the next day."

Jim nudged me and burst into wild laughter.

"Seriously, Jim," I said trying to hide my embarrassment. "When Mr. Rami and Miss Lux came to help, they always worked together, very closely, all the time. Now don't tell me these are city folks symptoms. Our helpers always isolated themselves from us and formed their own team project. They laughed softly and talked quietly. I could never hear what they were saying. Had I known better, I would have listened better. But at the time I was too busy pushing the stupid dirt to the pile."

"Just as well, Lizard. You didn't need to eavesdrop on them."

"Why not. We could have known much sooner and had fun for quite some time already."

CHAPTER 22

"Oh, shut–up, Lizard," Jim scolded, but his cynical eyes laughed at me inwardly, and I wanted to knock him down. "Well. At least, now, I can say that the excavations were well worth the trouble," he declared.

"Is Mr. Rami going to Germany, or is Miss Lux staying here?"

"For now, I understand, they are staying here until Mr. Rami's commitment to the government is terminated. Miss Lux wants to poke around here and do some of her own digging. After that, who knows. It's their problem."

Jim spoke with glee. He hummed and danced his way to the restaurant like a happy bear. I watched him as he moved in nimble steps and eased himself, first to the right, then to the left, and then forward again.

Chapter 23

Peasants never marked their calendars; they had incredible memory. In addition, events like Mr. Rami and Miss Petra Lux's wedding needed no calendar. They were grand marks in the history of the village, just like the year of the flood. The day of the big wedding, the town's wedding, approached. Parents volunteered to decorate the schoolhouse, the designated place for the wedding. They made plans to cook the wedding meal, sing the appropriate traditional songs, bring the proper instruments, the most talented poets, the cavalry, the noise makers. The list grew longer each day. After Mr. Rami had given the people the liberty to organize his wedding, especially since they begged him to allow them the honor of putting it in their hands, he felt that the preparations were now getting far out of hand.

Nervous, responsible villagers constantly stopped Mr. Rami on the street and asked him what he would think of colored lights to cover the facade of the school, three hundred loaves of taboon bread to serve with the wedding meal, thirty–three trays of rice, each covered with roasted pine nuts and heaped with a whole lamb, head and all. The directory of the wedding turned into an encyclopedia; it grew at a steady pace.

Mr. Rami walked into the guest house, a few days after the villagers took over the wedding plans and collapsed in one of the chairs and covered his face with his hands. Abu–Zeid sat down facing him with a disparaging grin.

"Weddings are tough, Mr. Rami, aren't they?" he said. "When my turn comes, I'll go to the Capital and come back with my bride, all married and everything. Of course I'm not as popular as the teacher. If I marry here, I would probably have a much quieter wedding."

"This is ludicrous. I have no more power to convince the folks to take it easy. They even want to build a throne for the bride and the groom to sit on during the wedding. Can you believe that? How do I tell them to slow down?"

"You don't. They were going to take it into their own hands anyway. Just get out of the way an let them do it."

"But it's my wedding."

"It's their wedding too. They are your family and owe you that much."

"Nobody owes me anything, Abu–Zeid. I owe them plenty. I hardly ever buy my own meals anymore."

"Lucky you."

Um–Sleiman walked in with a load of bread to deliver at the Guest House. Abu–Zeid had ordered it for a group of tourists due the next day. When she spotted Mr. Rami, she walked straight to his table and sat down.

"Well, Um–Sleiman," said Mr. Rami. "I've got to hand it to you. You are a great fortune teller."

"Told you so; didn't I," she said proudly.

"You sure did. I hope you're coming to the wedding."

"You mean I'm invited too?"

Chapter 23

"What do you mean are you invited too. The whole town is invited. Didn't you know that?"

"The town has limits, you know, and I kind of live out of town, just like this Guest House. Is Abu–Zeid invited?"

"Of course he is." Mr. Rami gave Abu–Zeid an inquiring look. "You are planning to come aren't you?"

"Whom do you think is assigned to bring the baklava?" said Abu–Zeid with a big grin on his face. The teacher shook his head and covered his blushed face again.

"I'll see if they need more taboon bread," said Um–Sleiman. She got up and pushed her chair under the table. "Excuse me, but I have work to do." She hustled out the door as if the wedding were to take place the next morning. The two remaining characters at the table stared at her. One shook his head again, and the other burst into laughter.

"Come on, Mr. Rami. What's another helper. A man doesn't get married every day. It's once in a lifetime," said Abu–Zeid.

Meanwhile, Jim puttered alone most of the time in his corner. The help he had received from the happy couple diminished as the wedding day approached, so he depended on me to spend more time with him, for his day was approaching too. He wanted to finish up and leave the excavations in a moderately presentable fashion, so that visitors could stop by and enjoy his ancient platform and capital of the Nabatean pillar. He had given up on the caves and told me with frustrated words that he had no interest in renewing his residency, and when I asked him why, he said, "I had waited too long, Raji. This is a project for a young man like you. After you become an archeologist, I hope that you would consider it again and remember me when you find the happy site. I shall leave my books with you, and all the information I had gathered about the caves."

"But can't you renew for another year? What's another year?"

"It is more than I can handle, my boy."

"I'll help you, Jim, and I'm sure Mr. Rami and Miss Lux will help you once they settle down. They'll be here next year."

"But I won't, young man. I've had a good eventful year, discovered a few things, and that's enough for an old geezer. It's time to go home and write. There is so much to write. This year had given me enough material to keep me writing till the day I die."

"You said several times that this is your home sweet home," I protested in a childish tone.

"Home sweet home is where you set your own pillow and mundane treasures. My home is here now, and it will be somewhere else when I choose to move it."

Jim had made up his mind, and I couldn't get anywhere with him. He was done. Soon there would be a wedding and shortly after, a farewell. I abandoned my cave and spent the time helping Jim finish off his work. I joined him for a few hours every day after school and all day on weekends. He grew quieter each day and I, almost dumb. We limited the words to polite and formal errand expressions, "hand me this tool, please;" "gather up these fragments of pottery;" "push the wheelbarrow off to the side;" "what do you think we should do with these missing pieces;" "tomorrow we'll clean up the corners."

We worked quietly and diligently like a couple of slaves under a horrid spell. On the last day of school, we were dismissed early for the second time this year, but the command this time came from the authorities, from the villagers, for they had to get real busy now. Mr. Rami's wedding – their wedding would take place in two days.

Chapter 23

Jim and I went to the Capital to buy wedding presents. He wanted to find something very American, and I didn't know what I wanted to find, for I had never bought a present in my life before. I sensed from Jim's comments that a dozen pigeons would not be quite appropriate for a wedding present. I had no clue what in the world would fit for such a present. When I told Jim about my perplexity, he said we would get plenty of ideas once we enter the right stores in town.

"There are many good stores in town. We'll roam them one by one until you find what you like," he said. I remained silent. When a person is crude and ignorant, or, in other words, when a person is a peasant, the best way to prove himself refined, civilized, and educated is by keeping his peace, I thought. My tongue felt comfortable in my mouth.

When we arrived in town, Jim directed the taxi driver to a residential area where no shops were in sight. Then the driver pulled over in front of a house. Jim paid him and motioned for me to get out.

"I thought we were going to the stores?"

"Later. We'll go to the stores for your gift; for mine, we come to this place."

"What place is this?"

"There is an American teacher who lives in here. I met her at the International Church a while back. She teaches at the American school and happens to be a great artist also. She's part native American, and she makes beautiful jewelry with turquoise and silver. You'll see. I want to buy something very American, something the teacher and his fair bride would remember me with when they use. If I buy them a pot or a pan, they would use it day after day along with a hundred other gifts and never remember who gave them what. An old archeologist prefers his gifts to be more memorable."

We knocked on the door and were received by a charming young lady with dark hair, dark eye lashes and blue eyes. I had thought that blue eyes belonged to fair people only, but this was a superior combination. She must have been part native American, like Jim said, and part Scandinavian or French. I had never seen such beauty before. Her eyes were piercing, worse than Aisheh's, and they radiated against the dark background.

"Jim! It's so good to see you," she shouted and embraced the old man hard enough to embarrass me. I squirmed and moved away, trying to find a comfortable corner. But then, Jim caught me and introduced me to her. We shook hands, and I continued to remain quiet.

"It's good to see you, Tami," said Jim as she ushered us into the house. "What are you up to these days?"

"Just getting ready to fly back home for the summer. School is out," she said firmly. "What brings you to town this time? More supplies?"

"No. It's a wedding, my dear lady, and I need a wedding present, a very special wedding present, which no one can furnish but you."

"I suppose you're talking about the jewelry."

"That's the very thing I'm talking about."

"Let me see what I have left, Jim. Most Americans who wanted to give gifts this year wanted something very American. They've been digging in my box at a steady pace. Next year I hope to bring a bigger supply."

She left the room and came back with a large box and set it in front of Jim. Then she asked Jim if we would enjoy a glass of ice tea and Jim said yes.

Ice tea! I thought. Now that's a first. I always drank my tea hot, the desert way, the hotter, the better no matter what the season was. Never in my life had I or even heard of ice tea. I frowned at Jim's negligence to my taste but decided to maintain my peace.

Chapter 23

In the box, there was a variety of pieces of jewelry. Some were very colorful, and some were plain silver that looked very much like the silver jewelry of the desert people, twisted, twined, braided skillfully. I liked what I saw from a distance.

After some discussion, Jim chose a round turquoise charm that looked like the sun. He said it was the symbol for the sun, a very common native American symbol. It was inlaid in silver and attached to a dainty silver chain.

"Miss Lux would like that," he said. "What do you think, Raji?"

I nodded, and Tami smiled at me.

For Mr. Rami, there wasn't much choice, Jim bought the last belt buckle that was left in the box. But it too was stately, and its colors matched the colors of the sun symbol. It was a great gift, I thought. Jim bought it and guzzled down his ice tea. I took a few sips of mine and struggled to swallow them. They went down, but my stomach dared me take another sip. I set the glass down on the end table and made sure that my chair hid it well from sight.

Jim called for a taxi, and this time we wheeled in front of a large house supply store. Jim was right. There were all sorts of gift ideas. He and the store keeper tried to help me, but it was too late. I had been thinking.

"A set of Turkish coffee cups or a set of Arabic coffee cups would make a good gift, Raji; don't you think?" asked Jim. The store keeper brought out samples of different designs, and continued to bring out samples of other gift ideas, salad bowls, condiment sets for the famous city meal, the maza, crystals, silver bowls and things I would never guess what their purpose in life would happen to be.

"I had been thinking, Jim," I finally said. "Your very American idea gave me a clue."

"What's that."

"I too wish to give them something they would remember me with wherever they went."

"Well then, get them some Turkish coffee cups. They would be exquisite in Germany."

"No, Jim. I want to give them something that is made in our village?"

"Your village? You mean Wadi Moussa?" The store keeper chuckled and tried to hide his disparaging smile. It made me sick, and I told Jim I'd like to go back home immediately. "But, what is there to be bought in the village?" continued Jim, "Raji, don't be overwhelmed by the city. Why don't you just calm down. We'll go eat lunch, talk things over, and then you can make up your mind." He shook hands with the store keeper and told him we would be back after lunch. When we stepped outside the store, I told Jim that I had already made up my mind. I wanted to go back to the village. He was quiet.

After lunch, we took a taxi and headed toward the desert.

"May I ask what your mind is set on?" asked Jim after a long silence.

"I'll show you when we get there."

Nothing else was said until we arrived at the village. When we left the car, I led Jim to Aisheh's brother's store. He had his back turned to us when we walked into his shop. Jim looked at the hanging sheep wool rugs and smiled with satisfaction. "I see," he whispered. The big man turned around as soon as he heard our noise. He smiled at Jim, but when he saw me, his eyes studied me with a slight expression of confusion.

"We would like to buy a wool rug," I said politely, "a wedding present for Mr. Rami and his bride."

The man's smile returned to his face, and he waited on us with utmost politeness. Jim helped me choose a nice, rug, about one and a half meters square. Its design embraced three different shades of brown, all natural wool colors. The light color formed the plain mass in the background, while the dark and the medium colors were stitched in the shape of a star within a star. The small dark star decorated the center of the rug, and the medium brown star, the one that matched Aisheh's skin color, reached the ends of the rug. The wool was fluffy and soft. Jim and I ran our fingers over it and caressed the different colors; each had its own touch. A sudden thought of Aisheh struck me, and I held back my tears.

"It's a beautiful rug," whispered Jim.

It smelled like home.

Chapter 24

Unlike city weddings, a village wedding could never be diluted by pretentious and excessive civility, nor could it be fettered by black ties and cufflinks. People came to express sincere wishes in robust music, vivacious dances, and never ending songs. They dressed up in all colors and costumes, from old, traditional, heavy and engulfing clothes that buried their wearers from head to toe, to modern but conservative outfits. Traditional dresses had disappeared from the cities and were even confined to the older people of the villages, but they were still there to tie the past with the changing times.

People brought with them the reed pipe player and the aoud player. The aoud was the traditional string instrument, the original version of the lute which made its way to England a few centuries ago and became a "British" instrument. It usually helped maintain the exuberant spirit of the village wedding. Young men and women danced in lines, and then in circles, first around the bride, then around the groom, and when the official ceremony was over, they danced around the bride and the groom together to reinforce a life–long bonding. Then everybody settled down for the Dal'ouna song, which consumed at least an entire hour.

The Dal'ouna was another one of those traditional, historical songs that started way back by Adam and Eve and was added onto throughout the years until it had collected as many verses as the stars in the Milky Way. In addition to the "original verses" which varied from country to country in the Fertile Crescent, and sometimes, even, from town to town, new verses kept cropping up during each individual wedding with deserving words to suit its people. Some of these added verses were filled with romantic poetry; others engaged the singers and the audience in silly merriment, and others were embossed with repugnant, crude, and naughty discourse. Verses of all types, however, became so famous that they were added to the "original" and helped maintain the incessant growth of the original version. The initial verse, usually, was well refined. The refrain, as I recall, went something like this:

Ala Dal'ouna Ala Dal'ouna
Blow, O air of my tender-loving country

Then the singers would take it from there. Each person would remember a few traditional verses and sing them while all the attendants repeated the refrain. And then, another one would take over and sing a few more verses, and so on until all the known verses were consumed. At that point, the talented and the ambitious individuals would take over and start making up their own verses to suit the situation, and situation they had, for not only was it a wedding, but a special wedding of two strangers in a small, tight and remote community. The added verses began to crop up from mouth to mouth, and they grew with the hours of festivity. Um–Sleiman sang,

Ala Dal'ouna, I saw it coming.
I peeked at the dregs

of their sweet coffee. There,
stood a man and a woman,
soft as silk, white as milk,
sweet as honey.
Then sang Abu–Zeid,
Ala Dal'ouna, that poor old teacher
is no longer so, my dear friends,
customers and neighbors.
Before our very eyes,
he found himself a bride
and fooled us all
before our very eyes.

The cavalry had mounted their horses and surrounded the building where the wedding took place and fired gunshots into the air to announce the beginning of the celebrations. They fired gunshots again to let those who were late hustle and join the party. And then they fired again to let the world know that a wedding was underway and then again to proclaim the end of celebrations.

Older women walked around the tables and chairs and chanted, in a special verse, sincere wishes and silly, teasing rhymes to the happy couple and followed each set of verses by a cry of alleluia, the oldest and most traditional cry of joy in the history of the country, if not the world. One could scarcely see the tongues of these alleluia women. The tips of their tongues rattled from upper to lower lip at the speed of light. Some of the older and more experienced women shaded their mouths with their hands as they let out their alleluias; others used their index fingers to help rattle the lips as the tongues accelerated. I tried to do that a few times and ended up with numbed lips.

The alleluia chants usually started with the cry of joy, "Aweea" and ended with the Alleluia cry. Verses of all nature became audible. One of the students' mothers chanted,

Aweea, See him, the history teacher
Aweea, See him; he's the groom
Aweea, He joined the excavations
Aweea, Take a look at what he struck . Aloulouloulouloulie.

And another one responded,

Aweea, Between one and three something happened
Aweea, One: We were all indoors
Aweea, Two: Two people found each other
Aweea, Three: Today is their wedding day. Aloulouloulouloulie.

Then came the blessings,

Aweea, May the blessings of the Lord surround them
Aweea, May their house be filled with children and noise
Aweea, May they recount the memories of this very day
Aweea, to their great great great grandchildren. Aloulouloulouloulie.

Some people joined the chanting women; both men and women joined in; others began a response verse, so that the chanting shifted from one side of the room to the other. Sometimes, the men responded to the women's verses, and the two sides became men versus women, and when they finished all the happy wishes they could come up with, they started on each other and chanted naughty, and teasing verses against each other, and they all had a happy time anyway.

The visitors also had a happy time. Hans, the Schnellers, and the Breners arrived early in the afternoon, right at the beginning of the celebrations. Although the language barrier hindered their involvement at first, the joyful sounds gradually penetrated that barrier, and the guests began to tap their feet, clap their hands and hum the tune of the Dal'ouna with all their might, even though their voices were still smothered by the extroverted sounds of the excited villagers. The school children picked on Hans or he on them.

Chapter 24

They tried to teach him how to sing and dance and eat in the traditional way. His round belly had become part of the wedding scene. It bounced and twirled and bumped into people as they came and went around the place.

The school was decorated inside and out. The villagers had brought all the glitters they could put their hands on and covered the walls, windows, and doors; they made a special, elevated seat for the bride and the groom and covered it with satin and lace; they pushed all the desks against the walls, all around the school, and made ample room for dancing and maneuvering. They set up small tables for the food and brought all the chairs they could find.

The ceremony itself took little time, early in the afternoon, but it was rather interesting, more of a representation of several religions, Christianity with its diverse denominations, Islam, and Archeology. Mr. Rami and his bride exchanged their vows in front of a number of religious people. Each thought that the authority invested in him was the official one. There was Sheik Hamdoun, who was known to be a fairly open minded and respected man in the southern communities where he had served most of his life. And there was Father Nicholas who came from Kerak, a mostly Christian town. Father Nicholas was an acquaintance of Mr. Rami. And then there was Reverend Whitman, the British preacher who had lived in Jordan longer than anyone could remember. He had learned the Arabic language fluently and served in many communities, mostly in the south. And, of course, there was Jim, the official sacerdotal representative of archeology.

After the exchange of vows, the Sheik, the Father, and the Reverend spoke briefly, each took a turn and blessed the wedding, and then Jim talked. He stood up, adjusted the glasses on his nose and cleared his throat. His eyes turned back and forth in half circles. He studied the people in the room carefully. An older woman sat on his right. He winked at her and nodded as if to communicate. Then he focused his attention somewhere in the corner, where the preachers and the bride and the groom were seated and began to talk.

Although Jim spoke with confidence, his tiny, restless eyeballs and his wide range grin revealed a mischievous, elfish character, hiding behind an otherwise, sagacious looking old man. "Archeology is a mysterious faith," he said, "for it had led a young maiden to leave her home place in Germany and travel all the way to Jordan in order to discover a young man in a small village at the edge of the desert." The smiles appeared on many faces in the school room, and people looked at each other and nodded and continued to smile. Even Reverend Whitman managed to smile, but the Sheik and the priest remained serious. It could have been their shallow understanding of the English language, and then again, it could have been their lack of faith in Archeology. "Although the discovery is not antique by the archeological standards," continued Jim, "but within this discovery lies an ancient kernel, a seed that is shared by people of all nations, young and old, and to that discovery, I say, Alleluia." With that, Jim gave a signal to the older woman on his right and she took off with a shout of alleluia that shook the ground beneath our feet, and the room roared with applause and boisterous jabbering and singing again, and the festivities continued on.

There was enough food and drink to fill the population for several days. Volunteer village women had prepared large special trays, heaped with rice, chicken and lamb cooked in yogurt sauce and topped with roasted pine nuts and almonds. They were carried to the wedding site at a steady pace. Children ate and danced and ate again until the juice dripped down their elbows. Then, some men walked in with trays of baklava on their heads. The baklava was ordered from the Capital by Abu–Zeid himself, and his waiters served it to all the wedding guests, the young and the old.

Jim floated in a sea of people with the same grin that never left his face. He visited, ate and drank, and when some men approached him and asked him to join the line of dancers, he stood up and danced like one of the villagers. Then he was tired and sat down for a while. A few minutes later, an older, heavy–set woman approached him, put her hand on his shoulder as if to give a blessing and began to chant her verses of good wishes to Jim. And the entire room resounded with the alleluia part. Even Jim's tongue began to rattle. I couldn't tell how much noise came out of him, but I saw his tongue go up and down in the right direction. When the woman drifted off toward another victim, Jim thanked her by saluting her with both hands. Her departure left a gap between me and Jim, the gap I'd been waiting for so I could reach him. I slipped through the mass of bodies, and when Jim saw me, he made room for me to sit beside him.

"I've got something to show you; I had forgotten all about it. You must see it." I said.

"Something good, I hope," said Jim. His look said it all. He was having a great time and did not want his evening ruined by anybody or anything.

"I've been excavating in my cave," I said.

"Look Raji," he interrupted.

"Just listen," I hollered. Some people around us heard me in spite of all the singing and the commotion. They stared in surprise. Jim lowered his eyes, and I did the same. "I just want to show you something I found in my cave that's all. It's very small."

"Where is it?"

"Right here." I pulled the tiny carved rock that I had found in the chink out of my pocket and put it in his hand.

He lifted his hand up toward the light and studied the rock for a long time. I thought I would never get a word out of him that night, for he seemed so engrossed in reading the little rock that he never noticed the people who began to stare at him and wonder what he was doing. The rock nestled in the palm of his hand, and he gently rubbed his fingers over it, first three fingers, then two, and then one. He felt each groove with the tip of his index finger again and then touched it with the tip of his tongue. I had seen many archeologists do that. Some told me that licking rocks helps identify the minerals in them; others said that if a person moistened ancient pottery (and I suppose, in a desperate situation, a person could use his saliva), the moisture should disappear immediately. Aged pottery was supposed to soak up the moisture instantly like a dry sponge. Jim did all that and then some. He began to look like a moron.

When I gave up on him, I heard him call my name, "Raji," he said.

"Yes."

"Tomorrow, I will climb up to your cave!" he said. His eyes were remote. They had gone through the little rock and then beyond it, back to the people who had carved it and used it in their daily life. The words came out of his mouth as soft as a whisper in still air, but I heard him. I heard him, in spite of the singing and the screaming and the gun shots that resounded outside the building, announcing the end of the wedding celebrations. All I had to do was look at Jim's lips. I'd been waiting for these words to come out of that mouth for a long time. Jim decided to climb up to my cave. I needed to lay down the red carpet. I had work to do before he changed his mind. He looked me in the eyes and carefully set the rock in the palm of my hand.

"Now, you take good care of this," he said.

"Yes Sir." I tucked the rock deep in my pocket, stood up and left.

It was eight o'clock when the celebrations came to an end, and the knot of bodies finally dissipated. The bride and the groom worked their way toward the decorated jeep, just outside the school building. The school children, led by Jim had done a good job pasting runners of bright colored crepe paper on the old jeep. The couple was escorted by singers, dancers and alleluia chanters. The horsemen fired their guns in the air, one shot after another until the musical and non–musical sounds blended into a roaring noise, loud enough to reach the stars in the darkness of the naked sky.

The jeep roared through the village streets and headed south on the main highway, toward the resorts of Aqaba on the Red Sea. The villagers sang their way to their homes, and Jim, Hans, and the rest of the guests headed toward the Guest House. Everybody disappeared in his own den and allowed silence, dead silence, to hover over the village again, and the music, the noise, that had filled the air a few minutes ago, ascended beyond the range of the human ear.

Chapter 25

It had been proclaimed that the visitors of Petra either fell deeply in love with the place or feared it. Some reported that the extraordinary monuments, the carved cliffs and their surroundings had formed an attractive and exotic paradise, while others mistrusted its existence. They described it as a depressing place of isolation, sinister, full of mysterious and evil spirits, because of its unusual looks and setting; however, all guests agreed that no place else in this world would match Petra. To me, it was home, and, although at the time I had not ventured much outside it to know the difference, it was still incredibly attractive at times, and then there were those moments when it felt depressing and sinister. When the place became a rut, a valley of ghosts from the past, the far past and the near, its bright colors turned into flames, and the carved shapes evil spirits, powerful forces, that haunted the inhabitants and chained them to the rocks of hardened sand, colored, hardened sand.

My cave continued to be the only escape for me. It was a place to climb out of the rut and come closer to the skies, even though, high as it was, it never took me anywhere outside Petra's boundaries, the elevation had always lifted my spirit and offered a ray of hope. Now I knew why the sun was so important to the Nabateans. Their most astounding worship places were up in the high places where the sun rays gave the light of freedom to those chained to the cold rocks.

With my recent discovery, the place also offered company, the kind only I chose to have, first Aisheh and her goat, the crude archeologist that kicked the mouth of the cave enough for us to discover it, and now, Jim, the real archeologist. I had to get ready to receive Jim into my own private home. I arrived at the cave early in the morning and began to prepare the most convenient route for Jim, if ever there was such a route.

The rocks at the bottom of the hill were, wide, sturdy, and fairly easy to climb. But the higher the person climbed, the steeper, more rugged, and impossible they became. I never had to study the route that closely, and I never noticed how difficult it could be for an old man like Jim. His visit was going to be exciting as well as nerve racking, I thought.

I spent the morning clearing an imaginary trail, rough but passable. It was imaginary, because, nobody could really see it, because it really was not there, carved and ready to tread. It was rather in my mind, for I knew exactly where Jim should set his foot safely for each step. I just had to tell him that, and he had to obey me or else stay up there, hanging in the rocks like a fossilized goat, waiting for someone to discover him. When I was done with my fictitious trail, I climbed down to see Jim.

The cheerful music which Jim had played during the picnic, when Mr. Rami invited Miss Lux to dance with him on the newly discovered platform, could be heard from a distance. When I reached Jim's place, I tiptoed to the half open door and quietly peeked through and saw him dancing with a cushion, his arms wrapped softly all around it, his head tilted upward, and his eyes half closed in a remote reverie. His feet were moving in nimble steps, more graceful and agile than Mr. Rami's ever were. I never thought the old demon could dance so well. I waited until he had his back turned to the door, sneaked in and turned off the tape player. The music ceased sharply, and the old man stopped with a crude jolt that tripped him over his last graceful step, and he almost fell to the ground. When he saw me, he shook his finger at me and collapsed on his bed. He huffed and puffed, and, when he was able to catch his breath, he said, "What did you do that for, Lizard."

"Did what? You were dancing with a cushion for heaven's sake."

"At my age, it is more convenient, Lizard, and more comfortable, believe it or not."

I waited for his breath to settle and said, "Are you ready to go?"

"Go where?"

"To my cave."

"Oh yes, Raji. See, I even have my light pack all ready to go."

"I'll carry your pack for you, Jim. You just worry about getting yourself up there."

"That bad heh?"

"At your age, Jim, everything is bad."

He nudged me with his fist and then rubbed the heels of his hands together as if ready for an attack. "All right, Lizard. Let me show you how badly I can climb," he said.

"I already know, Jim," I whined, failing to hide my nervousness. "Let's get this show on the road."

He walked, or I should say, he almost danced his way to the edge of the hill. I had never seen him in such good spirits. The man couldn't have been in love, and, if so, with whom, for all the women that were worth loving in our daily life had chosen other males, richer, younger, and, God knows, better looking than this piece of antique. The only favorite woman left that I could think of was my mother, and Jim couldn't have been in love with my mother. I knew that much. For one thing, she spoke very little English, and he spoke no Arabic, although he thought he could say a few words, when in fact they sounded more like gas bubbles back firing at him after a meal of garbanzo beans.

"All right, where is your easy way up," he said when he reached the top of the last easy boulder.

"Here. Put your foot in this crack, right here, and hang on to the end of this boulder."

"You know. Even huge boulders can come tumbling down, Raji."

"When they are on top of a castle, yes, but when they have been half buried in the hill for centuries, it is not likely, Jim, unless an earthquake happens by, and this area hadn't had one for centuries. Earthquakes seem to concentrate on southern Turkey these days."

"With my luck, we'll get one today."

"With your attitude, we will. You know, the old folks at the village say that if you don't think of bad things, they won't happen to you, but if you keep calling them, they will come. Bad things are like evil spirits, waiting to be called. Don't bring them onto yourself, old man."

"Oh, Raji. You're a pain in the neck."

"Thanks. So are you."

Jim stopped to mop the sweat off his forehead. I gave him a sip of water from his canteen and showed him his itinerary through the most rugged part. He saw that it was also the shortest part of the journey, and that gave him some courage.

"There is a good place for each step," I said. "I have cleared a sturdy path for you, Jim, and don't you forget it."

"I won't, Lizard. How could I ever forget."

CHAPTER 25

He continued to obey me like a sweet little lamb. He followed my instructions with trust, pleasure and determination. It was hard to believe. I had begged him for an entire year to take this trip, and he refused it adamantly. I had tried every diplomatic approach I could think of to con him into climbing the steep hill, but he wouldn't. Now, all of a sudden, and after his term had approached the end, he decided to visit the cave with such esprit de corp; it puzzled me.

It took about an hour to clear the rugged part of the journey. We stopped repeatedly, first to take a drink and then to dispose of it and take the next one. Water seemed to flow through the man like a rapid after heavy rains. The scene had become embarrassing and ludicrous. He watered the trail all the way up to the cave.

When we finally came to the clearing in front of the cave, he looked at me and asked, "where next?" He had been so engrossed in climbing and never even looked up to see the semi camouflaged door to the cave. He just raised his head enough to look at me, with eyes, ready to absorb more instructions.

"Let's catch our breath, first," I said. "Sit down right here on this boulder. This is a good spot for a break."

He took a deep breath and followed it by a long drink. I sat down next to him, and we gazed at the valley and all the ruins below.

"Jim," I said, trying to wake him up from a daydream.

"Hum?" he answered, still dreaming.

"Was it the small, carved rock I showed you at the wedding? Was it the reason why you decided to come up here?"

"It helped," he said. His thoughts were still half lost, somewhere between the valley and another time zone.

"Aren't you going to stay until you find Dushara and his friend god Allat united into one god?"

"I think I found them, Raji. I think I found them."

"In that carved rock I showed you?"

"I don't know for sure, my boy. That carved rock is a stamp. The Nabatean design on it alludes to some sort of deity, a unity in the deity."

"The design has Dushara's eyes staring out of a river, doesn't it?"

"That's what I saw in it, but, who knows. It could have been a logo that belonged to a merchant or a caravan or a company of merchants from Petra.

"And it could have been the symbol of the unity of the gods."

Jim nodded. "Now, you lead me to that cave of yours before I change my mind," he commanded.

"Welcome, Jim," I said and pointed to door behind him. "You're sitting on the key."

Jim puttered outside the cave while I moved the rock and opened the door for him. He studied the surroundings and seemed to have the same hesitation Aisheh and I had before we walked into the cave for the first time. Closed, ancient places seemed to have their own aura; they released a protective, secret power that demanded reverence and installed fear; they stood there like Pandora's box or like the forbidden apple or the reinforced door in the enchanted castle that couldn't be opened by mortals. But they all provoked man's curiosity, and, leaving them alone, would be against the nature of man.

When Jim saw the pottery, he began to stutter. "Why didn't you ever bring it down?" he asked.

"Because it's huge, Jim. How could I possibly risk bringing it down without breaking it." He realized the shallowness in his question and nodded. "Besides, I didn't wish to reveal the source to anybody, Jim. I didn't want anybody up here, digging up and looting my home. This is my own home, you know."

CHAPTER 25

"Then why did you invite me here?"

"Because," I said and then encountered the complexity of the answer and hesitated for a second, "because, I believed, you were looking for this very place." I pointed to the tiles and the hole in the wall, the most probable entrance to a second cave. Jim's eyes widened and his mouth dropped open. "I just uncovered this part of the wall, Jim. It had been camouflaged with a layer of dirt."

We pulled the rest of the tiles out of the wall. The hole grew bigger than I had anticipated. We scraped the dirt off the wall and traced the tiles all the way down to the ground. We had uncovered a door, not just a small cavity – an entrance to a connected cave. It was more of a supply room, for it had traces of a spring that once flowed in the middle of the cave, and a dry stream bed had carved the cave and led a way through the hill on the left side. On each side of the stream there was a shelf carved in the rock and covered with pottery, countless pieces, all intact and well decorated. Very few were plain. Most pieces had delicate decoration in dark brown and/or black paint. The entire interior of each bowl was covered with designs of leaves, grapes, and wheat and surrounded by different shapes. There were circles within circles of black and white designs, and among these circles there were eyes that stared at us. Jim and I froze for a few moments. We allowed the cool air of the newly discovered cave to seep through our senses, while the eyes of the ancient god watched and waited.

In the middle of the stream rested an obelisk, the kind that the Nabateans had commonly set for the god of the sun, Dushara. His face was carved on the obelisk so that it greeted those who walked in through the mouth of the cave. It also greeted the sun, for the mouths of the entrance cave and the second cave were lined up so they would receive the sun at a certain time of the day, so that the sun rays, the sun god, would meet the spring, its waters, and its god, Allat.

The eyes on the face, carved in the obelisk, stared at us everywhere we went. We left the door and moved to the right side, and the eyes still stared at us. Then we moved to the left, and the eyes followed and rushed tingles through our limbs and weakened them. We moved slowly in silence; we shivered; we smiled, and we stared at the staring eyes. They were surrounded by locks of hair curled evenly around the face and down the sides of the neck. The beard on the face matched the hair, curly, tight, and even. The mouth was small and slightly open, and the nose had been chipped slightly, which made it difficult for a person to follow its bridge, but the eyebrows outlined the staring eyes and helped the eyelids form perfect cavities. The cheeks were delicate and the forehead smooth.

Jim and I continued to move, stare and say nothing for a long while, until finally, Jim lifted one of the small bowls off the shelf. He held it firmly with both hands and looked inside it.

"Imagine, Jim" I said. "Someone ate out of that bowl two thousand years ago."

"They must have had good table manners to eat out of bowls this thin and delicate."

"They had no silverware back then, Jim. They scooped their food with bread, like we, peasants, do, which wouldn't be as hard on fine pottery as metal."

"I bet you they dipped kh...kh.."

"Khamie."

"Khamie with their bread and scooped chunks of lamb or chicken out of this bowl."

"Jim, I have an idea."

"What's that?"

Chapter 25

"I want to set a table, Nabatean style, just to see how it would look like."

"I'll help you do that."

"And then we'll take pictures of each other, dining at the table and pretending to sip from the ancient cups. I brought my camera."

The time escaped us while we quaffed fanciful drinks, feasted on Nabatean khamie and set tables and reset them by using different items from the extensive selection that lay at our disposal. We moved around like two heavily intoxicated creatures, lost in time and space, for before us lay a thick layer of history. It had arrived from the past, stopped at the present and waited for us to do something with it in the future.

"Your home is the dream of every archeologist," said Jim finally, trying to recapture reality. "It's an archive, ready made. What are you going to do with it?"

"I don't want anybody up here," I said firmly

"Are you going to sit on all this for the rest of your life?"

"I don't know. I need your help, Jim. Maybe, between the two of us, we can come up with something."

"Let me think about it, Raji," said Jim. "I need to think about it."

It was dark when we stepped outside the cave, but the moon was bright, and the shadows of the colossal rock appeared like ghosts of all types, scattered everywhere in deep silence. Jim's face sagged. "I had hoped to be down before dark, Raji."

"Don't worry, Jim. You'll make it. I'll point out each footstep you should take with the flashlight. Besides, the moon is bright; it will help us too."

He moved slowly and said nothing until we reached the most difficult section toward the middle. Then he stopped.

"Here, Jim," I said. "Put your right foot here." But he stood there and did nothing. I moved the flashlight to his face and saw tears in his eyes. "Jim, let's go down now. Everything will be fine," I whispered.

"Everything will be fine," he repeated.

"Now, put your right foot here."

"I can't see where I'm heading, Raji."

"You don't have to, Jim. I know exactly where you're heading." He turned his back and decided to crawl down backward, while he hugged the hill. Then I had an idea. I took each step ahead of him, anchored myself with one hand and helped him down with the other, until he made it down to the easy boulders.

"You know, Raji," he said when he finally made it to safety.

"What?"

"I still think you're a pain in the neck."

"I know."

"Thanks," he whispered as if he didn't want me to hear, but the evening air carried the words in my direction.

"You're welcome," I said.

CHAPTER 26

Jim showed me how to pack each piece of pottery and care for it. It was worse than caring for a new born baby. The painstaking efforts that took to carry each piece down the hill had tested my patience, and there were times when I debated the worthiness of such labor. First, I filled each item with soft materials (the small items were filled with cotton balls and the large ones with rags) and then wrapped it carefully (the small items were wrapped in toilet paper and the large ones in special tissue paper which Jim had purchased from Amman). Jim had supplied all the packing material, and I did all the work, because it had to be done up in the cave. After filling each item with soft filling, the entire piece had to be wrapped in newspaper, and then I had to set it in a wooden box and fill in the space around it with more newspaper and carry it down, one step at a time, one boulder at a time. I counted every rock on each trip up and each trip down. Before this performance, the stones were all one whole step that I used to take in a slithering motion. Now, they outnumbered the stars in the sky, and when I complained to Jim he said, "That's what you get for being a lizard."

"But, face it Jim, I did enjoy places no one else dared to tread. Besides the view from the high places, especially when you're alone up there gives your ego a sense of superiority and pride."

"Now, enjoy paying for the view, young man. It's due time. In large cities you pay big money for a good view. You've been freeloading here long enough."

"Admit it Jim," I said. "I found you the bosom of the hill you were looking for."

"That is a funny place for a bosom, Raji. If I ever meet that French explorer, perhaps in another life, I would quiz him on the locations of certain parts of the body."

"You just didn't know which end was which; that's all."

"Oh, shut-up and work."

All the pieces made it safely to the bottom, even the huge water jugs. I was able to lower them down, one step at a time. Jim waited for me down at the easy boulders and then carried all the pieces slowly and surely the rest of the way to his cave. We worked diligently; we labored alone, for the rest of our team had gone, first on a honeymoon, and then the happy couple left for Germany to spend the rest of the summer there. Even Jim complained about their departure. "It would have been much easier had Mr. Rami and his girl stuck around a little longer," he mumbled one day.

"I don't know about the girl, but Mr. Rami is no acrobat either, Jim." I remembered the first time he crossed the Seeq with me. "I still would have done all the packing up here all alone while the three of you partied on the easy rocks."

"Ms. Lux would have joined you. She's adventurous."

Chapter 26

I guess I wouldn't have minded that at all, I thought. Maybe the pretty woman would have changed her mind about Mr. Rami and loved me instead. No, that was no coveting, just a thought, an intruding daydream. "Well. She ain't here, and you ain't much help," I concluded.

"Shut-up and work, Raji."

It took us a month to move all the items down and close the project – my project. After that, Jim's work began.

Between him and his contacts with several universities in the United States and the Department of Archeology in Amman, I was awarded a respectful monetary award for my discoveries and granted a choice of full scholarships including air fares and accommodations. I had my fair share of education, enough to bring joy and pride to my mother's heart and to surprise the villagers. I was still called goofball but with an addition. My name grew longer again, although it was easier to pronounce this time. It became, The Goofball Who Made It Big.

Aisheh was never thanked for any of this, nor was she ever heard of again. Many a time I thought of her as the goddess of this place, the only soul who knew more about these hills and valleys than any professional; her soul that still dwells in the caves, the ruins, and the wild flowers of springtime; the soul that sings to the passer by and consoles the lonely moon.

After Jim's visit to my cave, nobody except me has set foot in it. Now, after all these years, the cave and its god are still there. They are still mine, above and beyond the reach of the average man. After I die, someone, perhaps another Lizard or another Aisheh may discover them, but then, the cave will be empty of all the pottery. Only the eyes, the god in the obelisk, would receive the guest and the sun rays through the mouths of the caves.

Jim spent the rest of his retirement years writing a book on Petra. He had been allowed to take a few pieces of pottery with him to America to look at and admire for the rest of his life. Abu–Zeid also gave him something else to look at and admire. It was a passport picture of his royal highness, Abu–Zeid himself, not in an album, but pasted on the side of a bottle, a special bottle filled with layers of the colored sand of Petra. I told Jim he could turn the picture toward the wall, and the bottle would be a remarkable piece of art, for Abu–Zeid had asked Um–Sleiman to layer the sand for him in the bottle. It was the art of her gifted hands. Each layer of sand, each color, portrayed a section of the hills, valleys, wild flowers, and monumental ruins of Petra.

Jim ended his book with a special letter, a memo, hand written, to the pupils of archeology whose curiosity might lead them to check out the Nabatean country in the future. In his memo, Jim said,

I finally found the united Dushara and Allat exactly the same way they had been described in the old explorer's book. The gods had been molded into oneness, a holy spirit that arose from the riverbed and greeted the sun that rested on an obelisk. His eyes, though carved out of the rock stared everywhere. A person would think the eyes were looking at him no matter where he stood in that place.

It is not easy to describe the feeling, the shock, which the staring eyes provoke in a man's heart; however, I believe that the god is still there for you to see, for it had been decided that the shrine itself, the obelisk would be deprived of its power if moved away from its original place, because the place, the cave within a cave, were bonded together with the sun, the spring, the obelisk, and the face that housed the eyes. Therefore, although the pottery that served the god and the pilgrims had been removed, the god himself remained up there, and to visit it, a person would need strong will and determination, for the trip is a pilgrimage, rewarding but not easy. You may wish to seek some help before you climb up there. Ask for the man who might still be slithering on the rocks of Petra. His name is Rajaiddin Al Mohtadi, better known as Lizard Boy.